FORGING BONDS

THE ZAUBERI CHRONICLES

J. W. JUDGE

WORKS BY J. W. JUDGE

Fiction

Vulcan Rising (The Zauberi Chronicles, Book 1)

Seeking Sanctuary (The Zauberi Chronicles, Book 2)

Forging Bonds (The Zauberi Chronicles, Book 3)

The Murder Tree (A Short Story)

Non-Fiction

Write Your Novel One Day at a Time: How to Write a Novel While
Having a Career, a Family, and a Life

scarlet oak press

ISBN: 978-1-954974-08-1 (Paperback)

ISBN: 978-1-954974-07-4 (eBook)

ISBN: 978-1-954974-09-8 (Hard Cover)

Library of Congress Control Number: 2022909878

Published by Scarlet Oak Press (scarletoakpress.com)

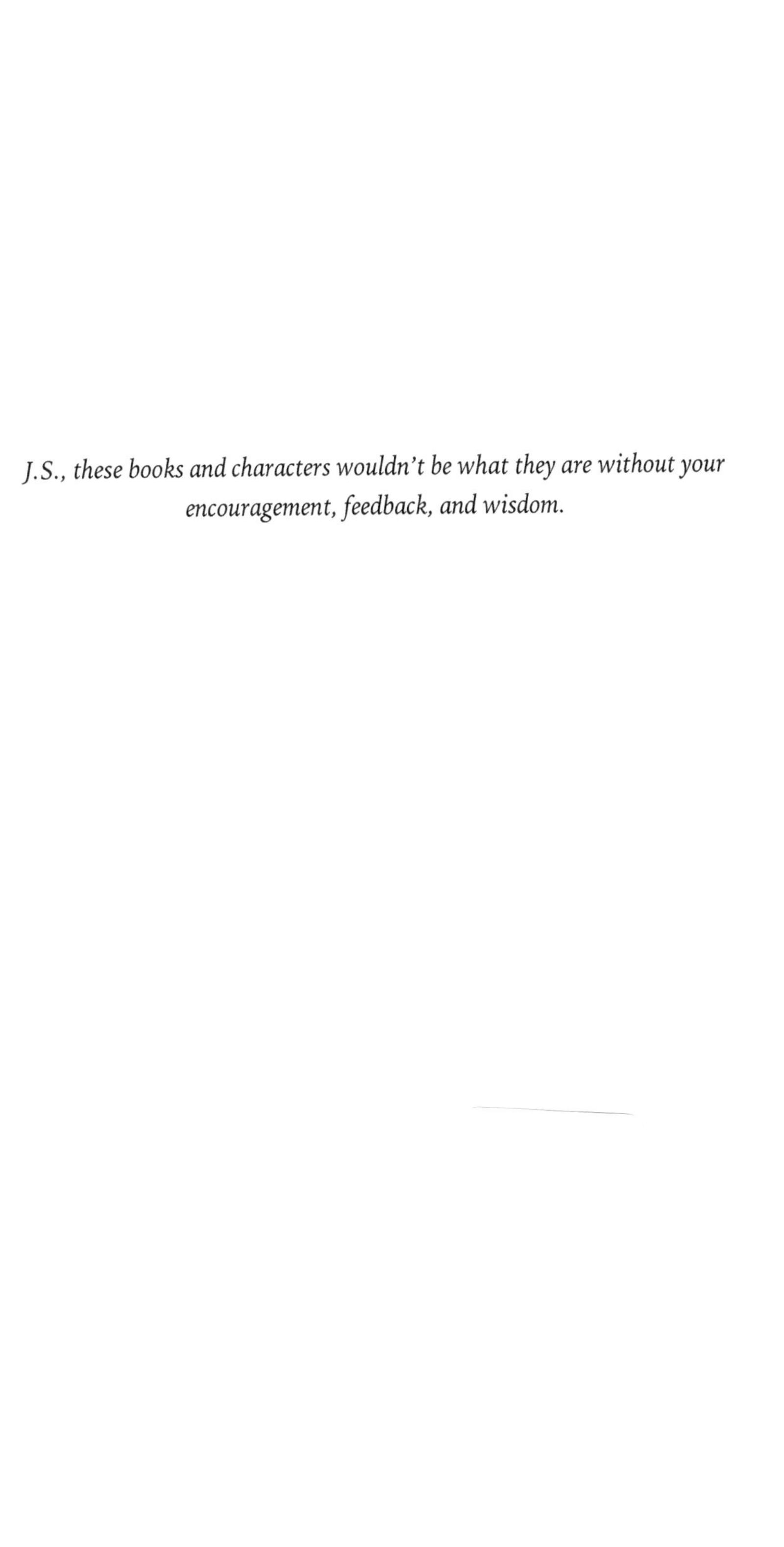

J.S., these books and characters wouldn't be what they are without your encouragement, feedback, and wisdom.

Darkness cannot drive out darkness;
only light can do that.
Hate cannot drive out hate;
Only love can do that.
Martin Luther King, Jr.

Now faith is the substance of things hoped for,
the evidence of things not seen.
Hebrews 11:1

The Zauberi Chronicles

FORGING BONDS

Book Three

1

AGATHA

AGATHA CLEARED HER BRUISED THROAT. Goosebumps prickled her cool, damp skin. At least the brisk temperature was a condition she could do something about. She took her time strolling the closest parts of the perimeter of the cavern where Vulcan had unceremoniously dumped her. Its ceiling arced upward toward a small hole some fifty meters above her. *How long ago did you start thinking in metric?* A few stars twinkled through the aperture.

A square kitchen table and solitary chair sat near the cave wall. They were plain in every way, but clearly crafted by hand. *When you're roaming the earth for a couple thousand years, I guess you have plenty of time to hone your skills. All of them. Kidnapping, murder, wood working. Just the usual stuff.*

On the table sat two gallon-sized jugs of water, a couple of bags of groceries — all boxed or canned — and her only source of light, an oil lantern. At least, the only source he'd left her. Agatha flexed her hands. She had her own means of lighting things up. She noted that the canned goods were all the pop-top variety. He would not give her so much as a can-opener that she might turn into a weapon. Agatha tilted her head to the side, thinking that all things considered, his omission was probably a good decision.

She picked the lantern up by its handle and took it with her on the short journey around her prison. No sense expending her own energy if she could help it. Agatha arrived at the cot and pursed her lips at it. Nothing more than a thin mattress that lay on a bamboo frame and slats. *Not much, but still better than cowboy camping.* A set of sheets and blankets sat folded at one end. *He could have at least made up the bed for me.*

The most curious thing in the space was easily the bookshelf that stood beside the bed. It held anything from Homer to Dan Brown. She inferred from the presence of the books that she should expect to be here awhile. *Going to be tough sledding making myself at home. This is spartan even by my standards.*

A rhythmic drumming permeated her consciousness. She revolved slowly in place, attempting to determine its source, but with no luck. The percussion reverberated as much in her feet as in her ears. It could have been coming from anywhere, or everywhere. She held the lantern above her head to expand the scope of the light. *This is stupid.* Agatha set the oil lantern down roughly, jostling the glass in the metal frame. She raised an arm overhead and sent a glowing orb aloft, bright enough to illuminate every cranny of the cavern. She squinted, letting her eyes acclimate.

A small inlet of water glittered back at her in a corner she hadn't made her way over to yet. It thrummed gently in connection with the drumming sound. Waves crashing against rocks, she realized. That was the sound. Agatha walked over to the pool, her light source trailing behind her. She squatted down and plunged her hand in, bringing a finger to lips. *Salty ... like me.*

And warm. Or at least warm-ish. That meant it was probably the Mediterranean, or one of the smaller minor seas within it.

She couldn't have identified them if her life depended on it … and hopefully, it wouldn't.

Too bad it's not fresh water, but this is something anyway. Where there was water, there was opportunity. Maybe she could get out the same way the water got in. Not likely. That would be too easy, but it would bear exploring later. She strode back to the cavern's center to finish taking inventory of her situation.

Aside from the chair at the kitchen table, the only other seat was the Savonarola that she'd been lashed to and dragged in on. The restraints had slithered away once Vulcan had dismissed himself through his portal, so the chair now sat in the middle of the room, looking mostly harmless.

Agatha struck out with her foot and kicked the ornate chair. It skittered several arm-lengths away and came to a rest. *Mostly harmless,* she thought to herself again, now wondering if she'd find *Hitchhiker's Guide* on the bookshelf. Would a space comedy make her feel more constrained than the feeling that the tight quarters were already imposing on her?

She reached out with the back of her hand, like she would with an unfamiliar dog, and touched her skin to the arm of the chair. Nothing happened.

Agatha jerked her arm away when water dripped from above, landing on her wrist. She scoffed at how jumpy she was. The water reminded her of the coolness she'd been contending with before taking her tour. Stepping backwards toward the foodstuffs, she raised her hand beside her ear and formed a ball of flame, careful not to singe her hair. Agatha shot the fireball like a free throw and landed it on the seat of the Savonarola. The orb burst into dozens of small fires and slowly consumed Vulcan's prize piece of furniture.

She burned it out of spite and loathing, and not a little bit of fear about what it could do. Had done. Both to her and to her sister more than twenty years ago. She would take her vengeance in whatever form she could get it. There was more to avenge. So much more. And she would attend to it one piece of kindling at a time.

For now, though, she would allow the chair to warm her. She stepped forward and raised her arms to the fire, tempering it. *Easy does it. Don't burn too fast. I want to savor this.* Agatha knew that as soon as the initial anger wore off, she'd have to attend to mourning her mother and worrying over Thomas. And she wasn't quite ready for either of those yet.

She looked across the flames at the scorch marks on the wall. The inverse silhouette of a titan was etched onto its surface. She made a sour face at the image. She didn't exactly regret having attacked Vulcan. What she found distasteful were her continual displays of ineptitude. It's not something she was accustomed to. Failure, yes. Sure. She'd had her fair share of that. But incompetence? Not never, but almost.

Yet every time she engaged Vulcan — her father, apparently, though she'd not quite come to terms with that revelation yet — it was one failure after another. First, Elle. Then, Joseph, which may not have been Vulcan directly, but his hand was in it. Her mother. And now herself.

Worse than the defeat and incompetence was Vulcan's awareness of it. His smug certainty. Even when he'd dragged her through the portal in that cursed chair. He had immediately loosed her bonds, the serpents uncoiling themselves from around her limbs and torso and retracting into nothingness. He backed slowly away from the chair, but not in retreat. More as though he were giving space to a child about to pitch a fit. She undoubtedly gave him what he was expecting.

Agatha leapt out of the chair and whirled to face her nemesis. Her mother's blood still coated his hands. Rage coursed through her, culminating in the fire that emblazoned her hands.

Vulcan said, "You cannot win, Agatha."

For once, he was not taunting her. There was no humor in his eyes. He spoke the truth they both knew.

Agatha was less concerned with winning than she was with vengeance. Her hands glittered with light and heat as she raised them up and set the heels of her palms against each other, letting loose a stream of fire on Vulcan.

As before, in the mines of Red Mountain, the inferno did little damage to the purported god of forge and fire. The cavern walls around him blackened. The flame that struck his apron disintegrated into embers that died on the cave floor, while his elephant-hide skin only grew pink against the blast.

Having withstood enough of her tantrum, Vulcan raised his hands to deflect the stream of fire to the side and strode toward Agatha. She backpedaled, wishing she still had the knife that was lying in the ruins of Gertrude's living room.

She scanned the room for anything she could use as a weapon, but came up empty. Vulcan watched her like a zoologist observing a newly caged tiger. He spoke over the roar of the blaze. "There is nothing here for you to use against me. I have prepared this place for your arrival. You are not the first to be held here. Nor are you likely to be the last."

She did not relent. Was incapable of doing so.

Vulcan both recognized and appreciated the lack of self-preservation. Her incapacity for concession. She was formidable. If only he could have turned her rather than making an enemy. He pounced, reaching her in one leap.

Vulcan snatched Agatha up by the throat. In her surprise, her fire sputtered out.

"Enough," he growled.

Agatha spit into his face. Through darkening vision and watering eyes, she saw that her spittle landed in the beard beside his lips. He cursed her before clenching the paw that grasped her throat. The world winked out of existence for a time.

Of course, she wasn't dead. Not yet, anyway. Agatha glanced over her shoulder at the table with its bag of groceries. From the looks of it, he didn't intend for her to die quite yet. She knew why, too. It hadn't taken her long to realize she was the bait. No different from a bucketful of chum.

But Agatha wasn't content to let things play out like Vulcan had in mind, which meant she had to figure a way out of this mess. No obvious solutions had presented themselves yet. She tilted her head upward. The stars were giving way to a graying sky that was gradually adding color to its palette. She must have been unconscious for a while. It had been well before midnight when she'd been snatched out of Hornberg and dragged into the cave.

She shook herself out of thinking about those events. She had to focus on her present situation. Still looking up, she decided there would be no climbing the walls that led to the opening at the top of the cavern.

Only the inlet of water gave her any optimism, but she kept even that at bay. Certainly, Vulcan had seen to that as a potential escape route. He had prepared this place. She had to assume he knew it well, particularly if he had detained others here, as he claimed.

Agatha rubbed absently at the crick that had formed in her neck. Being relatively still for so long had allowed soreness to creep into her bones and muscles. Her encounters with Vulcan had taken a toll. It didn't use to be like that. *Getting old ain't for the faint of heart.* She would have to recover herself a bit before exploring her only hope.

2

LEA

Luka he craned his head back to look at the Colosseum. "It's not as big as I thought it would be."

"We've all been there before, bud," Lea giggled. He was always setting himself up like that.

Despite his words, Luka had been wearing a look of awe as he gawked at the ancient stadium. But the expression fell away at the realization of Lea's comment.

Even Thomas, whose mood had been mostly dour for the last two weeks, grinned at the exchange.

"That's ... not nice," Luka said.

"Two things. First, you're protesting that it's not nice, rather than that it's not true."

"That's pretty damning," Thomas said, joining the fray.

That a boy, Thomas. Join in the fun. Lea passed a knowing look. "Second, I never promised I'd be nice, just that I'd be honest."

Luka looked bewildered. "When did you promise that?"

"Not to you, dummy," Lea said. "It's a promise I made to myself."

"Whatever." Luka looked back at the ruin, shading his eyes against the brightness of the mid-morning sun. "I'm just saying, if you're going to call it the Colosseum, it should be bigger than the futbol stadiums back home."

"You might be judging it by the wrong standard," Thomas said.

The trio stood gazing at the two-thousand-year-old arena. "I mean, it's still cool. I'm not trying to say it's not. I just thought it would be more … colossal, is all."

"I'm glad to hear that you're not disparaging one of history's great landmarks," Thomas said. "Because the Italians are pretty easy-going, but if you slander their tourist attractions, you might find yourself fighting lions like a gladiator."

"That would be awesome," Luka said.

"It's nice to hear that you think fighting is awesome *now*," Lea said, "because I seem to recall that when Thomas and I were struggling for our lives like a week ago, you and Finn were down in the basement playing thumb wars or whatever."

"Wha—" Luka protested, his face reddening. "That's not— we were trying to get out."

"Uh-huh," Lea said, feigning skepticism.

Thomas shook his head. "You're savage."

She gave him her biggest smile. "I know. It's a feature, not a bug." She might ought to ease up on Luka though. She couldn't afford to hurt his feelings right now and have him acting pouty while Thomas was still so sullen. Luka was the one who had to keep the other two from descending into darkness.

"You kind of remind me of my mom," Thomas said, with his head turned away from her, as if he didn't really want to say it aloud and would be okay with her not having heard it.

"I wish. She's a total badass," Lea said with a blush. "But don't think I'm going to cuddle with you or rock you to sleep. I know boys are weird about their moms."

Thomas' demeanor shifted, and the darkness he'd been carrying with him returned. "Okay. She's all yours," he said to Luka as he walked away.

Scheisse. Always a bridge too far. Always. Lea cringed. "Sorry."

"It's fine. Not your fault. It's just … you know."

"Yeah." If anyone knew, it was her. The night had once stripped her of her parents. And instead of being more sensitive to what Thomas was going through, she was as cavalier and callous as ever. She knew he needed from someone, anyone, more than she could give. Because, instead of dealing with the deaths of her own parents, she had just kept piling more dirt on them. It would be easier if he were like Luka and she could just distract him with fun and games. But that wasn't the world Thomas occupied. He was much too sincere for that. He kind of reminded her of Jem from *To Kill a Mockingbird*, except with super awesome können.

Steering away from the treacherous ground that Lea had led them toward, Luka said, "Hey, man, where is it you said we're going? The Roman bellybutton thing?"

"Umbilicus Urbis. The Shrine of Vulcan should be near there, but no one knows where it is for sure."

"So … how are we going to find it if people have been digging around there for two hundred years and never spotted it?"

Thomas stopped and spun to face Luka and Lea. "We are going to find it because we *have* to. Everyone else just *wanted* to."

Lea grabbed her phone out of her back pocket and flipped through her most recent text messages. "I've got the picture pulled up of that old map that Finn sent. Something called the Volcanal is supposed to be beside the Arch of Septimius Severus."

Thomas stepped back toward his friends, and the three crowded around the screen.

Lea pointed at the Volcanal on the map, right beside the Umbilicus Urbis, and asked, "You think that's it?"

Thomas shrugged noncommittally and turned to walk again.

Luka leaned toward Lea and whispered, "He's kind of moody."

"Well, yeah," Leah said, following behind Thomas so they didn't lose him in the throngs visiting the Roman Forum. "You'd be emotionally unsettled too if your grandfather killed your grandmother, then stole your mom, and your priest person turned out to be a serial killer. Or, at least, most people would be. I'm not sure about you. Sometimes I think you've got the emotional range of a jellyfish."

"Huh," Luka grunted before grinning broadly. "That stings." He started cackling. "You see what I did there?"

"Woof. That was bad. Are you sure you're not a 40-year-old dad?"

"I can't help it if I'm punny."

"Please stop. It's going to get really awkward if I have to break up with you."

Luka frowned. She watched the wheels turn in his head. He wanted to ask if she was serious. But he knew by now that she'd just double down on the threat she'd made, leaving him more uncertain than if he'd left the question unasked. To alleviate his concerns, she grabbed his hand and interlaced their fingers. "Come on. We've gotta catch up a bit. I don't want to lose him in these crowds. He's too focused on finding this shrine to pay any attention to us."

They picked up the pace, making their way past the Arch of Titus and fighting the crowds to the three pillars that remained of what had once been dedicated to Castor and Pollux. From there to the western wall of the Temple of Saturn, before coming to a stop in front of the Arch of Septimius Severus.

Thomas peered around the northern end of the arch, hampered by fences that restricted his ability to see. Lea tugged at Luka to join her inside the arch. "Look at the panels to see if there's anything about Vulcan."

"I don't even know what I'm looking for."

"Like a guy with a hammer or anvil or whatever."

They stood hip-to-hip, studying the hundreds of images that had been carved into the stone nineteen hundred years earlier. Tourists bustled all around them. Shutters clicked while people posed. A dozen different languages assaulted their ears. The jostling and distractions did nothing to ease their task.

Lea spun in sudden irritation. "Somebody just grabbed my butt."

Luka turned his head with a grin.

Her irritation did not lessen. She was not amused. She pinched a plug of skin at his midsection. "Listen to me, Luka. You know that I'm usually like what's mine is yours, and what's yours is mine."

Luka grimaced with discomfort but bobbed his head in acknowledgment.

"But now is not the time. Agatha is going to die if we don't figure this out. So you're going to have to quit being such a hound dog for a few days. Got it?"

Luka blushed and nodded. He gestured at the arch. "It's all about some war or something, I think. There's nothing about any gods here."

"Yeah, I noticed that too. Let's check in with Thomas."

Luka turned to the right and picked his way through traffic while Lea traveled in his wake. Rounding the corner from the arch, he encountered what looked more like a big broken pizza oven than any kind of monument. Three words had been etched into a stone tablet on its side: Umbilicus Urbis Romae.

"That's it?" Luka asked.

"What did you expect?" Lea said dismissively. "It's basically a big distance marker."

Luka pursed his lips as he considered it.

Lea pointed past him toward Thomas. "What's he doing?"

Thomas leaned over a railing, squinting at something. Luka

and Lea shuffled along the railing and sidled up on either side of him. "What's up?" Luka asked.

Thomas shoved his finger toward the entrance to the Umbilicus Urbis. "There's something in there."

Luka tilted his head to the left. "I don't see anything."

Thomas huffed. "Get on the other side of me."

Luka squeezed between Thomas and Lea. She pointed to a piece of paper that was rolled up and pushed into a gap in the stonework.

"So we're looking at a piece of paper?" Luka said with the inflection of someone who was certain they were missing something but had no inkling what it might be.

Lea wasn't sure it was more than a pamphlet either, but Thomas was as determined as a hunting dog that had treed a squirrel, so she wasn't going to try to dissuade him. She pulled her phone back out and retrieved the map. "So what Finn sent us says this is where the shrine to Vulcan should be. Like, right where we're standing."

She and Luka looked at the ground around them, then up at each other. Nothing. There was nothing indicating anything about Vulcan. Lea put her hand on Thomas' arm and, in the softest tone she could manage, said, "I think this is a dead end. It made sense as a starting point, but it was never going to be this easy."

Thomas pulled his arm away and vaulted over the rail. He dashed forward and snatched the rolled-up paper from the hole in the marker's entrance.

"Stop!"

Lea jerked her head around. Several meters away, a Carabinieri was storming toward them. When she turned back to Thomas, she found that he was back on the correct side of the railing, and instead of yellow paper in his hand, he held a map. Luka stood beside her with his mouth hanging open.

"Scusi. Scusi," Thomas said. "I dropped my map, and it went back there." He gestured behind himself with his thumb.

The Carabinieri scowled at him. "Do not go past rail. Signs everywhere."

Thomas lowered his eyes and held his hands in front of his chest. "Sorry. It won't happen again."

The officer grunted and stalked off, looking back over his shoulder once as he went. A stunned silence settled among them until Luka broke it. "Well?"

Thomas returned the map to one back pocket and pulled a crumpled piece of beige paper from the other. His face remained stoic as he unfurled and read it. Lea watched him for any signals but received none. When he had finished, he handed the note across to Lea.

Dearest Grandson,

I told you to search out the places of the old gods. Instead, you have come to a profane place. One where they gave me only a shrine, while Castor and Pollux were worshipped at a temple. It's good for Pollux that he was killed in battle, because if it weren't for his death and his brother begging for his resurrection, there'd have been no story to tell about him. He was entirely unremarkable.

But, I digress. The sand in the glass continues to run, and you are no closer to your mother. Seek me in the old places, Thomas. I stand alone to the west, where I am well regarded as the god of conflagration.

Yours truly,

V

Lea handed the message back to Thomas, who folded it and tucked it into his pocket.

Luka voiced the most pressing question, "What does that mean — standing alone in the west?"

Thomas shook his head. "I don't know. Here," he said,

pulling the paper back out of his pocket. "Take a picture of it and send it to Emma and Finn. They can help us figure it out. We need to go check out of the hostel and get to the train station."

"Where are we going?" Luka asked.

"Don't know. We've got some time to think it through before we have to buy a ticket."

"One request," Lea said. "Can we maybe choose somewhere that doesn't have bedbugs?"

Thomas smiled in spite of himself. "They promised they'd take care of it."

"Smashing them all over the walls and bed covers wasn't really what I had in mind."

Luka said, "For what it's worth, they also said the bed bugs only cause mild irritation."

"Luka, can you handle finding us a place to stay?" Thomas asked.

He nodded. "Once we know where we're going, I'll be on it." Turning to Lea, he added, "I guess you'll want somewhere without lice, too?"

She ran her fingers through her raven hair. "I don't know. I've always kind of wanted to go Sigourney Weaver and chop it all off."

Luka's eyes narrowed in disapproval.

"No?"

"I mean, if you look like Natalie Portman in *V for Vendetta*, I'm all for it. But you might just come off looking like a refugee. And like the late Tom Petty says, 'You don't have to live like a refugee.'"

Lea groaned, and shoved him to the side as she skipped to catch up to Thomas, who had already bailed on the conversation.

3

THOMAS

THOMAS CHECKED his email on his phone to make sure the tickets were in his inbox. When he found the message, he said to Luka, "So Finn really didn't tell you why we should go to Naples?"

"No," Luka answered. "He said they really think it's Naples, and we should call once we're on the train."

"You didn't press for more information than that?"

Luka shrugged. "No. Why?"

Thomas needed Luka to step up in a way that he hadn't been doing so far. They'd only been on this journey for a few days, but Luka's weaknesses were making themselves far more visible than his strengths. And Thomas didn't have the patience for it.

"Hang on," Lea interjected. "What platform are we going to?"

Thomas checked his screen again and pointed to a sign just ahead that read Napoli Centrale 15:45. "Fourteen. Leaves in ten minutes. We're fine."

"Let's get a car with a compartment so we can talk to Finn without an audience. No sense drawing attention talking about finding a long-dead mythical god." Lea made a rolling gesture to

"

Thomas and said, "Now, you can tell Luka why he should have asked more questions."

The trio navigated the turn from the terminal to the platform, being briefly split up by a bustling family of seven bound in the opposite direction. When they reassembled, Thomas said, "I'd like to know how they arrived at their conclusion, so I can decide if I think they're right. Because I'd rather not get on a train going an hour-and-a-half in the wrong direction, if we can help it."

"Makes sense."

That's all the concession he was going to get for the time being. Thomas scoured the windows of the train cars, looking for one with compartments. Since this was a commuter train, those were scarce. When he pointed one out, Lea led the way, navigating through clusters of people and luggage before entering the train. Luka fell in behind her as she ascended the steps. When he didn't do anything inappropriate, Thomas asked, "Nothing? You're not going to do anything to her that gets you in trouble?"

"New rules. I'm trying to behave."

"How long is that going to last?"

Luka considered the question as he hoisted himself up. "I wouldn't wager any money on it that you aren't willing to lose."

"Sounds about right," Thomas said, nodding his head toward Lea. "Looks like she found us an empty one."

Once they shut the door and stowed their bags on the overhead racks, Lea asked, "What were you two hens chirping about?"

Luka donned his most pious expression as he sat beside her. "We were discussing what a fine young lady you've become."

Lea jabbed on the underside of his thigh with her claw-like fingernails, causing him to yelp in pain. "Don't lie to me," she said.

"Alright, alright," Luka complained as he rubbed his leg. "You know, I don't have to take this kind of abuse."

"I know."

"That's it?" he asked with surprise.

"Pretty much. Yes, I know you don't have to, but I also know that you will."

Thomas tugged at the coarse hair on the side of his head, making it stand out like in old depictions of Wolverine. "Are y'all about done with couples' therapy, or should I go shove my head under the train?"

"Done," Luka said eagerly.

The train lurched forward, carrying them away from their first failed effort to locate Agatha. It picked up speed after it left Roma Termini and began its southward journey. Thomas stared out the window as the landscape evolved from its urban center to gradual countryside. All the cities were the same in that way, densest in the center and becoming increasingly less concentrated as you edged outward until it was nothing but pastures and the occasional small town.

Those outlying towns made him miss Hornberg, which had long ago become home. He hardly even remembered Birmingham anymore. He'd been so young when they left, and they'd never gone back. It was a part of his life that he rarely thought about and which mostly resided behind a closed door. One that Agatha never wanted to open.

Luka leaned forward and tapped Thomas on the knee, pulling him out of his miasma of thoughts and memories. "Can you switch seats with me? I get motion sick facing backwards."

Thomas stood, and they swapped. Lea adjusted her position and re-crossed her legs to give Thomas more space. Luka flashed her a smile from the other side of the compartment.

She scowled. "If you moved over there just to check out my legs the whole ride, I'm going to punch you."

"Not *just* to do that. I really do get motion sickness. You said

I couldn't touch, not that I couldn't look. Besides, you should take it as a compliment."

Lea's eyes flared with anger. "Let's not have you telling me how I should feel about you objectifying me, or this is going to go from lighthearted and fun to problematic real quick. So why don't you get Finn on the phone so we can figure out if we're going to the right place, and I can have a minute."

Luka pulled his phone out and punched at it several times. He held it at arm's length as it rang on the other end. His face lit up when Finn answered. "Whoa! You look terrible."

"Nice," Thomas said.

"What? Look at him," he said, turning the phone around.

Thomas and Lea waved at their friend, who smiled sheepishly through a still-swollen and disfigured face. Finn said, "The heilerin they have me seeing is kind of woo-woo. She was talking about how the physical marks mirror the spiritual wounds from this kind of trauma. So we need to give everything time to heal congruently with each other. Or something. I don't know. So in the meantime, I'm covered in bruises. Look who's here."

Luka pivoted the phone to show Emma. Thomas grinned at the sight of her, though a pang of guilt accompanied it. He hadn't called her the night before like he'd said he would. He couldn't stomach retelling his disappointment at not finding Agatha or Vulcan. So he'd begged off with a couple of text messages.

Lea took charge of the meeting. "Put your phones where we can see everybody, so we don't have to do this taking turns thing. Luka, pull out the tray to prop the phone on it, and come around here."

Once everyone had rearranged themselves, Thomas asked, "Why are we going to Naples, Finn?"

"I should think that would be obvious — Mt. Vesuvius."

"Of course," Lea said, smacking her forehead. "I should have thought of that."

Finn continued. "Beyond the obvious that it destroyed Pompeii and three other cities in 79 AD and has been active for stretches ever since — in fact, since 2018, scientists have been saying it should erupt—"

"Finn," Thomas interrupted. "Focus."

"Sorry. I've been getting really nerdy on all this volcano stuff. Anyway, it also fits the description in the note. Pull up a map."

He waited while Thomas searched his phone for a map of southern Italy.

"It's a mountain that stands alone in the western part of the country, and it's certainly renowned for its fires."

Thomas nodded, then handed his phone to Lea. He took Vulcan's message out of his pocket and unfolded it. After reading over it, he pinched in on the map in Lea's hand so he could see more of it, and started shaking his head. "I'm not sure you're right, Finn. The message doesn't say *in* the west. It says *to* the west."

Finn looked at Emma, who shook her head slightly. "I don't think we follow what you're saying, Thomas."

"The note reads, 'I stand alone to the west where I am well regarded as the god of conflagration.' *To* the west is different from *in* the west. Naples is southeast of Rome, not west of it."

"That's being very particular," Finn said. "You don't think you're reading too much into that difference?"

Thomas shrugged and hung his head. His voice was muffled when he said, "I don't know. We don't have much to go on, and I don't want to get it wrong. We can't afford to."

A prolonged silence fell over them, with the other four being uncertain how to proceed.

True to form, Luka asked, "You really think he would kill her?"

Emma covered her face in surprise. Lea's mouth gaped as she turned to Luka.

"What?" he said defensively. "We're all thinking it."

Lea said, "The rest of us had the good sense not to say it out loud."

"It's fine," Thomas muttered. "I don't actually think he would. At least, not yet."

"Why?" Finn asked.

"He wants me. It's always been me. Everyone's dead because of me." Thomas' face reddened as he collapsed under the weight that he'd been carrying. He buried his face in his hands, and his chest heaved as his breath came in ragged sobs.

Lea rubbed his back until Luka got up, knelt in front of him, and reached out to hug his friend's neck. Thomas slid onto the floor and clung to Luka's embrace. The grief he'd been repressing for a week, and which had clung at the periphery of his life for the last twelve years, poured out of him.

After a time, Thomas sat up again and wiped his eyes with the backs of his hands. He croaked, "Well, that was embarrassing."

"On the bright side," Luka said, "Finn's not the only one with a splotchy face now."

"Right," Finn agreed, "but mine has the distinction of being multicolored — purple fading to green at the edges — where his is only red."

Thomas cleared his throat. "Okay. Like I was saying before my little come-apart there, Vulcan wants me. His only shot at that is if he can hold something over me. So my mom's not any use to him dead. And unless he kidnaps one of y'all too, that's all he's got. But he gets kind of impulsive when he's frustrated — and by impulsive, I mean he kills things — so that's not something we can count on indefinitely. Everyone needs to be on your toes so you don't become bait and make the problem more complicated. Especially you, Emma, if he knows that we're, you know, together, or whatever."

"I'll keep an eye on her," Finn said, then added hastily, "Not that you need some guy to protect you. You're very capab—"

Emma laid a hand on his forearm. "It's okay. I know what you meant."

Thomas nodded. "We all need to be watching out for each other. It has nothing to do with male or female, strong or weak. We're dealing with an enemy who's more wily, experienced, and determined than any of us. It's going to take all of us at our best to pull this off. And honestly, it will be a miracle if we come out of it in one piece."

"Well, that was grim," Luka said.

"It's the truth," Thomas added. "I'm not here to cheerlead anyone or paint a pretty picture of it. This is my mother and my problem. Any of you can walk away at any time, and I won't hold it against you."

"Yeah, man, that's not what I meant."

"No one is walking away," Lea said fiercely.

Thomas sighed. "I'm just saying—"

"No," Lea said. "No one is walking out on this. We all understood the risks when we decided to get involved, and we still understand the risks." Lea looked at each person to watch them nod their affirmation. "Thomas, we are going to find Agatha, and we are going to kill that kidnapping mothe—what?!" Lea said when the compartment door slid open.

The ticket inspector held up the device in his hand. "I must check your tickets."

A trickle of laughter escaped from Luka as the tension was sucked out of the room. Thomas passed his phone down. The inspector scanned it and handed the phone back. "Grazie," he said, closing the door behind himself.

4

THOMAS

DESPITE HIS DETERMINATION not to enjoy any part of this because of how inappropriate that felt, Thomas couldn't help but be impressed by the beauty of the scenery that unfolded around them as their ride ascended Mount Vesuvius.

The small taxi pulled to a stop at the Ristorante Vesum, and the trio piled out. "It's not very nice to get dropped off in front of this restaurant when we're about to go hiking instead of eating," Luka complained.

"It's not even open yet," Lea said. "You ate breakfast right before we left. How are you already hungry?"

"Muesli and yogurt is not breakfast. It's barely a snack. Basically goat food."

"I'm starting to wonder if you're not the American, instead of Thomas."

Thomas meandered to the left of the restaurant, where a gravel path and sign marked the trailhead that overlooked the valley below them. The top of the sign read "Il Fiume di Lava." Surely, if Vulcan had anything in mind for them on this mountain — an actual volcano — it would be on the river of lava, right? He whistled at the other two, who broke off their argument and congregated around him. He pointed at the markers. "The trail goes through the woods for a bit before opening up on the lava flow."

They nodded, and Thomas walked ahead of them down the gravel path until it gave way to dirt and entered the woods, beginning its descent. The footsteps behind him fell into a rhythm, one set more of a thud than the other. "Maybe you should have worn sneakers?" he suggested to Lea.

She looked down at her Doc Martens. "These are better for stomping on snakes."

"You know that even if you see one, it isn't likely to be venomous, right?" Thomas said.

"Oh, I won't be waiting long enough for you to have a conversation with it about its intentions. If it crosses my path, I'm going to stomp it."

Thomas shook his head. He'd have to keep a lookout, particularly on the lava flow where they might be sunning, and warn off any snakes he saw.

The trees canopied over them, but it wasn't the dense vegetation and mammoth trees of the Black Forest. There was undergrowth here, but nothing lush and burgeoning with life. These plants all looked like the stragglers that were left behind when the others were either killed or immigrated away from the volcano that emptied its wrath onto them every few centuries.

From the back of the line, Luka called, "So exactly what are we looking for?"

Thomas stopped abruptly, and Lea nearly piled into him. "I don't know," he said. "Anything. Nothing. A sign. Vulcan himself. I don't know."

Luka raised a hand to his chin and rubbed at the hairs that he had allowed to sprout there. "So, how will we know it if we come across it?"

Thomas sighed, letting his exasperation show. "I don't know. And that's probably going to be my answer to most anything you ask right now. So maybe quit asking me so many questions." He didn't intend to direct his frustration at Luka, but his inquisitive friend bore the brunt of it. Only songbirds interrupted the silence that stretched out among them.

Lea glowered at him. "I'll take overreactions for four hundred."

"I know. Sorry. I'm sorry," he said, looking Luka in the eyes.

"No worries, man."

It was good to have an unassailable optimist in the group.

"Look. We know Vulcan isn't subtle and that he wants us to find him. This is all a game to him. So if there's something here, he will make sure we see it. I don't think it will be another note. He's done that twice now. Of course, that doesn't really narrow down the field of things that it could be."

"But what if there's nothing here?" Luka asked.

Thomas grunted and turned away. Lea interceded. "This trail is like two kilometers out and back. If we don't find anything, we'll just go to a different trail and start there. One of the other trails was called the Valley of Hell or something, so if he's not on the lava flow, then the Valley of Hell sounds like his kind of place. Okay?"

"But how do we get there?"

Lea stepped closer to him and lowered her voice. "No more questions. I understand you have lots of them, but no one has any answers right now. We're just taking this one step at a time. And right now, we're hiking to a lava flow, yeah?"

Luka huffed in annoyance and said nothing.

Thomas resumed walking down the path on the side of the volcano.

What a difference a few weeks made. A month ago, he and Agatha were content in their little sanctuary. Life had been normal — or what passed for normal when you lived in a community of people who had superpowers, even if that's not what they called them. Then Agatha had found a dead body, and everything had come unraveled pretty quickly after that. But really, it had already been unraveled. They just didn't know it yet. Vulcan had known where they were. He was biding his time, waiting for Thomas to grow up. What was a decade when you've lived for millennia?

The trail wound into an s-curve in a kind of meadow that housed picnic tables. Through the trees, he could see the tens of thousands of homes below that people had built in the shadow of Vesuvius. It seemed crazy to live so close to an active volcano that was always spitting out steam and had erupted again within the last hundred years. But he was living proof that people can get acclimated to just about anything and go on with their lives trying to make the best of it.

"Does anyone need to stop for a rest?" he asked.

"We've only been going for like ten minutes," Lea said.

"Just checking to see if your clunky boots had given you blisters yet."

"If they got gangrene and were about to fall off, I wouldn't tell you about it."

Beyond the meadow, the path narrowed and threatened to be overtaken by ivy and other undergrowth. Just enough foot traffic disturbed the worn dirt trail to keep it clear. Did that bode well for them? Would Vulcan take a chance on putting a clue in such a remote place with so little chance of it being found? Was he counting on Thomas looking in just that kind of place? He might as well have been playing one of those claw machines at the arcade that were designed for you to lose. This time, though, even if he won, the prize was a date with the devil.

They passed a trail marker that had once said something in Italian, but was now so weather-worn that it was no good to anyone, except to serve as an indicator that you were still on a designated path. Thomas led their descent into a forest that was not pretty. If there weren't a lava flow and the hope of a clue on the other side of it, he would have turned back long ago. He raised his shirt to wipe the sweat from his face.

Ahead of them, the hue of ambient light grew less green as the trees thinned out. In short order, the landscape shifted dramatically. Grasses and stunted shrubs replaced the ivy and overhead foliage. They had gone from a forest to a desert within a few meters.

"Look," Luka said, pointing at a rock outcropping just above them. "That's igneous rock. I bet the lava flow is just around the corner."

"Look at you with the science words," Lea teased.

Luka smiled. "I like geology. It's kind of my thing. Want to know what my favorite rock is?"

"Umm, not really."

"Come on. Ask me," Luka pled.

"Fine. Luka, what is your favorite rock?"

"Mica."

"Okay," Lea said, shaking her head in confusion. "Glad we can move past that. I'll be sure to write it down in my notebook of your favorite things."

"Do you—no, never mind. Now ask me why," he said, wiggling his eyebrows at her in anticipation.

Thomas smiled, knowing what was coming. "Go ahead. Ask him."

Lea crossed her arms and sighed, shifting her weight to one hip and taking on her sassiest posture. "Luka, so help me, if this is something dumb ... why is mica your favorite rock?"

"Because it has cleavage." Luka burst out cackling before he even finished saying it.

Lea rolled her eyes. "Oh, my gosh." She took off down the trail at a quickened pace, calling over her shoulder, "If I find Vulcan first, I'm going to ask him to go ahead and kill me. Whatever's on the other side has to be better than this hell I'm stuck in with you two."

Luka cupped his hands around his mouth and yelled, "I hate to see you leave, but I love to watch you go."

Lea made a rude gesture without looking back. She only stopped when she came to a railing just before the trail would have taken her around a bend beyond their view.

"Guess we better catch back up," Thomas said.

"I really do like her a lot," Luka said, as if he were confiding some great secret.

"Then how come you spend so much time irritating her?"

Luka shrugged as he started walking. "It's how I show my affection. Besides, she enjoys being irritated. It's like her default state."

"If you say so."

As the boys pulled up on either side of Lea, Luka slid his arm around her waist. Without breaking her gaze on the horizon, she slapped the hand that landed on her hip and shrugged it off.

Thomas smirked and shook his head. They seemed content with their dysfunction. It's certainly not something he could sustain. He needed more stability than that. One thing he liked so much about Emma was the lack of drama. Though he could do with more assertiveness from her at times. But it wasn't like you got to toggle the features you preferred. You have to find the person who best suits your needs and try not to mess it up. Maybe she was that person for him. But maybe it was too early to be thinking about stuff like that. The two next to him certainly weren't thinking along those lines.

From the railing where they'd stopped, the lava flow pointed the way down Mount Vesuvius onto the coastal plain and into the Gulf of Naples. It was an amazing sight, but it's not what he was here for. He was having difficulty not begrudging his friends taking pictures of the panorama. So he turned and headed across the gray jumble of rock that resembled pictures he had seen of the moon's surface, except that this was interrupted by goldenrod, small purple flowers, and bramble that had gained purchase in its cracks over the decades since the last eruption. He looked up the mountain toward the cone. Tendrils of steam vented into the sky.

Thomas' phone rang. He snatched it out of his pocket and looked to see who was calling. Emma.

"Hello?" he answered.

"Hi, Thomas. What are you doing?"

"You know, just hiking on the side of a volcano, looking for any clue that might lead us to my mom or her captor."

Emma paused on the other end.

"What is it?" Thomas prompted.

"It's just … I don't think you're going to find anything there."

"Y'all are the ones who sent us here," Thomas complained, scuffing his feet and kicking at a loose rock.

"I know," Emma said meekly. "But something's happened — I've had another vision from Elle."

"Oh," Thomas said with a sudden shift in his demeanor. Still anxious, but hopeful now. The last time Elle had visited Emma, she had warned them that Vulcan was coming back. "What did she say?"

"Vulcan is waiting for you."

"Where?"

Behind him, Lea and Luka rounded the bend in the trail in search of him. Thomas turned and summoned them over as Emma explained what she knew, and what she and Finn had put together.

Thomas hung up the call with a click of the red button. "Alright, we're out of here."

"Just like that?" Lea said in astonishment.

"Just like that."

Luka leaned in. "So … that means we can eat now, right?"

5

EMMA

Emma looked around at the newly foreign surroundings. She suspected someone else was taking over her dream. *Can that even happen? I guess you don't think so until it does.* She was finding it increasingly difficult to rule anything out as impossible.

The color palette shifted like her eyes were suddenly seeing the world differently. The others in the dream weren't familiar any more, as those people she knew at all appeared slightly different. Taller and slimmer. A nose that was not quite the same shape. Eyes the wrong shade of blue. It was subtle, but the perspective had shifted.

Are you supposed to be this aware in a dream? The only times she remembered ever having been aware that she was dreaming was when she fell asleep on the couch — *always when I'm napping, never at night* — and knew that she was asleep, but she was trying to wake up. She couldn't. Her body was paralyzed. She could see herself as though her spirit had detached from her body and was looking down at her. No matter how hard she strained, she couldn't make anything move, imprisoned in her own skin, until finally something gave way.

As terrifying as those episodes were, they weren't half so

strange as walking around inside someone else's dream. Or was it still hers that had been hijacked? She walked through the town she had known her whole life. Or thought she'd known. The last couple of weeks had taught her that while she was well acquainted with its exterior, what lay within the shell was dark and venomous. Perhaps that was over-simplifying things. Maybe it could be insidious, but wasn't always.

The buildings around her drained of their color, the tones shifting from the vibrant storefronts of Hornberg to sepia and then monochrome, as the color slid from the buildings into the gutters. After the last of it had dissipated, the buildings themselves melted, morphing from wood and stone to wax that drooped and collapsed into a lumpy, ashen soup. Only the road that she stood in the middle of remained unaltered. Its storm drains clogging with gray goo that piled up against itself.

Someone approached. She sensed it before she saw it. The person crossed the bridge over the Gutach. Emma clenched her jaw as the figure drew nearer. When she got close enough for Emma to identify the George Strait shirt, Emma's breath caught in her throat. This was so much different from her other dreams with Elle had ever been.

The shirt looked strange on her. It was probably fine when she was in her twenties. But now she was … a woman of a certain age. And it was just weird. And why that particular shirt? Was it what she'd been wearing when he'd taken her? The rest of her had never recovered from that, had never come out of it. Why should her outfit?

Emma walked forward to meet Elle. "Guten nacht," Emma said. "It's nice to finally meet you." She didn't add, *Thanks for not wearing my body like a Halloween costume this time.*

"He is not with her."

"Who … oh, Vulcan. He isn't with Agatha?"

Elle nodded her head.

"Where is he, then — no, where is she? That matters more."

Elle broke eye contact, looking away. Where her eyes landed, even the molten gray landscape that remained evaporated.

Everything seemed suddenly ephemeral. "Stay with me, Elle."

Elle's attention snapped back to Emma. Her eyes were forlorn and vacant. The void that consumed the town accelerated. "I do not know."

"Fine. Where is *he*, Elle? Where is Vulcan?"

Nothingness swallowed Hornberg. Emma grabbed Elle's hands as the terror and tremors overtook her. All these years later, he still consumed her.

"Where is he?" Emma asked again.

"He awaits them in the valley of his temple."

Even as Elle became translucent while the void tore at her, she grew suddenly fierce, flinging off Emma's hands and grabbing her shirt. "He wants the boy. He must not have the boy. It would be better that he was dead, that we all were dead." The last of her ebbed away as the words died in the air.

The darkness gripped Emma, groping at her. Trying to pry her mouth open and crawl inside. It coveted her life and thrummed with the desire to extinguish it.

⟁

Emma gagged as she awoke. She ran to the toilet and wretched black bile out of her belly. It felt like tar in her mouth, but as soon as it hit the water, it sizzled and desiccated before evaporating

When she was done, she sat against the wall and cried. Not sobs or wailing. Just quiet tears. Being sick always made her cry. It didn't help matters that whatever her body had just expelled confirmed that what had just happened was no mere dream.

A soft knock on the door. "Emma, are you okay? I heard you being sick."

She wiped her cheeks and eyes with the heels of her hands and cleared her throat before answering. "Ja, mama."

"May I open the door?"

Emma pushed herself up off the floor and stood up. She checked to make sure nothing of her sickness was visible and pulled the door open. Her mother stepped in and put a hand to Emma's forehead. "Are you pregnant?"

"No!" Emma balked. "What? Why is that the first thing you thought?"

"Because, my little mouse," she placed her hands on Emma's cheeks and pressed their foreheads together, "you are a teenage girl with a boyfriend, and you're being sick early in the morning. When I was in my first trimester with you, I was miserably sick every day just before dawn."

Emma pulled her face away. "First of all, we don't even — you know what, no. I'm not talking about this now. I want to brush my teeth. What time is it?"

"Almost six. I wouldn't go back to bed. You'll only feel worse. You know you can talk to me about anything, right?"

"I'm not pregnant." *And I absolutely can't talk to you about anything. You have no idea.*

"Okay. Well, I'm here if you need anything."

Emma grabbed the door handle and slowly closed the door, forcing her mother to retreat. As she brushed her teeth, she pulled Elle's words back into her mind, afraid she would forget them. *Vulcan is waiting for them in the valley of his temple. What does that even mean? And is that more or less urgent than figuring out where Agatha is?*

Emma shuffled back to her room and let herself fall into bed. Her arm flailed off the side of the bed, her fingertips strumming her phone. That sparked an idea. Her eyes flitted open, and she picked up the phone. She was going to need help figuring this puzzle out. With her thumbs, she typed out a note of everything she could remember about the dream. It took longer than she had expected, and when she read it back to herself, it sounded no less bizarre.

Emma opened up her text messages and went to Thomas. What to say? He was dealing with enough right now — should she burden him with this, too? Not yet. She wanted to give him answers, not more questions: *"Hey, I think you're in the wrong place again, but I don't know where to tell you to go yet, and I'm basing this on some crazy fever dream that your aunt appeared in."* That didn't seem helpful.

Clicking back to her other recent messages, Emma punched Finn's name. He would be up working still, so she didn't have to worry about waking him up. "Come over when you get off work. I don't think the others are going to find anything in Naples. I have a clue about where V is. Sort of. More when you get here. 11:00?"

She immediately received a thumb's up in response. That's it. She'd sent a super cryptic message before the sun was even up, and all she got back was an emoji. Boys were so dumb. Emma laid the phone back on the floor and rolled onto her side to try to catch a few more winks.

◊

"Well, what do you think?" Emma asked after she finished telling Finn about her dream.

He said, "Whatever you ate before bed, I would probably avoid that from now on."

Emma glared at him before her expression changed to one of surprise, realizing she had never told him about what happened with Elle before, either the other dreams or beside the river. She grimaced. "There's one more thing. This isn't the first time something like this has happened. Somehow, I have a connection with her, or ... I don't know, really. She's appeared in my dreams before. And while you were being held captive—"

Finn winced when she said it.

"Sorry," she said, reaching out and touching his arm gently. "Is there a better way to say it?"

He shook his head. "Just go on with what you were telling me."

"Okay. So Thomas and I went to visit her at the nursing home, and she grabbed my arm and — I don't know — took over my body to tell Thomas that Vulcan was coming." Emma shuddered at the memory. "It was weird and scary, and I made Thomas promise not to tell anyone."

Finn mulled over the new information for a while before saying, "You know what you are, don't you?"

She looked away. This was a weight she wasn't sure she could bear. It wasn't even a matter of desire, but one of capacity, capability. She nodded her head slightly. "Please don't say it out loud. The thought occurred to me after Elle spoke through me, but so much happened right away that I kind of forgot about it. Until now. I don't think I can do it, Finn."

Finn scooted around to where she sat with her back against her bed. He placed his hand on hers, and she clasped his fingers lightly.

"Our können are not burdens. They are gifts for us to use in the service of others."

Emma slid her hand away and crossed her arms. "That's very academic of you. Because it sure feels like a burden when some woman invades my dreams and then a void tries to consume me."

"Well ... yeah," he said, stumped. "You may not know this about me, but I am sometimes better with books than with people."

Emma leaned to her left and nudged her shoulder against his. "We were in the same nursery together. I know most everything there is to know about you," she said with a smile. But she caught a look in his eye before he looked away that suggested she may not know everything. To avoid anything getting weird, she diverted back to the earlier topic. "I thought … oracles were a können whose time had passed."

"Every age has its own oracle," Finn said.

She regretted the diversion. She still wasn't ready to be some kind of medium or prophet or whatever else the new development entailed. "Let's dig into our other problem, then. What should we start with, where Vulcan is or Agatha?"

"Vulcan. Agatha's location is too cryptic. We don't even really have a starting place for it yet. Besides, Vulcan seems to be the more immediate issue, and he can tell us — no, tell *them* where Agatha is."

"It is *us* though. This is going to take all five of us."

"You and I are not part of them," Finn argued. "We aren't in any danger sitting here in our houses. Well, I'm not, anyway. I don't have ghosts shoving stuff down my throat. I'm just logistical support. 'Hey, we need some information. Call Finn. He can help.'"

Emma took a deep breath. She hadn't expected this. Finn was always so even-keeled. "Do you know what Agatha says to Thomas when he's pouting about something?"

Finn did not hide the offense he took at being told he was pouting, but shook his head anyway.

"Buck up, buttercup."

He looked at her expectantly. "That's it?"

"Yes."

"What does that even mean?"

Emma shrugged. "I'm not sure exactly. But it's like we've got things to do, so get it together. You and I, we have things to do. We are the only ones who can do them, because we have information the others don't have. So you need to get it together."

"Okay."

"I don't know if that's a sarcastic 'okay' or not."

"It means I'll get it together."

"Okay," Emma said with a smile, glad that her chastisement had held his self-pity in check. "Grab your tablet out of your bag, and let's see if we can sort out what Elle meant by saying Vulcan is waiting in the valley of his temple."

Finn leaned over and dragged his canvas messenger bag across the floor.

Emma said, "Maybe with some of that money you're making, you can get yourself a nicer bag."

Finn looked affronted. "What? I like this one. I got it at any army surplus store."

"It looks like something the Soviets abandoned in East Berlin on their way out."

"I like it," he repeated. After clicking around for a few minutes, he said, "Look here." Finn tilted his screen so Emma could see. "I searched for temples of Vulcan. There really aren't very many. There's the one in Rome."

"Well, we know that's not it," Emma said.

"Right. And I think we can rule out the one in Alabama."

"I sure hope so, or they're going to have to make some new travel arrangements."

"Besides," Finn said. "It's on top of a mountain, not in a valley."

"It's not really a temple. Thomas says it's just a big statue."

"That too. The only other notable temple in Italy is in Sicily."

"Umm." Emma covered her face in embarrassment. "I can never remember which one is Sicily and which one is Sardinia."

"Sicily is the one at the end of the boot."

"So they aren't that far away?"

"Yes and no." Finn pulled up a map of Italy. "They're not that far, but they'll have to fly into Palermo, then take a train down to Agrigento. A train ride from Naples would take forever."

"Alright, but Thomas may not take this very well since we

just sent him to Naples for no reason. How confident are we about this?"

"Pretty confident, I think," Finn said. He pointed at Rome. "This is where they were when they found Vulcan's note that told them to go west — which we misinterpreted. And the Vulcan temple at Agrigento is in the Valley of Temples. So it seems to fit all the criteria."

"I'll call Thomas then."

6

LEA

RAIN PLINKED at the roof of the train and ran in rivulets down its windows. Lightning crackled in prolonged bursts, revealing the sleepy Sicilian hill country. Without looking up from her book, Lea said, "I need a bath. I feel like I've been cooped up for days."

When she didn't get a response, she looked over the top of her e-reader. Thomas dozed across from her with his hood pulled up, shrouding his face. Luka's tablet illuminated his face as superheroes fended off a villain and his earbuds muted the outside world.

Lea sighed, pushed the power button on her e-reader, and laid it on the table. She pushed herself off the seat and swiveled, straddling Luka on her way to the aisle. His tablet clattered to the floor, and his expression told Lea he couldn't have been more surprised. She stayed there a second longer than necessary, his hands pinned to his legs, before shifting her weight and sliding off. Before she walked off, Lea leaned down and popped his earbud out. Touching her lips to Luka's ear, she whispered, "Bathroom in the next car. Two minutes."

She heard his breath catch. Lea smiled as she walked away. She swayed with the rocking of the train. She could get used to this kind of travel. In the space between destinations, time seemed to displace itself. Especially on the Italian trains, which were far more laissez-faire about arrival and departure times than the German counterparts.

As Lea unlatched the door and stepped into the space between cars, she wondered how many accidents happened where someone fell through and got run over. She entered the next car and went into the WC that was just inside, closing the door behind her without latching it. It wasn't particularly clean, but it wasn't a disgusting mess either. It would do for what she had in mind, anyway.

She propped herself up on the countertop, which turned out to be a little less dry than she had thought. It made an uncomfortable groaning sound as she settled. Lea winced and prepared to vault off of it, but the structure held.

She unbuttoned the top couple of buttons on her shirt — *just enough, but not too much* — when the train door opened, followed by the bathroom door. She flung her head so that her hair draped over her shoulder on one side.

A gray-haired man stepped in, lurching to a stop in the threshold. He leered, looking her up and down. Lea swung a booted foot in his direction and said, "Get out, perv!"

She heard a muffled, "Excuse me," from around the corner as Luka edged past the man who was ambling away. He, too, froze in the doorway. "You accommodating all the patrons?"

"Shut the door, dummy."

He turned partway around and fumbled for the door, not wanting to look away. Afraid that he'd miss something.

She waited on him expectantly, and was caught entirely off guard when Luka furrowed his brow and said, "Hold on, now."

Lea raised her eyebrows in a question.

Luka crossed his arms. "I thought you said there wasn't going to be any making out or — I don't remember what else you said."

She appreciated the vain effort to show some backbone. She shrugged and said, "I'm bored."

"You're bored? So … what? I'm just your play thing for when you need some amusement."

She shrugged again.

"I don't think I like how that feels," Luka said with more truth than either of them cared to inspect at the moment.

"Well, if you'd rather not," she said, sliding down to the floor, "we can head back and read our books."

"Wait. That's not what I said."

"That's what I thought. Now, come here, and let's see if we can sort out those feelings."

◊

When Lea and Luka slid back into their seats, Thomas still leaned against the corner with his hoodie covering his eyes. Moving nothing other than his lips, he asked, "Did you two get yourselves sorted out?"

Luka wore a bashful look. "What? We were in the bar car."

"Uh-huh. What did you have?"

"A high roller," Luka said with confidence before faltering and whispering to Lea, "Is that a drink?"

She shrugged. "Don't know. Don't drink."

Thomas slid his hood backward. "You don't?"

Lea shook her head. "Addictive personality. My aunt — before she quit fighting it and became a junked out shell of herself — said she spent her whole life feeling like she was jumping from one full-speed train to another one going in the opposite direction and just hoping the landing wouldn't be too rough. Right now, this one here," she said, pointing a thumb at Luka, "and chasing bad guys are about all the vices I can stand."

"Why didn't you ever tell me this before? I mean, I thought you used to party and … you know, all that stuff."

"When would we have talked about this? In one of our long heart-to-hearts? That hasn't really been our thing. Look, it's fine. When you talk a certain way and dress a certain way, people make assumptions about who you are and what you do. It doesn't matter that they've never seen you do the things they talk about, and if they asked the right questions, no one else has actually seen it easier. It's just your reputation. And it's kind of like a river. You can fight it if you want, and you might gain ground for a while, but eventually it's going to do its thing and the current's going to get the better of you. So it's easier just to go with the flow."

"That's not fair to you, though," Luka said.

Lea laughed harshly. "Fair? Look at any part of my life and tell me what you think is fair. Besides, there's no such thing as fair. That's just what we say to justify whether we got what we think we deserved." *Well … that was unexpected. I guess that had been building up for a while.*

"Whoa," Luka said. "That's heavy."

"Emma's the only one who bothered to inspect whether things were as they seemed. She was my only real friend for a long time."

"Y'all did seem like an odd pairing," Thomas said. "Makes more sense now."

"Even you two only came to be friends with me through her. And our friendships were pretty shallow until recently."

"Turns out a missing friend and facing a serial killer adds some instant depth to relationships," Thomas said.

After a prolonged silence, Luka added, "I'm sorry. I know you said it's fine earlier, but it's really not."

"You're right. It hasn't been fine, but it's getting there. In a weird way, all this terrible stuff has helped put things into perspective a bit. And it's drawn us all closer. I mean, I wouldn't wish it on anyone, but I don't regret it either."

Thomas' face grew dark. "That's because your grandmother wasn't murdered, and it's not your mother we're looking for."

Lea covered her mouth with both hands. "Oh, Thomas. I'm so stupid. That's not what I meant."

"I know," he said, standing up. "I'll be back. I need some air." He slipped out and slunk toward the back of the train car.

Luka gloated, "I've gotta say, it feels fantastic not to be the person who said something monumentally dumb." When Lea punched him in the ribs, Luka grunted, but his smile didn't falter. "You really didn't think that through, did you?"

Lea opened her mouth, then closed it, dropping her head. "No. I did not. Since you have more experience with this, I guess I should ask, what do I do now?"

"I normally try to deflect with humor."

"Does that work?" she asked.

Luka shook his head. "Not really. It usually makes things worse. But then they get mad about the not-funny thing instead of the hurtful thing. Or maybe it's both. I don't know. I'm not very good at de-escalating."

"That was very helpful. Thanks."

Luka turned to the aisle, looking over his shoulder to see if Thomas had stayed in their car. He turned back to Lea and asked, "You think I should go talk to him?"

"No. I think I should."

"Are you sure? No offense, but you're kind of the reason he left."

Lea gestured at Luka to get up. "That's exactly why it should be me. Now, let me out."

"You don't just want to climb over me again?"

"No."

"Oh," Luka said, not hiding his disappointment. He stepped out into the aisle. Lea scooted out and past him, heading in the direction Thomas had gone. She traversed several cars without seeing any sign of him. Finally, she came to the last car, which housed the bicycles and oversized luggage. Lightning flashed, showing rain streaming off the back of the train like condensed contrails. *It's going to be fun finding our way to the hostel if this doesn't let up.*

"Hey," Thomas said.

She spotted him propped against the wall between two boxes.

"Hey," she returned the greeting as she walked in his direction. "Scooch."

Thomas moved to his right, and Lea slid down beside him. They sat shoulder to shoulder on the floor, backs against the side of the train.

"You know, it's not that long ago that you wouldn't talk to me because I accidentally set Luka on fire. And now you're scrunched up beside me on a train in Sicily."

"I'm sorry about what I said. It was dumb and insensitive."

"No worries. I know what you meant. But I gotta say, I'm not really accustomed to apologetic Lea. Where did snarky Lea go?"

"Oh, she's still around. Don't worry. She's just trying to contribute more to conversations than sarcasm these days." She put a hand on his forearm. "So, in the spirit of turning over new leaves — do you want to talk about your mom or oma? I had no one to talk to when my parents died. And that could have been helpful. Maybe snarky Lea would have had less of an edge about her. Or maybe we can talk about what comes next?"

Thomas looked into her eyes. She felt a little fluttery inside and pulled her hand back. A lot was going on behind those eyes. Their intensity was nearly overwhelming. She'd never seen him in this way before. No wonder Emma was so taken with him. It was very compelling.

"This is the place. I can feel it," Thomas said.

Lea bit her lip. She held plenty of doubt in reserve, but that's not what he needed right now. "Guess we'll get to test that feeling tomorrow. I hope you're right."

7

AGATHA

AGATHA STOOD at the edge of the inlet of water, considering. Her reflection stared back at her impatiently. Swimming had never been her thing. She *could* swim, just not well. But that wasn't really what restrained her from exploring the blue waters below. It was the idea of getting lost under there and drowning.

Of all the deaths she could imagine — and she had seen men die in an extraordinary number of ways — drowning seemed one of the most terrifying. You were aware of what was happening to you. The fear of being unable to surface. Then the decision to fill your lungs with the water that would kill you. Or was it a reflex at that point, your autonomic nervous system overriding your will? How long did the pain last before your oxygen-starved brain clicked off forever?

Agatha shivered and turned away. Not today. She hadn't reached the necessary level of desperation. Besides, she should do it when the tide was lower. That way, she'd have less water to traverse. *There you go.* Now she could attribute her decision to logic rather than cowardice.

At the table, she poured herself a cup of water. Less than two gallons left. She drank in sips. Even though she'd been limiting herself to only two cups a day, she watched obsessively as the jug's contents continually diminished. There was still plenty for now. But how many days since he had left her here? She looked at the marks she'd made on the wall with one of the charred remains of the chair she'd burned.

Ten days. Each an eternity. Eight days to a gallon. That gave her two more weeks down here before she ran out. She could reduce her rations further, but she was already feeling the effects of dehydration. Lethargy tugged at her, and even small expenditures of energy bore a cost. She could not cut back yet. She would re-assess in a few days.

Agatha's belly grumbled at her. Thirst wasn't her only problem. On the bright side, though, she'd cut those extra pounds that had been nagging at her. All it took was a little imprisonment with finite food resources that had to last an unknowable amount of time. *Easy peasy. Maybe this is my million-dollar idea.* "First, there was the Atkins diet. Then, there was keto. But those don't hold a candle to the results you'll get from the Agatha Plan. Just take yourself down to your basement and lock the door. Then swallow the keys. Enjoy the taste because it's the last thing you get to eat."

Agatha clapped a hand over her mouth. She couldn't start talking out loud to herself. Not yet. That felt like a threshold she'd rather not cross.

To distract herself and deal with one of her other pending problems, she shuffled to the table and sat. She sorted through the canned goods, settling on green beans. The top popped off easily enough, and she flung it blindly over her shoulder. It gave a satisfying series of pings as it clanged against the other discarded items.

She ate the beans one at a time, hoping that by savoring each one — though they could do with a bit of salt — her stomach would believe that it was being sated. It didn't, and growled at her more defiantly instead. *Don't worry, tummy. I'll drink the juice when I'm done too. Or maybe I need to save that for later.*

A bird squawked as it flew overhead. Agatha looked upward by instinct, though her narrow angle of view rarely allowed her a glimpse of the things that funneled sounds down into her cavern. She had begun to think of the cavern as hers, even with the occasional indicators she found that others had resided there before her. *Wild what a week-and-a-half will do.*

Movement caught her eye as something bounced off the rim of the hole atop the cavern and fell in, crashing to the floor with a wet thud.

Agatha shoved her chair backward and ran to it. A reddish purple object about the size of a small onion lay crumpled on the ground. She got down on her hands and knees to inspect it, nudging it with a finger before picking it up to look at the flattened side. It had split from the impact, and Agatha peeled it in half. A fig. A badly bruised fig. The bird must have dropped in on her way over. *Too bad the bird didn't fall in. Then, I could have a proper meal. Stop. Be thankful for what you got, girl.*

Agatha devoured the first half of the fig, not having had fresh food since the day she'd been ripped out of Hornberg. She thought it might be the best thing she'd ever eaten in her life. She had an epiphany — Fig Newtons didn't do justice to figs, and if people had a different entry point into figs, it'd be a much more popular fruit. Agatha looked down at her left hand and briefly considered saving the second half for later. In her present state, though, she had no interest in mustering the self-discipline necessary for such restraint.

With a mouthful of fig, Agatha had a second revelation — if things could fall into the hole, things could fly out of it. She smacked herself in the forehead with a sticky palm. "Dummy," she said aloud. In a different mental state, this would have occurred to her much sooner.

She stood from where she had been squatting and traipsed

over to what she thought of as her watering hole, despite her inability to drink from it. She rinsed her hands and washed the stickiness from her face, then shrugged her shoulder forward to wipe off her mouth and cheek.

With her eyes toward the craggy opening at the top of the cavern, Agatha strode up the small precipice that was the highest point on the cave floor. The night sky shone stars at her, daring her to create her own constellation.

This could be her salvation. A flare would certainly draw attention if anyone was within miles. She raised her hands overhead. They quaked with anticipation. Agatha closed her eyes and breathed in deeply to steady herself. She formed an orb of fire in her hands, evaporating the remaining water from them and leaving only salt crystals.

Small waves of heat radiated toward her face. With her eyes still closed, she propelled the ball of fire upward. It rocketed toward the opening. Agatha opened her eyes in time to see her conflagration splatter against the roof. *Well, obviously, that wasn't going to work. Still, that hole's the size of a car tire. Shouldn't have missed that wide.*

While the first attempt had failed, it released the jitters. Just to be sure, she gave her hands a good shake before gathering herself for a second effort. Butterflies erupted in her belly as she readied herself. "Alright, settle down." One big, slow breath in. She held it for a beat, knowing she would fire on the exhale, just like discharging a pistol. She squinted her left eye closed to aim with her right. Exhaling slowly, Agatha allowed the energy to grow and swirl around herself before collecting into a sphere of light and heat that burst from her hand.

It flew toward the opening. When it reached its target, the orb dissipated into a thousand sparkling droplets that fell back to earth like a meteor shower.

Agatha collapsed to the floor, landing hard on her knees, and putting her hands out to catch herself as she fell forward. He'd done something to keep anything from getting out. She should have known, but instead, she'd allowed herself to hope. Hope that she could escape. That she could get back to Thomas, wherever he was. That they could finally end this. No more running. No more hiding in quaint little towns with a false sense of security.

But that hope had just been quenched. She should have known better than to conjure it in the first place.

Her ears perked up at a shuffling sound at the far end of the cavern. She didn't look up. She didn't need to.

8

AGATHA

V ULCAN LEANED his hulking frame against the cavern wall. "Agatha," he said, feigning disappointment. "You need not have signaled to get my attention. Are you that desperate for it? I know I've been an absentee parent, but there's no need for theatrics."

Taunting, always taunting. She purposed in her heart not to rise to it. He expected her to lash out. It's how she always responded to him. How could she do anything else when he had taken so much from her? But she must not. She had to be restrained, strategic. It was her only chance. She had already established — a couple of times now, and at great cost — that she couldn't beat him by sheer force of will.

When Agatha remained on hands and knees and neither moved nor spoke, Vulcan said, "I'm not angry, just disappointed. It's been ..." He looked down at his watch and then back at Agatha before gesturing at something on the wall that had caught his attention. "Ah, I see you've got your own calendar going. It took you ten days to attempt to escape. I would have expected that to have happened much sooner. What with you wanting to avenge your mother, and with your sweet little boy out there scouring the earth, trying to find you."

She looked up. "Thomas?" Agatha asked, finally breaking her silence.

"Yes, Thomas. Who else? But he's been looking in all the wrong places. I left him a note, trying to give him a clue. But maybe I was unclear."

"Where is he?"

"Italy. Looking for the Roman god of fire and forge. But I'm not Roman, am I? No, I'm a good bit older than that. The Romans just appropriated the cultures of those who came before them."

Agatha played along. It seemed like the only way she might get any information. "To be fair, you do go by your Roman name. I assume you think it sounds better than … come to think of it, I don't know what the Greeks call you."

Vulcan shifted his weight and crossed his arms.

Agatha barked a laugh, "You've had like three thousand years to get used to your name and you still don't like it?"

"Hephaestus," he said glumly.

"Alright, Festus, where sh—"

"Don't," he warned. "I have very little good will toward you to begin with. You are little more than a snare so the boy can have a choice in his fate."

"You have kind of a skewed perspective of free will, don't you? But whatever. If I'm not in Italy, where should he be looking instead?"

"Oh, come now. You didn't think it would be that easy, did you? So disappointing. Maybe I should have stolen *you* away instead of your sister all those years ago. She was always the smarter one, wasn't she? She would be more fun to play games with. More of a challenge."

Agatha pushed herself up to standing. He was right, of

course. Elle was the brains. She was the muscle. Force was always her first option. She had lived her life by the idea that if force wasn't working, you weren't using enough. *And look where that has gotten you.*

"I need more water," she said.

He looked to his right. "You have sufficient supplies for now. It is not my intent for you to die here. Well, that's not entirely true. I do not intend you to die of natural causes. Yes," he said with a nod, "that's a more accurate statement."

"Is he okay?" she asked.

"Of course he is." Vulcan said dismissively. "I have grand plans for him."

"To be a part of your army?"

"No. I am done with armies and underlings. Too much hassle. And as you have seen for yourself, too much incompetence and opportunity for disruption. The boy will be my apprentice. I will raise him up to be greater than myself. To use his powers to control legions and ascend to heights that few are capable of. And when he is ready, he will crush me because I am an obstacle to his ascension. It is the natural order of things. The lion kills his father when he senses the elder's weakness and is prepared to command the pride."

"And you?" Agatha said. "Did you kill your father?"

"No," he said, his voice heavy with regret. "He met his demise at the hands of others. My raising was ... atypical for my kind."

Agatha's curiosity got the better of her. She engaged, despite her intentions to do otherwise. "Oh?"

"You do not know my story?"

She couldn't tell if he was genuinely surprised or putting on a show. "Can't say I was ever curious enough to dust off my history books." She knew it would hurt his pride that she cared so little. She wasn't trying to gain any tactical advantage with it, just being petty.

"Well, you have time now," Vulcan said.

"I might rather you just kill me," she said smugly.

With a sudden coldness in his voice, he said, "Keep it up, Agatha, and I may accommodate your request."

She had pushed the envelope far enough, and it was wobbling precariously on the edge. She shifted her demeanor, becoming acquiescent. More important than running her mouth was staying alive to see her boy again. "Alright, let's hear it."

"My parents were Zeus and Hera—"

"Hold it. Timeout."

Vulcan grumbled in frustration. "What?"

"Like *the* Zeus? You're not just messing with me?"

"Yes. And I thought you weren't interested?"

Agatha tried to reign in her curiosity. "Well, I wasn't until you started telling me that my grandparents were the king and queen of the Greek gods."

"It wasn't like that," Vulcan fussed defensively. "You know as well as anyone that we're not gods. The stories got a little carried away with some accounts of things over the years. Some, but not all."

"Fine," Agatha said. "Get back to whatever it is you have to tell me."

"When I was born ... I was hideous and lame."

"Oh, you're definitely still lame."

Vulcan leaned in with a reddening face. "Last warning. If you insist on making snarky comments like a petulant child, I can just kill you and be done with it."

Agatha shrugged, trying to seem indifferent, though the subject of her own death was one of the few topics she was decidedly not apathetic about. Still, Vulcan stared down at her with quiet intensity, waiting for a more committal response.

"If you're waiting for an apology from me," Agatha said, gesturing around the cavern in which Vulcan was holding her captive, "we're going to be here a hot minute. But I will keep the sniping to a minimum."

Vulcan continued, "I was born lame in one leg, and I was terrible to look upon."

Agatha couldn't help but look down at his legs.

He shook his head. "I have had several millennia to resolve the problem. But I have not told the whole truth. It has never been clear to me whether I was born lame or if I became lame when Hera cast me out as an infant because she couldn't bear to look at me. She left me to die—"

"Harsh," Agatha mumbled. "I guess that sticks with you for a while."

"Indeed. I got my revenge, but it's fair to say it influenced who I have become."

"Oh, you think that had something to do with you being a supervillain?"

"I have more to tell, if you would hear it," he said with reproach.

Agatha could see his irritation in the way his lip snarled. She did not relent in prodding at him. "Yes, please, tell me more about your justifications for having become a murderous bastard." *You can't quite rein it in, can you?*

"Fine." Vulcan spun on his heel and opened a portal.

"Wait," Agatha said, a little more desperately than she would have liked.

Vulcan paused and looked over his shoulder. Agatha mimed zipping her lips and throwing away the key, just like Thomas had done when he was little. He raised an eyebrow at her, and Agatha sat cross-legged and made an X over her heart.

With his frustration assuaged for the moment, Vulcan continued his story. "After I was cast out and left for dead, I was taken in by a sea nymph and a titan. They raised me in a hidden cavern on the edge of the world."

Agatha opened her mouth to ask a question, but thought better of it. She raised her hand and waited to be called upon.

Vulcan waved her off. "No, not this one."

She lowered her hand.

"As I got older and stronger — and frankly, more bitter and devious — I plotted my revenge against Hera. Even after she took me back in once she realized my skills with the forge and woodworking, I schemed and waited. Eventually, I built a golden throne that I presented as a gift to her. She should have been suspicious of it. But she was too much of a narcissist. As soon as she sat on the throne — well, you can probably guess what happened next. You've seen that episode before. Once she was bound up, I carted her off to a cavern that I had prepared for the occasion."

Agatha's arm shot up again.

"Yes, it was this one. May I proceed?"

Slowly, she withdrew her hand from the air and placed it in her lap. *Hell's bells. I'm in the same prison that held a goddess. No, not a goddess. Someone else like me but with different können. Just, you know, a few thousand years ago.* Agatha looked around in awe, wondering if she had missed anything that previous occupants had left behind. She had a thousand more questions, but it was more important to accrue whatever information he was willing to give her than to risk not finding out something because she interrupted him too hastily. She nodded her head.

"I left her here for days. First, the others begged me to release her. Then they threatened. Particularly, Zeus. He was ... displeased. He had a reputation to uphold, after all, and having his castaway son imprison his wife didn't fit within that framework. After none of that worked, they made promises, offering me riches and a seat on Mount Olympus. None of it mattered. I had been planning this for decades. I was content to let her rot here."

After an inordinately long pause in which Agatha thought he

might not finish the story, she prompted him, "So what happened?"

"Do you know the story of Sampson?" Vulcan asked.

"The strong guy in the Bible. Sure, I guess."

"Do you remember how the Philistines finally captured him?"

Agatha was a little fuzzy on the details. "They cut his hair?"

"Yes, but to do that, they had a woman seduce him into telling her his weakness. It's a tactic as old as time itself. Because it's effective. And it worked on me. Aphrodite got me drunk and talked me into releasing Hera."

"I get the … uhh … commonalities and all, but why are you telling me this?"

Vulcan shrugged. "Aren't fathers supposed to regale their children with stories about the past that the kids don't really care about? Besides, I don't frequently have a captive audience."

Agatha's mouth fell open. "Are you — are you making puns about my imprisonment?"

He grinned wryly and gestured, opening a portal to his left. "Is there anything you'd like me to tell the boy?"

"Wait. What?! You're leaving, just like that?"

"Yes," Vulcan said.

"You're going to see him?"

"Clearly, he will not find you on his own. He needs a little guidance. And maybe it's better that I go to him in Italy rather than let him catch your scent. And maybe I have a little proposition for him."

"Stay away from my son!" Agatha roared.

Vulcan laughed and turned away from her. "Or what? You're as impotent here as a eunuch."

Agatha jumped to her feet, summoning an extraordinary amount of energy and unleashing it at Vulcan, who ducked with the instincts of one who is accustomed to evading attack. The giant ball of fire crashed through the portal and delivered a thunderous explosion from the other side. Vulcan sprang back upright and turned to Agatha with widened eyes. "Adio, Agatha." Vulcan leapt through the portal, lithe as a lynx, and closed it behind himself.

Agatha slumped back to the ground, exhausted, and buried her face in her hands.

9

THOMAS

Lea cast a sideways glance at Luka. "Umm ... why are you putting your bag on the same bed as mine?"

"I thought it would be nice?" he answered.

"No. First of all, these are twin-size beds and there are five more of them in this room. Second, unless we are in danger of hypothermia, we are absolutely not sleeping all cuddled up like a nest of squirrels. Only monsters sleep where they're touching another person. Third—"

"Alright, I get it already," Luka complained.

"I'm not done. Don't interrupt me." She paused to see whether he was going to comply. He crossed his arms and stared at the floor, but said nothing. "Third, don't be so presumptuous."

"Done?" Luka asked, his anger clear behind his reddening face.

Lea nodded. "Yeah, I am."

He picked his pack up and threw it over his shoulder before walking to the furthest bed in the room and dropping it there. He opened it up, making a show of concerning himself with the contents of his toiletry bag.

"So things are going well, then?" Thomas said.

Lea sighed. "We need to work on our boundaries. Just because I want to make out sometimes doesn't mean he has an open invitation to get into my bed."

"Make out? I thought y'all …" he considered the most politic way to say it, "were more involved than that."

"Didn't we just talk on the train about making assumptions?" she said defensively.

Thomas apologized and said, "It's just the way you talk about things, I thought … you know. Besides, we also talked about Snarky Lea chilling out for a bit."

"One thing at a time." She added more quietly with flushing cheeks, "I talk a big game, but that's about it. My therapist says it's a defense mechanism. If people assume the worst already, I can't disappoint them."

An awkward silence fell over them like a fog. Thomas didn't know how to find his way out of this, so he just let it lie.

When Lea had enough standing there looking at the worn toes of her boots, she asked, "So you got any ideas about how to deal with him?"

"Have you considered being more direct and using words to express how you feel — like you just did with me?"

"Ugh," she grunted.

"That's what I figured," Thomas said. "Let me just offer this as someone whose mother wasn't always super expressive: sometimes words are helpful."

"Whatever."

"Well, I need you to go make nice so we can go out to the temple and do this."

"Tonight?"

"Yes, tonight. I don't want to wait until tomorrow."

Lea pointed to her wet hair and damp shirt. "It's still raining."

As if to emphasize the point, thunder rumbled outside.

Thomas shrugged indifferently. "You won't melt. Wear a poncho."

"What's a poncho?"

"It's a rain jacket that you pull over your head. You see people wear them at futbol matches when it's raining."

"When do you think I last watched a futbol match?"

"That was more of a general *you*," he said. "Luka, help me out. Do you know what a poncho is?"

"Are you sure it's not too intrusive if I answer that question?"

This is what Thomas had been afraid of from the start. It would have been a minor annoyance if they'd been home and were separable, and Emma could help him mediate things. But here, when he needed both of them to have their heads in the game, it was going to be really problematic. Under his breath, he said, "You have to fix this."

"Yeah, yeah," she muttered, walking across the room. "Hey, dummy, we need to talk."

Thomas turned to his backpack and tuned them out. Either they'd sort it out or they wouldn't. He just hoped it didn't come to a point that he had to choose which one to keep and which one to send home. There might be no coming back from that.

He unzipped an interior pocket of his pack and pulled out the two notes from Vulcan that were scrawled on yellow paper. *We can't miss anything else.* The only part of the first note he'd found at Oma's house that seemed to matter read "… you will have to seek out the places of the old gods. Maybe then we can attend to our unfinished business." There was little doubt about their unfinished business. It wasn't often that a schopfer came along, and Vulcan had plans for Thomas. Plans that Thomas had no intent to succumb to. It was the part about the old gods that had him flummoxed. They hadn't gotten that right yet. They were missing something, but he didn't know what.

Thomas laid the message on the bed and unfolded the note they'd found in Rome. He had it more-or-less memorized by now. Again Vulcan mentioned the old places, but he was more specific in this letter than he'd been at any other point: "I stand alone to the west where I am well regarded as the god of conflagration."

Luka and Lea walked over and stood on either side of him. He asked, "What was Emma's message from Elle?"

Lea pulled her phone out of her back pocket and tapped on her most recent message from Emma. "About Vulcan: He's waiting for you all in the valley of his temple. He wants T. Elle says you can't let that happen — we'd all be better off dead than T joining V."

"Finn and Emma think this is the place," Thomas said. "Anyone disagree?"

"No," Luka answered. "But I think we should do it tomorrow instead. If he's waiting like she said, make him wait longer. He might have set traps we can't see in the dark."

Thomas finally looked up from the papers. "He's not the only one waiting. I don't know what he's doing to her. But I do know that Elle never recovered from it, and she was only there for a few days. My mom has been there ..." He looked down at the date on his watch.

"Ten days," Lea said.

"Ten days," Thomas repeated.

Luka raised his hand.

Lea said, "Do you have a question?"

"Yeah. What happens if he's there at the temple? What do we do then?"

Lea looked at Thomas. "I believe that one is for you."

"I'm not really sure," Thomas answered as he picked up the notes and folded them pack into quarters. "He must have some kind of weakness, but I don't know what it is."

"Is there something we can trade him?" Luka suggested.

"What he really wants is me. That's what all this has always been about. So I don't think anything else will do. I've been thinking through it for days now and haven't figured anything out yet. I guess we'll just have to wing it."

"I have just one more question," Luka said.

Thomas headed it off at the pass. "Yes, we're going to eat before we go to the temple."

"Oh, good. That's been weighing on me. I know I signed up for Vulcan hunting, but I can't very well go fighting baddies on an empty stomach."

Lea raised an eyebrow at him. "Oh, you're going to fight him, are you?"

Luka flexed his biceps. "That's why I brought these guns along."

"Oh, geez."

Thomas smiled. Luka did bring a much needed lightness, even if it was sometimes misguided or obnoxious. Thomas grabbed his tablet off the bed and brought it to life. A map of the Valley of the Temples appeared. "We are directly north of the park now. We'll get a taxi to drop us off at the Temple of Zeus, which is basically in the middle, then follow the trail northwest to the Temple of Castor and Pollux." He dragged his finger across the screen. "Over here, off to the west by itself, is the Temple of Vulcan."

"Why does it say 'Efesto' out beside his name?" Luka asked.

Lea said, "That's the Italian translation of his Greek name, Hephaestus."

"Wait, Vulcan isn't Roman?"

"None of the Roman gods are originally Roman."

"If my name was Fester, I'd go by Vulcan too. I'll have to ask him about that," Luka said.

Thomas closed out his tablet and shoved it in to the pack. "Is that before or after you fight him?"

"Before, for sure. I'm not sure he'll be in any condition to answer questions afterward," Luka answered with a bravado that he tried to wear confidently.

63

10

THOMAS

THE TRIO STEPPED out of the car into a torrent of rain and wind. "At least we're on top of a plateau, so there's no protection from the elements," Luka yelled to the others as their ride's taillights wandered away from them into the night.

Lea pulled Thomas close. "Which way do we go?"

He pointed at a glow emanating through the trees to the west. They hustled across the road and onto the trail until Thomas stopped and hollered, "Dagummit!"

Luka hurried back to him. "What happened?"

Thomas lifted his foot and said, "Stepped in a huge puddle. My foot is soaked."

Luka shrugged with a frown. "Maybe don't startle us with your wet feet when we're monster hunting, yeah?"

Lea wagged one of her Doc Martens toward Thomas. "Should have worn boots."

Thomas cinched the hood of his jacket tighter around his face. Not that it mattered. The wind drove the rain sideways so that it invaded everything that wasn't sealed. He jogged down the path toward the quarry and piles of limestone blocks that were all that remained of the Temple of Olympian Zeus.

A burst of lightning crawled across the sky with thunder chasing after it. The sudden darkness that ensued left Thomas seeing phantoms. He slowed to a walk, using the railing to help him navigate the path around the quarry. The volume of rain lessened by several degrees, and the wind faltered from a howling gale to a gusting inconvenience.

"That's weird, right? For it to just change like that," Luka said, not having to yell this time.

Thomas held his hands palms up.

"Maybe the storm just blew itself out?" Lea suggested.

"Maybe," Thomas said, as he watched Luka futilely attempt to use his wet sleeve to wipe the water from his face. "You didn't do anything?"

She shook her head. "I can create weather events, but only small stuff."

"That tornado in the woods a couple of weeks ago didn't feel small."

Lea's pride showed through on her face, even though it was mostly encased in shadow. "Relatively small, then. I can't unmake a storm … I don't think."

They made their way westward out of the grove of trees that huddled around Zeus' fallen temple. A clearing gave them an uninterrupted view of the four upright pillars at the northwest corner of the Temple of Castor and Pollux.

As they crossed the open ground, Thomas noticed that the steady rain petered to a drizzle, then all but stopped. Even the gusts of wind grew still. He pushed his hood back off his head and turned, catching Luka's look of surprise as he too realized that Lea wasn't walking with them anymore. Looking back the way they'd come, they found her with her arms upraised and her face toward the sky. Wind and rain funneled around her.

Luka said with awe, "She looks like Storm."

"From the X-Men?"

Luka nodded.

A last burst of lightning illuminated Lea as she pushed the storm that she pent up, and it hastened its way eastward.

"Should we order her a costume?" Thomas suggested.

His friend's head bobbed up and down enthusiastically.

After the wind became a whisper and the clouds broke up, Lea lowered her arms and strode toward them. "So that's a thing I can do, apparently." There was a ferocity in her eyes that had never been there before. Thomas recognized it as the discovery of a well of power within herself and the feeling of invulnerability that accompanied it. She'd learn soon enough that the sense of invincibility was misplaced. *No need to wreck that wave she's riding right now, though.*

At the Temple of Castor and Pollux, the trio took a trail that led north and brought them to a gully spanned by a rickety wooden bridge. Now that they were in the most remote part of the park, the lighting had given out and submerged them in darkness.

"Could you maybe shed some light on the situation?" Luka asked.

Thomas looked around. Considering the storm and the late hour, there was really no chance that any other people would be around. He flung out an orb of light that floated ahead of them, illuminating the bridge and the planks it was missing. Luka turned around and shared a smug look, making sure everyone knew he had a good idea. Lea pushed him ahead, cutting his moment short.

After getting their bearings, Thomas directed the light to trail them so it could light the way a short distance ahead of them without obliterating their night vision.

On the other side of the bridge, stone steps showed every bit of their two thousand years of usage. The steps gave way to a rough trail that ran northwest for a couple hundred meters. A small sign reading Temple di Vulcano pointed west.

"Look," Luka said. "It's pointing right at that porta-T. This guy can't catch a break. His name is Fester, and people confuse his temple for a toilet."

Lea and Thomas shook their heads in unison and walked past Luka without further acknowledging his observation. The new path carried them back up a grade and toward a railroad track that lay atop a steep embankment. Thomas extinguished the flame. Darkness descended on them again, but it wasn't as complete as before because the nearly full moon had peeked out from behind the breaking clouds.

"We're getting close," Thomas whispered as they arrived at the bottom of the embankment. "If he's here, I don't want our light to give us away. Let's just take a minute to let our eyes adjust."

"What are we about to get into?" Lea asked.

"Once we go up this embankment, there will be a railway platform with a set of stairs leading down to the right. We'll go down those stairs, then take the path to the left. There will be a building, and on the other side of the building will be Vulcan's temple. During the day, you'd be able to see two pillars standing up over the top of the building, but I don't know right now. There's another building kind of perpendicular to the first—"

"Dropping geometry words into regular conversations now, are we?" Luka jibed, trying to lighten the mood a shade.

"In what world is this a regular conversation?" Lea said.

When Luka shrugged in response, Thomas heard the rustle of clothing and sensed movement, more than he saw the gesture itself. His eyes weren't ready yet.

"Also, I thought you just told us at Mt. Vesuvius geometry was your thing."

"Geology," he corrected. "Rocks, not shapes."

"Whatever. Are we ready to do this?"

"Hang on," Thomas whispered coarsely. "You need to know what we're walking into. Who we're expecting to meet. When he kidnapped me, I saw him ..." Thomas' words choked off as images that had long been held at arm's length came crashing back in.

"Take your time," Luka said gently, patting his friend on the shoulder.

"Time is what we don't have," Thomas snapped. "He crushed a pegasus' skull with a hammer just to make a point. He broke his own guy's neck because he made a mistake. And he killed dozens of children — people and creatures — because they didn't have the powers I have. This isn't some crazy priest. He's an actual monster who will do whatever is necessary to get what he wants. So don't go doing anything heroic or you'll just wind up dead ... like everyone else."

Lea stepped toward Thomas and spoke with anger in her voice. "I find it kind of insulting that you keep trying to warn us off. If you think we came all this way just to let him snatch you up, you couldn't be more wrong. So if you're done telling ghost stories, we'll just get on with it."

Thomas clenched his jaw. He appreciated the support, but he didn't want to have more blood on his hands. They were already stained red from a dozen others, including his dad and grandmother.

Luka stepped in too. He covered his mouth with his hand and said, "I agree with her, man. But my dinner had a bunch of garlic and onions, so I'm uncomfortable saying too much with us all standing this close."

Thomas shoved him backward lightly as a smirk tugged at his lips, though the smile fell away quickly. He didn't know whether they really understood what might happen here. "It's just—"

"Enough," Lea growled, grabbing him by the shirt. "We might die. We are all friends, and we love each other and all that. We get it. Okay?"

Thomas nodded.

She let him go and stepped back. "Good. Let's go do this."

Luka spun in a tight circle. "She said she loves me."

"I don't think—"

"Shh," Luka interrupted. "It counts."

Lea scrabbled up the embankment to the railroad tracks above. Thomas and Luka followed in her wake. The rocks that trickled down the hill sounded more like an avalanche in the post-storm silence. Even the birds had not begun checking in on each other yet. Perhaps they were still holding their breath, sensing that while one storm had passed, another lay ahead.

11

LEA

ONCE ON THE RAILWAY PLATFORM, Lea waited for the other two to catch up and looked to the west with her hands on the railing.

"See anything?" Thomas asked when he joined her.

"Just a building." She found that hard to believe, though. All the clues had led them here. As long as they were interpreting them correctly.

Thomas led the way down the stairs. She had a sudden impulse to run from this place, from Vulcan. She had visions of the rotting zombie children and burning creatures that Thomas had told them about. It almost overwhelmed her purpose for being here. But she was the one who terrorized bullies, who put them in their place on the pecking order. Now Vulcan might be a different situation, but she wasn't going to bail. *Agatha, we're coming for you,* she murmured to herself, needing the reinforcement.

The trio splashed through the mud from the sidewalk to the back corner of the squat stone building. Hugging it so closely decreased their field of view of what lay ahead, but it also limited their exposure to whatever dangers awaited them on

"

the other side. The first pillar of the Temple of Vulcan revealed itself as Lea crept toward the front corner of the building, Thomas taking the point position. A cloud slid in front of the moon, rendering her unable to decipher any details in the diffuse light. Regardless, they continued their forward progress.

When the second pillar came into view, a small, sharp glow emerged at its base. Thomas froze. The glow waxed and waned rhythmically and appeared to hover several feet above the ground. Tendrils of smoke reached upward.

"What is it?" Lea whispered as quietly as possible.

Thomas held a hand out behind him. *Stop.*

A jet of smoke puffed outward. Someone was smoking.

"It's just me, Thomas," Vulcan's voice rumbled. The boy stepped out from the shadow of the building. Lea stepped up to his right and saw Luka do the same on the other side. Her hands trembled, so she shoved them into her back pockets.

"But you are not alone, I see," Vulcan chided. "I am disappointed you would put others at risk like this."

Thomas held his ground and did not reply. *Good for you. Don't take the bait.*

"Well, let's not shout across the grounds like enemy combatants. Come over here and let's have a proper conversation."

Still nothing from Thomas. A kernel of concern planted itself in Lea's consciousness. Was Thomas being resolute, or was he petrified with fear? Not that she could blame him. It's just that it would be an insurmountable problem.

The cloud that had been obscuring the moon floated off to the east, exposing a hulking figure smoking a pipe at the base of the pillar.

Luka said, "That's Fester? He's not so big."

Vulcan stood from where he had been squatting on his haunches, revealing his full height and imposing frame.

"Oh," Luka muttered. "You can see how I misjudged that."

"You would do well to mind your manners, boy," Vulcan warned.

Luka whistled and said, "Fester has a temper."

He can't help but poke at bears. Lea turned to Luka and whispered coarsely, "Don't provoke him, dummy."

Vulcan cleared the ground between them in several large strides. "Thomas, maybe you should introduce everyone. I hate to kill a stranger."

Thomas stepped back. Luka and Lea shuffled backward too, falling in line with Thomas again.

"It's been a long time, Thomas. I'm surprised you don't have a warmer greeting for your grandfather."

Thomas roared in a sudden burst of rage and unleashed a torrent of flame at Vulcan, who reached out calmly and deflected the barrage with the palm of his gargantuan hand. Vulcan stepped forward, unfazed by the attack. As he closed the ground between them, magma rebounded off him back toward the trio, who were forced to retreat, almost in unison, until they bumped against the building.

Still, Vulcan advanced. Thomas cut off his assault, with his two friends huddled beside him in the shadow of their enemy.

Vulcan tilted his head as he gazed down at Thomas. "How did you think this was going to go? Not like this, I presume. You have allowed time to give you an inflated view of your abilities, though I will admit to having been surprised by the fire. I didn't know that was a gift you possessed. Your mother has both trained you well and done you a disservice. She should have told you that fire would have minimal effect on me. In fact, you should have known it yourself from our previous ... engagement. Perhaps you were too young to remember it."

"I remember it," Thomas hissed. "*All* of it."

Vulcan raised his arms overhead and, with a joyless smile, said, "He speaks! I was afraid that maybe you'd traded your voice for your new gift, like Ariel. But apparently not." He waited for Thomas to make introductions. When none came, an awkward silence fell among the group. Vulcan appeared to revel in the discomfort he was causing.

"Well, Thomas, if you're going to be rude about it, I will have to do this myself. I won't know your names, but I bet I can pin down your roles." He jabbed a finger at Luka, who flinched. "You are the loudmouth jokester of the group. You take pride in making the others laugh, sometimes at your own expense, and other times you go too far and hurt people's feeling. Laughter is where you find your self-worth because you're not as skilled or talented as the others. How am I doing so far?"

Lea was glad there wasn't enough light to see the color of Luka's face. It would be either as splotchy red as when he ran in the cold or blanched of all its color due to embarrassment.

"Not bad," Luka said. "Now it's my turn, Fester." Vulcan bristled at the nickname but didn't speak. "You have great powers, but you're petty and jealous and small — not physically small, obviously. You know what I mean. No one likes you. Not even the people who were supposed to be worshiping you. They were just scared of the giant rampage you would go on if they didn't build your temple. So they built it way out here, as far from town and the other temples as they could get. Literally, on the other side of the tracks." He paused. "How am I doing so far?"

Vulcan retained his composure, but his smirk had slid into a sneer. "Let me spoil the surprise for you, boy. The mouthy one always dies first. If for no other reason than the bad guy tires of hearing him talk."

Lea burst toward Vulcan. Lightning crackled at her fingertips and wind whipped around her. "Don't threaten him!"

Vulcan took a half-step backward before recovering himself. His mirth-void smile returned. "Looks like I touched a nerve. That's good to know. Now, put out your sparklers before you hurt someone, and let's talk about you for a second."

Lea chastised herself. She should have kept her cool and not given him anything to work with. He was trying to be divisive and cruel, and she'd handed him a can of fuel for the fire. She let the energy around herself dissipate. Thomas grabbed her wrist and pulled her back into line beside himself.

"I like you," Vulcan said. "You have an open invitation to come work with me whenever you want. Just like Agatha always did. You are very much like her, you know. I expect that is why Thomas is drawn to you. The anger inside you burns hot, and you have found nothing to quench it. I can teach you how to use it rather than put it out." He held a hand out to her. "Join me."

Lea spit onto his palm. "I would die first."

He left his hand out as the spittle sizzled and evaporated until nothing was left.

With coldness in his voice and a shake of his head, he said, "I may yet give you the opportunity. So much like Agatha. I have tried to kill her countless times — turns out it can be exceedingly difficult to kill your offspring — and every time, she fights. Even knowing she can't win. But suit yourself. "

Vulcan shifted his gaze. "Thomas, that brings us to you. You know the deal. Come with me. I have great plans for us. We can do things the world hasn't seen in several ages. It will be extraordinary, and that is an understatement. Or ... Agatha dies."

Thomas' voice was devoid of emotion when he spoke. Better than anyone, he knew what was at stake. She did not envy him this. He was not making his decision now. It had already been made. "Never."

Vulcan wagged his finger. "It would have been much easier if you'd said yes. But I won't lie. There was a part of me that wanted you to reject my offer. I'm going to enjoy the wreckage."

He turned to walk away. Thomas thrust his hands outward. The overgrown grass latched onto Vulcan and snaked up his legs. He stumbled and nearly fell, flinging his arms out to regain his balance. He raised his leg several inches and tried to jerk free of the plants. They held steadfast.

"Where is she?" Thomas demanded.

Vulcan reached down and burned the grass. It glowed briefly before becoming embers and ash that flaked away on the breeze. "It won't be that easy, boy. If you learn her location from me, you're going to earn it." Vulcan gestured around them. "And you don't have the resources here to pull off something of that magnitude. We'll do this again. One more time. One more chance, before I put an end to everything."

He turned back toward the ruins of his temple and opened a door to another place.

12

EMMA

EMMA GLANCED over her screen at Finn. The bruising on his face was mostly gone, leaving behind some pale greenish-yellow splotches that would have been hidden on a darker complexion. Her parents weren't keen on them spending so much time in her room, but they hadn't disallowed it either. So here they sat on the floor waiting on details from their friends about their escapades from the night before. Totally normal. She was irritated that it had taken until late afternoon for anyone to respond to her texts. But apparently, they'd all slept rather late after … she still didn't know *after what* yet.

When her phone buzzed in her hand, she wrinkled her nose as she read the message. "Apparently, the meet-up with Vulcan didn't go very well last night."

"Is everybody okay?" Finn asked.

"Yeah. She says Thomas is kind of a mess, though. They didn't really learn anything new. Vulcan threatened to kill Luka, so there's that."

"He has a very punchable face. Not that I've ever punched him."

"Or anyone else," Emma said, giving him a light shove on the shoulder.

"Fair. But I've wanted to punch him. And if he can elicit that impulse from me, imagine what a supervillain might want to do to him."

"I get it," Emma said. "He also said he was going to kill Agatha if Thomas didn't join him."

"What did Thomas say to that? He's got to know that he can't trust Vulcan to keep his word."

"I think he understands that. Lea says Thomas said 'Never,' and it sounded like it was written in stone. It made the hairs on her neck prickle. Oh, and when Vulcan threatened Luka, Lea lashed out at him, and he basically offered her a job."

Finn looked at her in confusion. "What?"

Emma turned the phone around and showed him the screen. "I don't know. That's just what she says."

The phone chimed at her again. "She has a question — does the name Hephaestus mean anything to us?"

Finn shook his head.

Emma put her hands to her face, feigning shock. "The brilliant Finn admits to not knowing something? Is the sky falling? Let me look out the window and see if the apocalypse is upon us."

"That's not fair," Finn said as his cheeks pinked up. "I admit when I don't know something. It's just that … I usually know the answers to the questions you all ask."

"Uh-huh," she said dismissively. She typed into her phone and after a minute, said, "According to the internet—"

"The internet isn't an entity. It can't—you know what, never mind. It doesn't matter. Go ahead."

"According to the internet," Emma repeated just to dig at the mildly overbearing know-it-all she was friends with, "Hephaestus is the Greek name for Vulcan."

"Oh no," Finn said. "You know what this means?"

Emma was disheartened by the new information. "I've got a pretty good guess — Agatha's not in Italy."

"Yeah. But knowing he's Greek doesn't help us narrow anything down."

"Why not? We can limit that clues we develop to things that fit Greece."

Finn shook his head adamantly. "We're not talking about modern Greece. Vulcan ... or whatever we're supposed to call him now, is several thousand years old. Ancient Greece was huge. It wasn't just Peloponnesus—"

"You're going to lose me here pretty quick. I'm a math and science girl ... who occasionally dabbles in talking to spirits. But I'm definitely not a history girl."

"Peloponnesus is the bottom part of Greece that looks like a paw. So there was that and the Balkan Peninsula and Macedonia and most of the coastline of Asia Minor. Not to mention a thousand tiny islands."

"That's not very encouraging," Emma said as she pushed her hands through her hair.

"So speaking of talking to spirits, what does Elle know? Can she help us?"

"Based on our last conversation, she doesn't know much. She couldn't or wouldn't answer questions about Agatha."

"Can you ask her again?"

"It's not like I can just summon her," Emma snapped.

"How do you know?"

"I ... don't."

"I think you should try," Finn suggested.

"How would I even do that?"

Emma could almost see the gears turning inside his head as he worked through it. Finally, a hopeful expression fell across his face. "If you're opposed to using drugs ..."

"I am," Emma said.

"You could try meditation. That might allow you to enter a state where your spirit can communicate with hers."

Emma raised an eyebrow at him. "I thought you said earlier that you could admit when you don't know something."

"Oh, I definitely don't know. I'm just throwing spaghetti at the wall."

"You're what?"

"Throwing spaghetti at the wall. You've never heard of that?"

She pursed her lips and shook her head.

"It's how you can tell if it's ready. If it sticks to the wall, it's ready. If it falls to the counter, it needs to cook longer."

"You could use a timer like a normal person. Anyway, back to the issue — instead of trying hallucinogens or meditation, maybe I'll just go visit her. That's how we had our first interaction."

Finn looked at his watch. "I can't go with you. I have to get to work."

"You weren't invited. I'm a big girl. I can manage on my own," she said defiantly, feeling a little like Lea as she said it. *Good, you could use a little more audacity in your life.*

"I know. That's not what I meant. We've been doing all this together, so I figured ..."

"It's fine. By the time I get there, it will probably be after regular visiting hours anyway. I'll be lucky if they let me see her. What time do you have to be at work?"

"About an hour," Finn said.

"I'm going to take a quick shower, and you can walk with me to Stephanus-Haus on your way."

"Sure, but how will you get home?"

"Walk. When's the last time something bad happened to a girl walking alone at night in a small town like this?"

Finn glared at her.

"Too soon?"

He nodded.

"Fine. I'll call my dad. He'll walk with me. Satisfied?"

He nodded again.

"Alright, I'll be back in a couple of minutes."

☙

Emma scrunched her hair dry with her towel, thinking about how absurd this whole thing was. Who were they that it was all landing in their laps? Her three friends scouring Mediterranean ruins in search of a woman who'd been abducted by a god. A Greek god, as it turned out. While she and Finn spent their days trying to solve seemingly impossible riddles.

She wrapped her towel around herself and opened the bathroom door. Steam poured through the opening. She liked showers her hot enough that it made her skin prickle. Emma smiled at her father, who was starting dinner prep in the kitchen, as she made her way to her room.

We have been spending a lot of time together. Since the other three had left, she and Finn had seen each other almost every day. *Is he getting too attached? Are you? No. Lea said he had a crush on somebody else. No, that's not right. She said he had a crush on someone, but she wouldn't say who.*

Emma pushed open the door to her room and reached to loosen her towel. She shrieked in surprise when she saw Finn.

He jumped up from where he'd been sitting on the floor. "Sorry!"

"Emma?" her father called from the other room.

"It's fine. Everything is fine." She crossed her arms over her chest while realizing how much of her legs were showing. She hissed, "I thought you would have gone to the other room." *And I noticed you didn't cover your eyes.* She wished for a bigger towel.

"I'm going," Finn said, hurrying out the door and closing it behind himself.

I only thought we'd been seeing a lot of each other. He was about to

80

see a whole lot more. Her cheeks flushed just thinking about the level of embarrassment that would have involved. *Obviously, I never would have been able to see him again after that. Probably would have had to move several towns over and change my name. Lea will absolutely die when I tell her about this. She probably would have just kept on with taking off her towel to see his reaction. She must be missing the part of her brain that involves inhibitions. Probably shouldn't tell Thomas, though.*

They parted ways when Emma turned right off Hauptstrasse to go to the nursing home. Long shadows crept across the grounds as the western sky evolved from blue to orange, with only the longer wavelengths of light percolating through the atmosphere.

Emma pulled at the door and found it locked. She pressed the button below the camera and waited.

"Ja?" a voice called through the speaker.

"I am here to visit Elle Strom."

There was a long silence on the other end before the speaker crackled. "Visiting hours have closed. Guten nacht." The crackle ceased.

Emma pressed the button again and did not wait for a response. "It is very important that I see her. Please."

The voice asked, "Are you Thomas' friend who was here a few days ago?"

"Ja, that's me."

The buzzer on the door leapt to life, and Emma pulled it open.

"Danke," she said, approaching the front desk. "Do I need to sign in?"

"For an after-hours visit? Nein. This will be between us. I haven't seen Thomas or Agatha in a couple of weeks," the attendant said, though her sentence was clearly a question.

"They ... went on holiday and asked me to look in on her while they're gone," Emma said, proud of her improvisation and hoping it was believable.

The woman smiled at her. "That's good of you. Do you remember where Elle's room is?"

Emma nodded.

"Go on back, mäuschen."

She made her way down the corridor to Elle's room, and upon entering, found her seated in her wheelchair beside an open window. The evening air was growing chill, so she closed the window and pulled a blanket off the bed to wrap around Elle.

Emma sat on the edge of the bed beside her. Taking a deep breath and leaning forward, she reached out and placed her hand on Elle's forearm. Nothing happened. The broken tension expelled from her in a stifled laugh.

She removed her hand and had begun to sit back when Elle's hand wrenched upward and seized her wrist. Emma gasped and felt herself sliding off the bed, but she was pulled into darkness before she could adjust her position.

When she opened her eyes, Elle stood in front of her. There were no notable surroundings, only a desolate void. Even the surface they stood on was absent of color or texture.

"You have reached me," Elle said.

That's a peculiar greeting. "I need help."

Elle stared at her, offering no response.

Maybe Elle didn't remember her. "Do you remember me from before?"

"Of course," she answered flatly.

"Why isn't everything collapsing around us like before?"

"We are in a more stable area. I chose our meeting place instead of you. Are these the questions you want to ask?"

Emma shook her head. "It's about Agatha."

For the first time, Elle appeared interested in the conversation.

"Did Vulcan take her to the same place he took you?"

The color drained from Elle's face, and she backpedaled several steps.

"Please, Elle. It's important. She's going to die," Emma pleaded, closing the gap between them again. "Where did he take her?"

"I remember only that it is in the cradle of life. Where it is neither warm nor cold. Where the sun is only a visitor."

She couldn't be more vague if she tried. "You're gonna have to do better than that, Elle. Agatha's life depends on you."

Elle shrugged, not with indifference but with hopelessness. "I cannot. The puzzle is missing too many pieces. I think some of them fell out when the box got shaken."

"I don't know what that means."

"It is not meant to be a riddle. My body was the box."

"Oh, right." Emma thought of a question she'd been pondering. "Why do you talk to me and no one else?"

"Would you prefer I not talk to you?"

"No, I'm glad you do," Emma said. She tried to place a reassuring hand on Elle's arm, but it went through the space where her arm appeared to be. Mist swirled as though disturbed by a breeze and re-formed in the shape of Elle. Emma retracted her hand. "Sorry."

"No apology necessary. It's a peculiar feeling, but I wouldn't call it unpleasant."

"Why do we only meet here?"

Elle looked around herself. "Because this is where I am."

"What do you call it?"

"This is the interstitial space. The place between realms."

Emma pressed the heels of her hands to her eyes and rubbed.

"Except for you, I have not spoken with anyone since ... that day." She shuddered. "I believe I am out of practice."

Emma forced a smile. "You're fine. It's just a lot to take in. Can I ask you another question?"

Elle nodded.

"Can you leave this place?"

Elle's eyes welled with tears that immediately spilled onto her cheeks before rolling off her jaw and dissipating in the ether.

"I'm sorry. I shouldn't have asked. We don't have to talk about it."

Elle waved her hands. "It's okay," she said through a constricted throat. She took a minute to settle and collect herself. "I haven't tried."

"In all this time?" Emma covered her mouth. "Sorry. I don't seem to have a filter today. Can't you go back to your body?"

Elle bit her lip. "It is a violated husk. I will not be confined to it any longer."

"But what happens when it ... you know ... dies?"

Finally, Elle smiled. "Then I will be freed from this holding place and go on to whatever comes next for me."

"And that's the only way out?"

"No," Elle said in a clipped tone. "It is not. But none of the gates are easy or safe." Elle looked around uncomfortably, the topic clearly making her anxious. "I must go now. I expect I will see you again."

"Wait," Emma said as Elle turned away. "Please find me again if you think of anything. About Agatha."

She nodded curtly.

An intense pressure caused Emma to wince. When she opened her eyes again, she sat in the floor of Elle's room beside the shell of a breathing person strapped to a wheelchair. The pretty face was a shadow of the one she'd been talking to.

WHEN THOMAS TOLD the driver to take him to the Temple of Olympian Zeus, the driver told him that the park did not open for several more hours. Thomas did not change his instructions. As the driver put the car in gear, he said something in Italian that Thomas did not understand, but he gathered from the tone that the language barrier might be best.

Headlights carried him south of town just as they had thirty-six hours earlier. He was glad to have gotten out without waking up the other two. He didn't want to talk about what he was going to do. Didn't want to have any arguments about it. And he certainly didn't want any company.

When the squealing brakes brought the car to a stop, Thomas paid the driver in cash and left a generous tip. The early morning breeze carried on it the tangy smell of salt from the Mediterranean. Thomas looked to the east and found the sky already changing from black to gray.

He set his jaw and took off at a run, remembering the route they had taken before. He vaulted down the steps at Zeus' ruins and sprinted across the grounds toward Castor and Pollux, where he hooked north.

When he reached the railroad tracks, Thomas scrambled up the embankment and hurried across the platform. He burst onto the temple floor between the two pillars where Vulcan had been awaiting them before.

His heart pounded against his ribs, fueled in equal parts by exertion, rage, and fear. He sent orbs of light in a half-dozen directions to illuminate anyone who might be there. No one and nothing emerged.

"Where are you now?!" he screamed. "Come fight me, you bastard!"

Thomas waited, expecting a response. He had assumed Vulcan would answer when beckoned, had assumed that he could sense being called. Maybe he could and maybe he couldn't. But he did not answer now.

"Have it your way then," he said, more quietly than before. The rage had not quelled, but it was transforming, focusing. Becoming a laser rather than a lantern.

The spheres hovered where he had left them. Thomas raised his arms out to his side and called them back to himself. They revolved in tight orbits around his hands, increasing in speed until they appeared to be wheels of light. He thrust his arms outward in the directions of Vulcan's pillars. The fire wheels smashed into them, followed by fountains of flame that poured from Thomas. He sustained the deluge with an intensity that he had never exhibited before. The heat that reflected back to him was almost insufferable. When he felt cool air strike his cheeks, he didn't know if it was the breeze or that he was pulling so much energy from the matter around him that he was actually lowering the ambient air temperature.

Thomas redoubled his efforts, driving away stray, intruding thoughts. The sandstone pillars shimmered where the assaults were most direct. The outer layers of stone at the pillar's rectangular base sloughed downward, forming molten puddles that flowed around disheveled blocks.

Still, he pushed the limits of his abilities. As its base eroded, the northernmost pillar sloped at an aggressive angle before tumbling off the pedestal into a pool of molten rock. The splash sent gobs of lava in all directions, and closer to Thomas than he was comfortable with. The super-heated rock consumed everything on the temple floor. Brushfires were its vanguard as plants and grasses burst into flame along its path.

Thomas looked over his shoulder and stepped backward onto a stone. From there, he hopped onto a larger block, then to the remains of a wall that led to higher ground. As lava overflowed his stepping stones, Thomas brought the heels of his hands together and poured all of his energy onto the southern pillar. Rather than toppling as its counterpart did, it collapsed into itself as if drowning.

With nothing left to burn, Thomas walked along the wall, noticing that the bottoms of his shoes had become tacky. Sweat poured off his arms and face, sizzling in the inferno below. He leapt from the wall toward a slope on the northern side of the temple and took the trail back toward one of the buildings. When he reached the sidewalk in front of the building, he looked down at his handiwork. Instead of joy or vengeance, he was overcome with exhaustion, followed closely by grief.

Thomas' shoulders slumped, and he sagged, pulling his knees up to his chest. He wrapped his arms around his legs as the tears began to fall. He rested his forehead against his legs and did not inhibit the pent-up feelings that burst out. The roar of the fire below him nearly drowned out his primal mourning sounds. The molten rock flowed to the outer walls and reached desperately for anything that would fuel its fire. Finding nothing, its surface cooled and coagulated, morphing from vibrant orange to gray slag.

"Thomas," a small voice said.

When a paw landed on his shoulder and a loud crunch

sounded in his hear, he raised up his head. "Ning," he whispered.

The panda bowed and plopped down beside the boy. He took another bite of the bamboo that he had brought with him.

"I had started wondering if you were ever real," Thomas said quietly.

Ning's mouth fell agape, and he turned his head to look at Thomas. "I have never been more insulted in my entire life."

"How old are you anyway?" Thomas asked with sudden curiosity.

"Well, I never," Ning protested. "After all this time, I come to check on you, and you hurl one insult after another at me. I will not stand for this ... but I will stand for *this*." He pushed himself up on his hind legs and shuffled to the edge of the sidewalk. From there, he extended one of the bamboo shoots over the still-molten rock. Thomas eyed Ning curiously as he waddled back.

"Toasted," he said. "It provides a delightful change of texture and releases a nutty flavor. I would offer to share, but I am still perturbed at my reception."

"My apologies, Ning."

"Apology accepted. Now, this is quite a scene you have caused. I do not expect it will go unnoticed."

"That was kind of the point. That he takes notice of it. I won't let him bully me into doing what he wants." Thomas' defiance asserted itself briefly until his fear resurfaced. "But I don't know how to refuse him without him killing my mom."

"Yes, that is a quandary," Ning said, nodding in a way that was overtly ponderous. "Have you considered talking to him about it?"

"Actually, yes. It didn't go well. Hence ..." Thomas gestured at the destruction below them.

"Ah. I am proud of you. Working through your problems with words is a sign of maturity. Of course, following it up with a gargantuan temper tantrum in which you burn everything to the ground …"

"What?" Thomas prodded. "Go ahead and say it."

"As best I can tell, it's a sign of humanity. Most of you are prone to occasional emotional meltdowns, as it were, particularly when under duress." Ning flicked an ear forward and said, "I will be right back," before winking out of Thomas' plane of existence.

When Ning returned with a pop, he vibrated with excitement. "Thomas, you appear to have drawn the attention of a number of other humans. The Carabinieri and vigili del fuoco are on their way here. It is time for you to go."

"Can you help me?"

"Thomas, I am a consolation creature and am disallowed from changing your circumstances."

With the sun peeking over the building to his left, Thomas hurried to his feet. He started making his way back toward the railroad platform. Ning padded along behind him. "If I can make a suggestion," he said breathlessly, "that might not be the best way to go."

Thomas stopped.

"Follow the trail that leads away from the temple. It will take you to the railway viaduct. There you will find a road. Take it to the left, and turn left onto the roadway it takes you to. At the first major intersection, go left again. That will lead back to town."

"Thank you, Ning. For everything."

"You are most welcome," Ning said with a smile.

"Will I see you again?" Thomas asked, feeling very much the six-year-old-boy he had been when he first met Ning.

"That is hard to say. I know a good many things, but not the future."

14

THOMAS

THOMAS WALKED into the common room at the hostel to find Luka and Lea on either end of a worn cloth sofa, staring at their phones. Next to Luka, three sandwiches sat stacked on top of each other.

"Thomas," Luka greeted him with excitement. "Look, they have stuff to make a lunch to take with you."

"You made one for each of us?"

A guilty expression passed across Luka's face, and the apples of his cheeks reddened slightly. Lea looked at Thomas with an expression that said, *You ought to know better than that. And really, you should be disappointed in yourself for the suggestion.* She accompanied her derisive look with picking up the two sandwiches that sat beside her.

Thomas nodded. "That makes more sense."

"Where have you been?" Lea asked.

"Went for a walk."

"That's a heck of a walk," Luka said. "You were already gone when we got up."

"Had a lot to think about. Is there any breakfast left, or did you eat it all?"

"There's some toast and boiled eggs, but the eggs smell like farts."

Thomas laughed.

Lea shook her head. "Do you have to work hard to be this disgusting, or does it come naturally?"

"Oh, it's definitely his natural state," Thomas said.

Luka grinned and nodded.

Thomas went into the adjacent room to grab some food. *He doesn't really care what kind of attention he gets as long as it's directed his way.* Thomas wished he lacked inhibitions in the way that his friend did.

He slathered some apricot jam onto a couple of pieces of cold toast and put two eggs on his plate. His belly rumbled at the prospect of food. It was a little vexed at him for having left it empty while spending such vast quantities of energy. He grabbed a third egg and a packet of salt on his way back to the common room. With Luka and Lea immersed in their phones again, he plopped down between them.

Luka leaned toward him and sniffed. "Dude, you smell like a campfire." He reclined again as if needing no explanation, then popped back upright and said, "Did you hear there was a fire at Vulcan's temple?"

Thomas sat up a little straighter before slumping and trying to pretend he hadn't reacted. He hadn't considered that the fire would make the news, and further hadn't thought about the news getting back to his friends before he did. "I hadn't heard."

Lea leaned forward and stared relentlessly across Thomas at Luka.

Should have known better than to think I would have gotten it past her.

"What?" Luka said defensively. "I didn't do anything. I told you it's the eggs."

"Do. The. Math. Dummy."

Luka was confused. He looked at Thomas for help, but

Thomas stared straight ahead and shoved an entire boiled egg into his mouth to mask his expression. Eventually, Luka's jaw dropped as his synapses drew lines to all the right dots. He whispered loudly, "Did you—"

"I don't know what you're talking about," Thomas cut him off. "I'm going to take a shower."

He stalked out of the room, eggs in one hand and toast in the other. He didn't look back, even when he heard the other two whispering fiercely to each other.

☙

It took two passes of soap and shampoo to clear the smell of fire. He'd have to wash his clothes before they left, or they would taint his bag for the rest of time. He wrapped a towel around his waist and ducked across the hallway to their room.

Thomas nearly jumped out of his skin when he found Luka and Lea sitting on his bed, hands in their laps, waiting for him. The surprise sent his hands up in a defensive posture, and he was glad he had tucked the corner of the towel firmly into place.

"I kinda thought we could talk about it after I got dressed."

"We're ready to talk about it now," Lea said. "Isn't that right, Luka?"

"Yeah," he murmured. "We're ready now."

When Lea turned her head back to Thomas, Luka shrugged and mouthed, "Sorry."

Without so much as glancing Luka's way, she said, "Peripheral vision."

Luka groaned.

Thomas gestured under the bed beneath Lea. "My bag."

She pulled up her legs and tucked them to the side. Thomas squatted down to slide his backpack out from under the bed. Lea tilted her head sideways and pursed her lips as she gazed down at Thomas.

"Don't try to look at his … thing," Luka protested, gesturing wildly at Thomas.

She looked at him with raised eyebrows. "You don't check out other girls?"

He stammered, "I don't—not, you know, in front of you."

In typical Lea fashion, she refused to concede the point and shrugged her shoulders instead. Thomas stood up with several articles of clothing in hand, mooting the issue for the moment.

"Are you going to turn around?" Thomas asked.

She shook her head and goaded him. "Do whatever you gotta do."

Thomas dropped his towel, causing Lea to squeal. Luka tackled her and covered her eyes. Through her cackling, Lea said, "I didn't think you'd actually do it."

"You can only push a man so far."

"Man? That's a bold proclamation from what I just saw," Lea teased through another fit of laughter.

Thomas had been feigning confidence up to that point, but blushed as he stepped into his boxers. The crew regained their collective composure without further incident while he got the rest of his clothes on.

Thomas sat down on the bed beside Lea. "So was there something y'all wanted to talk about?" he asked with a coy upturn of his lips.

Luka looked conspiratorially around the room. He showed Thomas a picture on his phone of a smoldering ruin surrounded by emergency personnel. "There was a small fire at a certain ancient world heritage site this morning."

Thomas lost his smile and said, "I might have lost my temper a little bit."

"You melted stone, Thomas," Lea whispered coarsely. "Did you know you could do that?"

"No more than you knew you could quell a storm. I don't know if it's something about that place, or if we're tapping deeper into our können. But I didn't go there for that. I went to summon him. To … I don't know. I didn't really have a plan."

Luka sat upright and pointed a finger at Thomas. "You should have taken us with you. You could have been hurt or killed. Or who knows what could have happened. That was stupid."

Thomas couldn't recall having heard that kind of anger in Luka's voice before. Anger wasn't an emotion that he dredged up all that often. As opposed to Thomas, who felt like anger was always simmering somewhere just below the surface. Like his mother. He had always sensed that about her as well, except hers was more than simmering. It was burbling, pressing against the crust, seeking a weak point to force its way out. She was always good about walking away before she got to the bursting point, going for long walks and returning once she had pulled herself back together. Like he'd done this morning. He hadn't put that together until now. He would have to ask her what she did on those long walks. If he ever got that chance again. He suspected now that it wasn't just casual strolls in the woods. Finally, he answered, "I just wanted to face him on my own."

"So what happened?" Luka asked.

"He didn't answer when I called for him. I don't know. I thought that if I yelled for him at his temple, it would be like the Bat-Signal," Thomas said. "But nothing happened. I guess it was a dumb idea."

"I don't think so," Lea said. "It may not have worked, but it kind of makes sense."

"So when he didn't show, I lit some stuff on fire … and it kind of got out of hand."

"'Kind of got out of hand'?" Luka scoffed. "That's like the understatement of the century. There's nothing left of that place. It looks like the lava flow on Mount Vesuvius."

Thomas couldn't help but smile. It had felt incredible while he was doing it, but now that the moment had passed, he had some concerns. "I don't know if there were any cameras on the buildings beside his temple."

"Let's hope not," Luka said. "We'll have … other problems, if that's the case."

"Might be time to skip town," Lea suggested.

Thomas agreed. "That's what I was thinking, too. Only one problem."

"Where to go?" she said.

Luka chimed in. "I thought we were going to Greece?"

Lea sighed. "Countries are made up of smaller units called cities. Cities are the municipal bodies that house airports and seaports. It would be helpful if we had some idea which city gives us our best opportunity to have a successful outcome."

"You don't have to be so mean about it," Luka said.

"I think it has to be Athens," Thomas said. "That seems like the most logical starting point anyway."

"What about Olympia?" Luka asked.

"Maybe? I don't know. How much did Vulcan have to do with the Olympics? Maybe we can have Finn look into it for us."

Luka looked really appreciative that Thomas hadn't dismissed his suggestion outright. It wasn't a win, but it wasn't a loss either.

"Has anyone talked to him or Emma yet today? One of them might have turned something up."

"Shouldn't you be the one to talk to Emma?" Lea said.

"Wow. You're just taking shots at everyone this morning, aren't you?"

"Well," she said, her eyes blazing with the orneriness that her voice projected.

"You might recall that I was a little pre-occupied."

"Have you been pre-occupied for the last several days? When is the last time you called her?"

Thomas huffed. "I don't know. I don't want to get into it right now. There's just a lot going on."

Lea shrugged. "Fine."

He was perceptive enough to know that *fine* didn't really mean fine.

Luka said, "Finn worked last night, so he won't be up for a few more hours."

15

AGATHA

AGATHA GINGERLY PULLED the charred can of carrots out of the small fire. Most of the label had burned away, leaving behind only the ribbed aluminum. The sight reminded her of her own worsening condition. Agatha put a hand to her side, where she could feel her ribs immediately beneath the skin.

She had saved the cooked carrots until she had few other options, and frowned as she poured the contents into the bowl. Reaching into the bowl using her thumb and forefinger as pincers, Agatha snagged one of the steaming carrots. *Who snatched this up out of the ground one day and thought, 'You know, it's all orange and phallic-looking, we should definitely eat it.'* Already, a gag grabbed at her throat. But her disgust was no match for her hunger.

She noted the accumulation of grime on her hands and decided she could give herself a minute longer to come to terms with eating the grossest of root vegetables while attending to some hygiene. Agatha set the bowl down and tromped over to the inlet.

Hard to believe it's come to this. Maybe when he comes back, I can just coax him into killing me. Agatha eyed her depleted water supply. *Of course, if he waits much too much longer, it's not likely to matter.*

She shook her hands, flinging seawater in all directions. In the absence of a hand towel and with clothes that were dirtier than her skin, air drying would have to do. She turned back to her fire and immediately registered the disaster.

"No!" Agatha yelled, as she flew across the cavern. With her foot, she nudged the melted ruin of her bowl out of the fire. Most of the carrots had fallen into the flame. She reached toward the bed and liberated one of the bamboo slats to use as a poker before coming to her senses and realizing this was her fire. It would obey her commands. She spoke it out of existence and looked down at the damage. "Roasted carrots? It might be an improvement, actually. At least they'll have a texture other than mush."

Agatha frowned as she reached down for the misshapen bowl that was now missing a significant portion of its side. It looked like a castle wall that had been breached by a barrage from a trebuchet. She pitched it onto the trash heap. Agatha slumped to the floor and began removing bits of debris that had attached themselves to the first of the carrots she picked up. Once it was mostly clean, she popped it into her mouth and picked up another.

Where the first carrot had been mostly oblong, this one was conical and reminded her of ... something. But what kind of something? She pinched it at the broad end and held it in front of her face, scrunching one eye closed.

The eye popped back open. "You idiot," she said as she stood up and strode to the trash pile. "You big, dumb, stupid idiot."

Agatha retrieved the bowl the fire had claimed and spun it in her hand. "Dummy," she said, shaking her head. She formed a concentrated blade of flame in the other hand and made an angular cut at the base of the bowl. Melted plastic slid away from the blade as she slid it slowly toward the bowl's rim.

Before she reached the edge, she turned the flame up and inward, then turned it back down again and finished her cut. Repositioning the bowl in her hand, Agatha mirrored her prior work. When the last stroke completely severed the new shape, the bowl fell away to the floor. Agatha held in her hand a spearhead.

A smile crept onto her face. "With any luck, I'll have fish for dinner instead of those awful carrots." Agatha sat on the floor of the cavern and while holding the spearhead at an acute angle, began scraping back and forth along the rough ground to sand away the plastic and form an edge. *Seventeen degrees? Twenty? Does it really matter for a plastic spearhead that feels more like a toy than a tool?* Oberhaupt appeared briefly in her head, talking about the importance of treating your weapons with respect.

"Alright, alright," she muttered.

She stood the edge of the spearhead against the floor at a ninety-degree angle, then halved the angle, and halved it again. *Twenty degrees-ish. Happy now, O?* It took several busted knuckles and bouts of swearing before Agatha found her rhythm.

After a seemingly endless amount of scraping, she raised the plastic spearhead to her face and blew away the dust. With her thumbnail, she peeled away the bits of clinging plastic that the friction had melted to the edge. She was pleased with her progress and grateful for a task to focus her attention on. She flipped the shard over and renewed her sanding efforts.

By the time she finished, her arms ached from exertion, and her belly growled at her as if reminding her of her purpose. Agatha took the spearhead and bowl to the bamboo slat that lay haphazardly beside the blackened place on the floor where she kept her fire.

She straightened the slat in front of her and lay the spearhead down so that the neck aligned with the end of the bamboo shaft. When she let go, the unsupported head of the spear tipped downward from its weight. Agatha sighed. *Can nothing go right the first time?* She pushed herself up off the floor and traipsed to the bed, removing another slat, which she then slid under the spearhead. *Now then.*

Agatha took the bowl and held it several inches above the joint of the spearhead and shaft. She summoned a flame near the side of the bowl. Its surface shimmered with the heat before it slid downward in a molten wave and dripped from the rim, soldering the plastic to the bamboo. She covered the neck of the spearhead entirely, letting it cool and harden before flipping it over to repeat the process on the back side.

When she had finished her work, Agatha looked up to find the sunny place on the floor. Her primitive clock. She'd been at her project — she very nearly thought of it as a chore, but it was so much more gratifying than any chore had a right to be — much longer than she'd realized. She hefted her spear above her shoulder. At less than a meter in length, it wouldn't be much good as a weapon of war, but it might work for fishing.

She wouldn't have enough light left for much longer. If she was going to try it today, she had to do so soon. With her spear at her side, Agatha walked to a rocky outcropping at the deeper end of the inlet of water and stood looking into it for a minute. Joseph's voice rang in her head, *Well … ain't no time like the present.*

She shuffled her pants off. With the weight she'd lost, she didn't even have to bother with unbuttoning them anymore. She pulled off her shirt and dropped it onto the pants. As Agatha hooked her thumbs into the sides of her underwear and was about to shimmy it off as well, she suddenly remembered a story about tiny fish in the Amazon or somewhere that could swim up your—*nope, nope, nope.* Her underclothes could probably stand a washing anyway. She shivered as though her body was trying to wick away the idea of that kind of invasion.

Agatha inhaled deeply and dove into the pool of water, the spear breaking the surface tension ahead of her. It was cooler than she would've liked. Underwater swimming with a spear in hand was going to take some getting used to. She swam down at an angle until she had to clear her ears from the pressure. Although the water was clear, the light fell off quickly, with no direct source of sunlight. She would have to try in the morning when the sun streamed directly into the inlet for a few minutes every day.

No fish swam within arm's reach of Agatha, and she didn't even see any that would have been worth the effort of trying to spear. When her lungs prompted her to surface, she rotated and kicked upward. It was darker toward the surface than she'd expected. Maybe the sun had already dropped below the point where it fed light directly into the cave.

Agatha kicked again, then threw her hands up in front of her face as she nearly struck rock. It spread out above her in all directions where the cavern had reached down below the water levels. Fear and adrenaline flooded her system. The dimming light made it difficult to make out which direction should she go. She couldn't make a mistake, but she couldn't see the right answer. Her lungs ached, demanding that she take a breath.

Using the rock for leverage, Agatha pushed herself downward again, though a part of her mind revolted at being further from air, but she had needed to widen her angle of view. She looked from side to side, before spotting what appeared to be a small lighter area where the dark mass of stone above her gave way. She kicked her feet and flapped her arms, propelling herself toward her hope.

Agatha broke the surface with a gasp. Her lungs heaved in great draughts of air. After bobbing for long enough to control her breathing, she doggy-paddled her way to what she thought of as her private beach and dragged herself out of the water, crawling onto land, flinging her spear down, and flopping over on her back.

That was fun, she thought, feeling validated in the fear she'd always had of drowning in a tight space. An interminable time later, Agatha pushed herself into a sitting position. Her energy was depleted far more than she would have liked. She'd already been burning more fuel than she had been taking in, and the underwater shenanigans only accelerated that. She stood up, discovering that a large volume of sand had glued itself to her. It wasn't the nice white sand from the Alabama gulf coast either. This was coarse gray stuff that was more like crushed rock.

Agatha waded back into the water, shuddering slightly. She reached around back and unclasped her bra, which was now supporting as much sand as it was flesh, then drew off her underwear for the same reasons. Even though she hadn't had a strictly Puritan upbringing, the idea of being totally naked in a non-private space made her feel weird. Of course, this wasn't really non-private, was it? It was about as secluded as she could get. There was no one within … how far? She didn't know. At least within earshot. She was darn sure of that. But it wasn't exactly homey either.

Agatha's teeth chattered as she exited the water and the cooling evening air wrapped itself around her. Fading orange light laced with purple filtered through the aperture at the top of the cavern.

As her feet touched stone again, Agatha summoned a ball of fire that she set in a spiraling orbit around herself, starting at her face and working its way to her feet. It took longer than a towel, but definitely did the trick. She wrung out her under-clothes and hung them on the back of the chair at the table. She eyed her remaining provisions covetously. But she shouldn't eat more today. On a ship, stealing rations would get you killed. And this wasn't altogether different. She couldn't allow her today-self to steal from her tomorrow-self, no matter how hungry she was.

With her orb of fire trailing her, Agatha wandered over to her discarded clothes and dressed, then shuffled to the bed and dropped onto it. Before her eyelids closed for the last time for the day, she caught a glint of light off the trash heap. An idea sparked. If she could melt plastic, maybe she could make the metal hot enough to form it into a weapon. Vulcan would have a nice surprise waiting for him when he came back. But that could wait until tomorrow.

16

LEA

Lea kicked an empty cup that littered the sidewalk. "I know we've been here for all of like twelve hours and most of those were spent sleeping, but I'm just going to say it — Athens is the dirtiest city I've ever seen."

Thomas said, "My mom was here the summer of the Olympics, but before they started. What year was that?"

"2004," Luka said.

"We weren't even alive then. How did you know that so quick?" Thomas marveled. "Do you have an encyclopedic knowledge of the Olympics stored away up there?"

"Actually, yes," Luka beamed. "I love the Olympics. It's probably my favorite thing … besides you, of course." He made an overly dramatic kissy face at Lea.

"Oh, gag me with a spoon," she said.

"Hang on," Thomas said. "Did you suggest we go to Olympia just because it's where the Olympics started, or did you think we might find something there?"

Luka began whistling and turned conspicuously away from the other two.

"Nice," Thomas grumbled.

"I wasn't really gonna let us go there."

Bored with the back and forth, Lea looked at her watch. Almost five o'clock. "Alright, let's head that way. By the time we get there, it will be closed and most of the tourists should have cleared out already."

The trio turned their backs to the Parthenon and toward the path that would take them to the base of the Areopagus. They took the steps to the top of the giant rock and stood overlooking the city. Luka pointed out the closest building to the northwest. It stood alone, surrounded on all sides by foliage. "That's it," he said. "The Temple of Hephaestus. Do you want a history lesson? I did some research."

"Umm, no thanks," Lea said.

"Too bad. It's dedicated to Hephaestus and Athena, which she couldn't have been happy about since he raped her and she had his son, Erichthonius. She kept the boy away from Hephaestus and raised him in secret. So it's kind of weird that they have a temple together."

"Well, at least we know he's been a creep for his entire existence and it's not a recent development."

"Is that reassuring?" Luka asked, confused.

"Sure," she said. "That way, nobody will have a crisis of conscience when it comes time to kill him."

"As if we can actually kill him."

"We can," Thomas said with quiet ferocity. "And we will. Let's go."

We'll see. Lea remembered the night a few weeks ago when Thomas had been unable to kill the priest. She's the one who had to spear him through the chest with a flagpole. And now she'd steeled herself for the same eventuality with Vulcan. Except with much smaller chances of a successful outcome. It was much more probable that they all three ended up dead, and Agatha too, since he wouldn't have any more use for her after that.

She followed Thomas and Luka down the ankle-wrecking face of the outcropping. The trail led in a generally northern direction past the leveled ruins of the ancient city. All that persisted on the remains were the footings and wall bases. Centuries of invasions and weather had been unkind to most everything.

One section of the trail was cordoned by caution tape where concrete had been poured. Luka eased up to it, stuck his leg under the tape, and pushed his foot down on the still-wet concrete.

"What the heck are you doing?" Lea said.

He yanked his foot up and whirled around. When he saw it was Lea, his look of dread at being caught evolved into a grin. "I'm immortal now. I've left my mark on Greece, like Hercules and Achilles."

She looked down to see the imprint of his Adidas. "You're an idiot."

He shrugged it off and sped up to catch to Thomas. Lea hesitated a moment before squatting down and pressing her hand into the cement beside Luka's footprint.

"Oy!" someone yelled from behind her.

Lea stood up and saw an official-looking person scurrying her way. She gave him the finger and took off toward Luka and Thomas, whose heads she saw through the crowd of tourists bobbing ahead of her. She pulled up beside Luka and grabbed his hands.

"Why are you so out of breath?"

She showed him her other hand that was lightly coated in wet concrete. "I got caught."

Luka looked over his shoulder but didn't see anyone following. He raised his eyebrows. "So who's the idiot now?"

"Shut up," she said, nudging his ribs.

As the trees gave way to a grassy field, a view of the Temple of Hephaestus opened in front of them. Lea took a deep and uneasy breath. Sober concern replaced the fleeting moments of levity she'd had.

"This temple is in a little better shape than the last one. Especially after fire fingers there got done with it."

"Yeah," she said. From this distance, it looked … well, not perfect, but close. All the marble columns remained in place, though some of the blocks that made up the shaft looked like a half-finished game of Jenga. The roof was almost entirely intact. Nothing they'd seen to this point matched it. "Does it seem like it's in unnaturally good condition to you?"

Luka shrugged. "They used it as an Orthodox church for a long time, and then it was a museum until about a hundred years ago. So I guess they had good reason to take care of it."

"Maybe," Lea said, a sense of unease clinging to her like a staticky blanket. She shivered.

"Are you jumpy?" Luka asked.

"No," she said defensively.

He kept looking at her, clearly not buying her answer.

"Fine. A little. Something doesn't seem right to me. Ask him."

Thomas stood a meter or so away, staring at the structure.

"Hey," Luka called.

Thomas looked his way.

"What do you think?"

"I think we give it a few more minutes."

The crowds had thinned considerably in this area of the park over the last several minutes, but there were still dozens of people milling around.

Luka suggested, "What if a sudden rain shower encouraged them to leave?"

Lea looked at the cloudless sky. "Wouldn't that be a little conspicuous? But maybe if the wind got a little breezy?"

He grinned, and Thomas didn't object.

"Alright, you two come stand in front of me." Thomas and

Luka stood side-by-side facing the temple. "Don't stand there with your hands in front of your junk. You look like you're posing for a picture."

The boys dropped their hands from in front of them. Thomas shoved his hands into his pockets, while Luka fiddled awkwardly. Lea redirected her attention to her task. She stood an arm's length behind them with her hands out, but not touching them.

A sudden burst of wind across the grounds sent foreigners scrambling for unsecured hats and maps that had blown away. A second gust set jackets to flapping, zippers assaulting their wearers. The unexpected winds were enough to empty the clearing and temple area of its remaining occupants.

Before Lea turned the shut-off valve on her können, a small panel of marble frieze blew off the temple and crashed to the ground, shattering.

"Might have been a touch heavy-handed," Lea said with a grimace.

"That was super weird," Luka said. "I could feel my guts rattling."

Thomas agreed, "Yeah, that's an experience I'd rather not repeat."

The trio walked across the grass to where the broken marble lay in dozens of pieces on the temple's east end. Lea reached down and picked up a shard. She examined it for a minute before sticking it in her bag.

"I thought you were done with that, Clepto," Luka teased.

"Souvenir."

"Hey, Thomas, did you take a 'souvenir' from Sicily — since I guess that's what we're calling theft of property now?"

Thomas shook his head and wandered toward the steps on the other side of the cable that roped off the temple itself from tourists. Luka and Lea followed. Thomas stepped over the cable and ascended the three steps to the temple floor.

"Are you sure about this?" Luka asked.

"We didn't come here just to look at it," Thomas said.

Lea ducked under the cable, because she was too short to easily step over it. "This is the only ancient site in the city that's named after him, so it seems like the best starting point."

Luka looked around before joining them at the top of the steps.

17

LEA

THE TRIO CROSSED the portico toward the heart of the temple's cella. Except for the polygon on the floor where the sun intruded through the western doorway at a severe angle, the chamber was entirely dark. Until their eyes acclimated from the bright outdoor sunlight, they could not discern any details.

They paused at the entrance, Thomas stepped through first. Lea inhaled deeply and followed. After Luka crossed the threshold and entered the cella, something ... happened. The light from the outside world was shut off. Darkness permeated everything. Lea grabbed hold of the boys' wrists.

Oil lanterns sprang to life. Four on each of the northern and southern walls. Lea was certain they hadn't been there a minute ago. And what they illuminated certainly hadn't been. The walls shimmered with golden light. A stone altar stood in the middle of the room. An iron brazier adorned with smithing tools sat on the altar.

The dancing light drew Lea's attention to two sculptures on the far side of the temple. A bearded brute of a man and an angelical young woman. Hephaestus and Athena. A man emerged from a door between the sculptures and strode toward the trio.

Thomas pulled free of Lea's wrist and immediately carried fire in his palms. The man who approached gestured, and Thomas' fire was extinguished.

"Scheisse," Lea whispered.

The three stepped backward almost in unison, finding their backs to the wall.

"Who are you?" she asked.

"You have used your mageia on our grounds," the figure accused, ignoring the question. Still, he approached, his tunic dusting the ground as he walked.

Luka leaned into her. "What's mag … what he said?"

Lea stepped forward and said, "It was me."

"I know. My question is not who, but why."

"Oh," Lea said sheepishly.

"Are you here to worship?"

"Worship?" Thomas scoffed. "Hardly. I need to know where to find Vul—Hephaestus."

The man's face blazed with curiosity at the brazen boy in front of him. "To what end?"

"He killed my grandmother and took my mother. After he tells me where to find her, I'm going to kill him."

So much for discretion. Lea had hoped they could gain more information than they gave to whoever this was, but it looked like most of their cards were on the table now.

"That should make things considerably easier," the man said.

Okay, that was unexpected.

Thomas said, "You never told us who you are."

"I am the overseer of this temple. You may call me by my title, Epitiritis. I am a priest. Of sorts. Our religion has passed on from this world. Nothing but Hephaestus remains of it."

"Dude, how old are you?" Luka marveled.

Epitiritis smiled but did not directly answer the question. "I am nearly as old as Hephaestus himself, but I may not be relieved of my duties until he too has passed on and I escort him to Hades."

"Whoa. That's grim," Luka said.

Thomas asked, "Why did you say it would make things easier since I plan to kill him?"

The priest took a minute to answer. "Because if you had intended to join him, I would have slain you."

"You could have tried," Lea said defiantly.

"I have many forms. This is but one of them."

Lea shivered as a wave of cold dread washed over her. She thought she saw the glimmer of a beast hover over him, but when she tried to focus on it, only the priest was there. "Whatever. So you're fine with us killing him then?"

"You will find that a more formidable task than the cavalier manner in which you speak of it. He has murdered each and every one of his rivals. He has thwarted countless assassination attempts. He is more wily and has more guile than any of the other gods. As to your question, I will not interfere, but neither can I aid you."

"He is not a god," Thomas said through gritted teeth.

"Of course he is not. We did not know what else to do with the ones in whom the mageia was so strong. So we pronounced them gods. But because they were depraved and insatiable humans, rather than gods, this exaltation served only to make them detestable. Even time has been unable to blot out their stain entirely."

"Do you know who he is?" Luka asked, pointing a thumb at Thomas.

"How would I know that?" the priest responded.

Luka shrugged. "I didn't know if maybe you were omniscient or something."

Epitiritis tilted his head and held Luka's gaze for a minute before turning his attention to Thomas. "Are you of significance?"

Thomas said, "No. I don't know. I don't think so." After taking a breath to collect himself, he said, "I am Hephaestus' grandson."

"Ah. That does not necessarily make you consequential. He has fathered many children, most of whom were — to his great displeasure — not worthy of any consideration."

Luka came to Thomas' defense. "Well, he's—"

His sentence ended in a grunt when Lea elbowed him sharply in the ribs and growled, "Shut up." *He'll complain about that later.* She'd hit him rather harder than she intended to, but he just wouldn't stop talking.

"It is best that you do not trust me with too much information. I do not have any loyalty to you. Thus far our only association is a tenuous connection based on a common adversary."

Lea asked, "How can he be your enemy if you're a priest in his temple?"

"I am its overseer. My duty is to the religion, not to the man. He has betrayed everything of substance in his life, including himself. The time for his reckoning has drawn near, but I am incapable of executing it."

"Who can?" Thomas said.

"That is unknown to me," Epitiritis replied.

"I'm going to do it."

"So you have said."

A prolonged silence fell over the quartet. The priest looked as comfortable with it as anyone Lea had ever seen. *When you've been around for that long, what's a few minutes of awkward silence?*

Thomas asked, "What do I need to know to pull this off?"

"As I have said before, I cannot aid you in your efforts," Epitiritis said. And although he stopped speaking, he didn't appear to be finished. Finally, he resumed, having apparently come to a conclusion. "But I can tell you he believes that he can only be killed at the place of his birth. You would do well to draw him there."

"Is it true?" Lea asked.

"I do not know."

"Then why does he think it's true?"

"My guess is that it's the only place he has ever slain those like himself. Therefore, he has come to assume that is the only place it can be done."

"But where is it?" Luka asked impatiently.

Epitiritis sighed. "It is my understanding that you have machines on which you can obtain all the information ever known by humankind. Is that correct?"

"Basically."

"Then I expect you will figure out where Hephaestus was born."

"It's Mount Olympus, isn't it?" Thomas said.

The overseer nodded with approval, cutting his eyes toward Luka.

"I have one more question," Thomas said.

"I will hear it."

"Vulcan kidnapped my mother. I'm not sure how. But I've seen him use a portal before, and I think that's probably how he did it. He says she is still alive, but we haven't been able to figure out where he's keeping her. He did the same thing with my aunt a number of years ago, and she lost her mind. She's been catatonic ever since."

"Why did he take her? What is his interest in her?" the priest asked.

Thomas said, "It's not her—"

Lea cut him off. "You have your secrets and we have ours. Do you know where he's taken her?"

The priest crossed his arms, clearly displeased at having information withheld from him. He huffed before answering. "He has likely taken her to the same place as he took Hera when he abducted her. Kidnapping powerful women has been something of a signature for him."

"You have not answered the question," Lea said. "Where is she?"

"Has anyone ever told you that you are exceedingly impudent?"

Lea grinned. "They don't usually use such polite language when they say it, but yeah, I've heard that before. So?"

"So … only Hephaestus knows the answer. You will have to take it up with him."

The fading sunlight reached out toward Epitiritis' foot as it crept across the floor. He slid away from it. "It is time for you to go," he said abruptly. "Be mindful of using your mageia in the ancient places. It can have unforeseen consequences."

He turned and walked away without another word. As he passed between the sculptures of Hephaestus and Athena, the light from the torches extinguished.

"Every bit of that was weird," Luka said.

"Thomas, give us some fire. I want to see something," Lea instructed.

"He *just* warned us against that."

"Right. Good call," she said. "Use your phone then. Shine it on the walls."

Thomas did as he was told. *That's what I thought.* Nothing was gilded any longer. No lanterns adorned the walls. She walked across the middle of the room, where a moment ago she would have had to go around an altar. On the far side, there were only bare walls. Not even an imprint on the floor where the monuments to the gods had once stood.

18

THOMAS

THOMAS TUGGED on his small pack and stood up. He rubbed his quads, which were already feeling tight. "It's a good thing the hostel let us check our bags into lockers. It would have been rough having to lug them up this mountain."

The new bags they'd bought in town had allowed them to reduce their loads to a few liters of water, an extra pair of socks, and a couple of extra layers in case the weather turned against them on the mountain. And snacks, plenty of snacks. Except for Luka, who had outfitted himself for an expedition. If they did find Agatha, she was going to kill him the first time she checked her credit card statement.

Lea sat on a boulder switching out socks.

Thomas paused, searching in his bag for an elusive Snickers bar and gestured at her footwear. "Are you glad you finally agreed to trade out your Doc Martens for some sneakers?"

"I had no idea how light shoes could be," she said excitedly. "My feet are like five pounds lighter. I think I could basically run up this mountain."

"It's about time, too. Those boots are pretty busted up."

"Easy," she warned. "I've walked more miles in those things than I've walked with any of you." Then, with a lighter air, she added, "They're basically a part of my soul. Besides, my calves look great because of them."

"Uh-huh," Thomas said, finding it incomprehensible how someone could be so attached to a pair of broken-down boots.

Luka squatted over a pile of pine straw, striking his new camp knife against a Ferro rod like he'd been doing for the last ten minutes, to very little effect. Sparks showered the kindling, causing pieces of straw to glow briefly before turning gray without creating a flame.

Luka grunted and swore. "Who knew it was so hard to make fire?"

"Most people?" Lea said. "That's kind of why we invented modern conveniences. Because the first ten thousand years of human history were kind of a drag."

Luka leaned in and blew on the pine straw. A tendril of smoke peeked out and a couple of embers glowed briefly, but still no flame emerged.

"Want some help?" Thomas offered.

"No, I don't want your help," Luka said defiantly, covering the pile with his hands as though Thomas might lob a fireball over his shoulder. "I can do this without using your dark magic."

Luka returned to scraping the metal and stone against each other with renewed vigor. Thomas knew it wasn't even about making fire as much as it was about proving his friends wrong.

Lea looked at her watch as she put her water bottle away. "If you're going to do it, you'd better get on with it. According to the trail map, we've got like four more hours ahead of us."

"Well, if *somebody* would have let us ride up to the car park and go from there instead of having to start in Litochoro, we could have been to the refuge already and had one of those giant bowls of pasta — did I show you the pictures? Maybe we could have even summited today."

Thomas didn't want to have to defend his decision again. It's not like he could explain it anyway. He had felt that it was important for them to take the entire pilgrimage up the mountain. They hadn't really argued with him about it, but he could tell from their expressions when he told them the plan, they weren't totally bought in either. But didn't it show even greater loyalty that they were willing to go with him without having to understand his reasoning?

They weren't here to summit Mount Olympus like a group of tourists. He didn't even know if they would summit. Whatever was going to happen could occur anywhere along the way. They had a purpose. A purpose that hadn't changed in the last — he checked the date on his watch — sixteen days. However and wherever that might manifest.

He wandered into questions about what Agatha had been going through for more than two weeks now. Elle had only been gone a few days, and when she came back, she was zonked out of her mind. His mother may not exist anymore. Not as he'd known her anyway. Even if they found her, she might be a shell of herself. Was it even worth doing at this point?

Thomas stood up suddenly and stormed away from the other two, angry that he'd even allowed the question. Behind him, he heard Luka whisper, "What was that about?" He didn't have to see Lea to know her noncommittal reply. They'd spent so much time with each other since they'd left home that they knew each other as well as they knew themselves. Or at least, it felt that way at times.

He walked halfway across the wooden bridge that spanned the creek where they'd stopped, and leaned over the rail. The water was as clear as if it had just rolled off a glacier, the same color as the Gutach in Hornberg in the earliest days of spring.

Luka rose to his feet and kicked his collection of kindling.

"Impossible," he grumbled. He shoved his fire-making kit and sheathed knife into the side pocket of his bag and pointed his palms toward his pile of charred debris, using his können to douse it and wash it into the creek.

"He should not have done that," a voice said from the other side of the bridge.

Thomas whirled to see where the soft voice had come from and spotted Ning scratching his back against the trunk of a Bosnian pine tree. Thomas rushed over to the panda. "What are you doing here?"

The creature groaned as he wriggled against the tree with his eyes closed. "I thought you would be happy to see me," he pouted.

"I am. Just surprised. You were gone for like twelve years, and now I've seen you twice in the last few days." Thomas paused as something occurred to him. "Can they see you?" he asked, gesturing at his friends.

Ning looked across the water. "Of course they *can* see me. But they have not noticed me. They are too preoccupied with themselves to be concerned about the likes of me."

Hushed voices and giggling carried across the water. Thomas didn't turn to see. He could guess. He asked again, "Why are you here, Ning?"

"I am here to tell you not to flaunt your abilities like that. It is an extraordinarily bad idea. They know you're here now. You should not draw further attention, though it likely will not matter. It is not as though they will forget."

"Who knows we're here?"

"The dryads who watch over these woods and this mountain."

"What are dryads?"

"You might know them as wood nymphs," Ning suggested.

Thomas grimaced and shook his head. "Like fairies?"

Ning rolled onto all fours and pushed himself up. "Not in

the sense that you mean. You would do well not to think of them as harmless."

Thomas patted his cheeks lightly, thinking. It sounded less than ideal that they'd drawn the attention of these dryads. Or maybe they could help. "Are they good or bad?"

"That question is irrelevant. The answer is too contextual. They are neither good nor bad. They are watchers. Whether you perceive them as good or bad is determined only by your relationship to the mountain. But that will say more about you than it says about them," he answered with a self-satisfied smile.

"That was … less helpful than you seem to think."

Ning signaled toward the trail. "It is time to move along, Thomas. You have assumed a congregation." Ning looked around and apparently saw things that Thomas could not. "And please do avoid drawing any further attention to yourself and your friends."

Hearing footsteps on the bridge, Thomas looked over his shoulder. Luka and Lea held hands as they made their way across.

"What are you doing?" Luka asked.

Thomas turned back to the tree before answering. Ning had vanished. "Talking to an imaginary friend."

Lea raised an eyebrow at him. "Alright, weirdo."

"If you're lonely, I can share Lea with you," Luka said with a laugh.

Lea dropped his hand and grabbed him by the shirt, pulling him close. Her cheeks flashed red with anger. "Am I a toy car that you share with your friend so he doesn't feel left out?"

A gust of wind whirled through the gully.

Thomas intervened with a harsh whisper. "Stop. No können. Not here."

They both looked at him with concern. Lea let Luka go and patted his shirt flat against his chest. She swiveled and headed up the trail, patting Thomas on the butt as she passed him. Thomas tensed up in surprise.

"Besides," she said over her shoulder, "if I think your friend needs some attention, I'll handle it myself."

Luka's expression turned from fearful to dour. "She didn't mean it," he said to Thomas as he followed after her.

19

THOMAS

Luka leaned back in his chair and patted his protruding, pasta-filled belly. "This may be my finest hour."

"I'll admit, it's impressive that you can shove that much food down your throat," Lea said. "Not the good kind of impressive. But it definitely leaves an impression."

"I think you're going to regret that come tomorrow morning," Thomas added.

"What? I'm carbo-loading."

Lea wiped her mouth and set her spoon into her soup bowl. "Yeah, I don't think that's how it works."

Before he spoke next, Luka sat up and looked around to see if anyone within earshot was paying attention to them. "What's the plan for tomorrow?" he asked quietly.

"We get up well before the sun and the rest of the hikers, and we head toward the peaks. We'll come to Skala first, and on the other side of it is Mytikas. At some point, we'll rise above the tree line and there won't be any cover for anybody to hide behind. I don't know if he will show up, but I expect he will. And it'll probably be when we are most exposed."

Lea asked, "What happens if he shows?"

Thomas looked away from them toward the sky that was mostly purple, though red and orange firebrands still flared out over the western mountains. He breathed out slowly and turned back toward them. He wanted to be looking at them when he answered. "I don't know."

"Of course you don't," Lea snapped before standing up abruptly and walking away. They watched her go to the north-facing railing and stand there with her arms crossed.

"I really don't know," Thomas said.

"I know."

"I've been trying to think of something. Of what we should do and can do against him, but I'm kind of in over my head here."

"I know. She's just worried. Mostly about you, but about us, too. She's not really mad. No, I mean — she is mad, but worried-mad, not mad-mad. You know?"

Thomas gave a half-smile. "Weirdly, despite your total lack of eloquence, I know what you mean. It's like when your mom used to get angry at us when we did something that might get us hurt."

"Like when you lit me up like a human torch?" Luka said, gesturing from his hip across to his shoulder.

"She said she wasn't mad about that," Thomas said in surprise.

"Of course, she said that to you. You already felt bed enough. And by the time you finally came over, that storm had already blown itself out. Also, can we not compare my girlfriend to my mom?" he said with a shiver. "Don't want to get any wires crossed."

Lea still hadn't moved from where she planted herself. Luka pushed his chair back and started pushing himself up. Thomas gestured for him to sit down. "Probably best if I go clean up my own mess."

"That's good," Luka said, patting his belly. "I was going to have to roll over there anyway. Too much pasta."

On the way from the table to the railing, Thomas racked his brain, trying to figure out what he could say that would make things better. But he just kept coming back to how little he knew what he was doing. Everything had felt like guesswork for weeks. And not even educated guesses. They'd been what his mother, in her more frustrated moments, called wild-ass-guesses. His world had been upside down basically since he'd met Pastor Stefan.

"Hey," Thomas said.

"Look," Lea said. "I just don't want to die on this mountain because we don't have a plan."

"So we're jumping right into this, huh?"

"I've had plenty of time to think while you two did rochambeau or whatever to decide who had to come deal with me."

Thomas chose his next words carefully, but he wasn't sure how they'd land. "Just so we're clear … you're okay with dying as long as we have a plan?"

She nudged him in the ribs with an elbow, but he had finally elicited a smile. She turned toward Thomas, putting a hand on his arm. "Real talk. You all are my family — you, Emma, Finn, and Luka. You are the family I chose, not the one I was born into. And that matters more to me than blood. I'll do whatever I need to for you."

Thomas looked away, suddenly flush with emotion. That was far more touching than anything he'd expected from her. Everything was so raw. It didn't take much for his feelings to break through to the surface. He cleared his throat before responding. "I don't know what's going to happen, but I don't think it's going to be some uncomfortable conversation again where he makes demands and I say no, and everyone walks away."

"I think you're probably right."

Thomas was quiet for a long time.

"I saw him kill a man with his bare hands. Just squeezed his neck until it crunched. What am I supposed to do against that?"

"We, Thomas. What are *we* supposed to do against that?"

"Fine. We. And I don't want to seem like that doesn't mean anything to me, because it does — it means a lot — but *we* don't have a chance against him."

"Maybe not."

He looked back at her in shock at the seemingly resigned response that defied the cavalier tone in which she had delivered it. "That's it? You walked away when I didn't have a plan, but now that I still don't have a plan and think we might not make it through this, you're just going to agree with me?"

"Would you rather I stand here and blow smoke at you?"

Thomas shook his head. "No, I wouldn't rather that." After another pause, he said, "Here's what I do know — we have to get up well before the sun so that no one else is around for a long time, so that whatever happens has time to play out."

"Alright, I'm going to let it slide that you already told us that part of the plan because it's all that you've got," she said, turning her back against the railing. "Let's get back to Luka before he creates things to worry about." As they walked, she laced her arm through his. "On second thought, I'll just give him a little something to fret over."

Thomas stopped, bringing Lea to an awkward halt. She looked at him quizzically.

"One last thing," he said with a smirk. "If we're your family, like you said, does that mean that you and Luka are committing incest?"

Lea shoved him with one arm and walked away. Over her shoulder, she said, "You two have been spending too much time together."

Thomas' pillow vibrated, pulling him out of a peculiar dream about zebras and the movie *Tremors*. The pillow buzzed again. He reached under it and pulled out his phone. A cheery, dancing alarm clock greeted him on the screen. Warmth and coziness tempted him to lay his head back down for just a minute, but he decided against it. He slid out of the bunk and put his bare feet on the cold tile floor.

Standing up, he turned toward the top bunk and rustled Luka, who farted loudly and groaned, but did not wake. Thomas shook him again, with even fewer results. Resorting to more extreme measures, Thomas yanked the covers off his friend. Luka rolled from his belly onto his side and curled his legs up. But he still didn't awaken.

Thomas conceded for the moment and went to Lea. He set a hand lightly on her shoulder. She grabbed his wrist and jerked upright, eyes wide.

"It's me. It's okay," Thomas said.

Lea released her hold on him and sat up. "Turn around." When he did, she flung the covers back and slipped on the pants she'd laid beside the bed.

"I couldn't get Luka to wake up," he whispered.

"I'll handle it." She went to the bunk, and stepping on the side of Thomas' bed, spoke quietly into Luka's ear. He bolted upright, nearly hitting his head on the ceiling. "Really?!" he said too loudly.

"No."

Luka slumped. "Oh."

"It's time to get up," she said as she stepped down and returned to her bed to put on socks and shoes.

They managed to get outside without rousing any of the refuge's other guests. Thomas was glad to see that none of them were making their start up the mountain quite so early as his little band.

The wind whistled past them on its way across the mountain. "Better put some layers on," Luka said. It was a fair bit colder than it had been the night before. They set their packs down and pulled out extra shirts and jackets.

"Which way?" Lea asked.

Thomas pointed. "The trail starts just beside that fountain."

There was just enough moonlight to let them make their way across the grounds. Before they entered the forest in which the ambient light was cut off, Luka asked, "Thomas, can you do us the honors?"

Instead of making a ball of light to guide their way, he handed out headlamps.

"Really?" Lea said, turning it over in her hand.

"Yeah. Use the red light so it won't wreck your night vision."

Luka and Lea did as instructed and started down the trail, which was now cast in a monochromatic crimson glow.

"This is kind of messing with my depth perception," Luka said from the front of the line. "Can't you just conjure something up for us?"

"No, it's not … for the best."

Lea and Luka stopped and turned, looking at him. Thomas put a hand in front of his eyes, shielding them from the lights. "Turn those off or point them down or something."

All three clicked off their lights. The darkness was even more oppressive than had they not been using the headlamps at all.

"Talk," Lea demanded.

"Do you remember what the priest said about using our können in these places with ancient magic?"

He could make out Lea's nodding head now through the darkness and sunspots. "Yeah, he said something about unintended consequences."

"How did you put out your fire yesterday, Luka?"

Luka covered his face with his hands, and a muffled response emerged. "I didn't even think about it." He dropped his hands. "But so what? Nothing weird happened."

"Apparently, we drew the attention of some dryads."

"Is that bad?" Lea asked, peering into the blackened forest.

"I guess we'll find out."

"How do you know all this?" Luka asked.

"I'll tell you as we walk. We've got to get moving."

Luka turned on his heel and clicked his lamp back on. The path was steep and unsteady. "You remember when Finn went missing, and I told y'all about Ning, the panda that was with me in the mines?"

Lea grunted her affirmation.

"Well, he kind of popped in yesterday … and a few days before that, when I melted Vulcan's temple."

"What!" Lea said. It was not a question.

"I probably should have mentioned it sooner."

"Yeah, probably so."

Luka called back, "Well, what did he say?"

"Not much. Basically, what I just told you. He's less helpful than you might think."

The conversation fell away as their breathing became more labored from the combination of altitude and the steepness of the trail. After several minutes of hiking, the trees became more sparse.

By the time they reached the first significant milestone, the only plants were grasses and stunted shrubs. Luka found a stone bench and sat down heavily. Thomas and Lea took their places beside him, huffing from exertion. The sky behind them had begun to turn gray.

"Let's eat something. I'm about to starve to my actual death," Luka said, slinging his bag around to the front and rummaging through it.

Thomas said, "We ate something before we lit out."

"First of all — lit out? Are we in a Western? And secondly — second? — secondly? Whatever. No one said we were eating."

Lea sighed. "Do you need me to breathe for you, too?"

"I mean, if you're offering mouth-to-mouth, then yeah, I'll take you up on that."

"Dummkopf," she said, but there was a laugh hiding behind it.

The eastern sky evolved from gray to purple as they sat. Thomas fidgeted impatiently but said nothing. They had another ninety minutes ahead of them. But maybe it was for the best that they would have some light before too long. The woman who ran the refuge told him that in another half mile, the trail would turn into a thin carving on a sloped shale field that they had to traverse for nearly a mile. It lacked any cover and was prone to rockfalls, but the good news was that this portion of trail would lead them to Skala, the first of the two summits they would encounter … unless something else happened first.

Wind howled around them, the chill piercing their layers. Luka stood up and, with a mouthful of food, said, "I can finish while we walk."

Lea and Thomas popped up off the frigid stone bench, and the trio headed west, guided by Luka's red beam and the growing ambient light.

20

LEA

LEA PULLED her sweater off and wiped her face with it. Despite the cool temperatures and breeze, she was sweating. Not glistening or whatever other nonsense terms girls used to avoid call sweating what it was. She was full-on dude sweating.

She felt like she'd been undersold on the degree of difficulty of hiking uphill on loose rocks while trying not to fall to her death off the side of a mountain. And that was if she was lucky. If luck didn't travel with her, she'd just be maimed and have to wait for hours until help arrived while she tried not to stare at the femur protruding through her skin with bits of muscle still clinging to it.

While she looked down the mountainside, trying not to envision herself as a tangled mess at the bottom, she noticed the mist hugging the valley floor that was still blue and ensconced in shadow. The sun that now warmed her neck would burn it away before too long.

Over the last half-hour, the trio had grown quiet. They weren't on a fun adventure any more. They never really had been, though they'd found enough moments of levity in the horror show they were living through. But the gravity of their circumstance always returned, pressing down on them relentlessly. The lyrics of the David Bowie song jumped into her head, but she'd rather not have that earworm the rest of the day, so she pushed against it. Not that pushing back ever worked.

It was not the circumstantial gravity that was weighing on her most now, but literal gravity. And this endless, uphill gravel trail. She returned to watching Luka's feet clop up and down like pistons. You needed someone like him leading. Someone whose pace didn't vary when their mind wondered. Someone who plodded along, their endless optimism driving them forward.

"I think that's it. Up there," Luka said, pointing.

She looked up and to the left. The trail seemed to reach the sky and stop as it curved. It could be the summit. She dared not put too much hope in that, though, as it might just be a place where the trail turned or leveled out.

The wind picked up as they neared the top of the ridge above them. Aside from a few small flowers that braved the elements, the surrounding landscape consisted entirely of shades of brown and gray.

When they hit the ridgeline, she saw that Luka had been right. Skala peak was in sight. The trail deteriorated into a jumble of broken rocks and boulders that they scrambled across. *It's a shame we don't have a heilerin. Somebody's bound to break an ankle.*

Lea looked back, checking on Thomas. He was the first of them to have become solemn as they hiked. She found him a few paces behind her, pulling himself through the narrow pass she'd just traversed. They made eye contact but said nothing. Desperate anticipation clung to them.

Luka broke through to the peak and halted. "Scheisse."

Lea nearly crashed into him as she turned. She tried to push him forward, but he didn't budge. She nudged him to the right and peered around him. "Oh." She whirled back around to

Thomas, her ashen face telling him everything he needed to know.

Vulcan squatted on his haunches on the broken ground above them, scratching casually at the stone with a chisel. Without looking up, he said, "You three made pretty good time."

Lea stepped up beside Luka, and Thomas came alongside her. She couldn't help but marvel at Vulcan. Even in this posture, he was almost as tall as her. And built more like a rhinoceros than a man. When he stood up and towered over them, her courage faltered. What were they doing here? Why had they ever thought they could do anything other than get themselves killed? He was the mountain atop the mountain. Vulcan leered at her, and she cast her eyes at the ground.

"That's right, child," he said, reveling in her reaction. "Look at her."

Luka and Thomas followed the instruction.

"I know that look," Luka said dismissively. "That's not fear. It's disgust. Have you seen your ugly face in a mirror in the last thousand years?"

Oh, no. Not this. Not now.

Luka kept going. "Isn't that why you got thrown off this mountain in the first place? Because you were too horrible to look at? News flash. Nothing's changed, dude."

Vulcan tensed, and his grip on the chisel tightened. All of his nonchalance had fled.

"You want to know why we're here?" Luka taunted. "To finish what your mother started when she tried to drown you."

Vulcan hurled the chisel at Luka. In his rage, he had lost precision, and it went wide to Luka's right, smashing into a stone and embedding itself. "You die first," Vulcan growled.

Luka took several exaggeratedly elegant steps to his right, as if he were preparing for a fencing duel. But Lea knew that having made himself the target of Vulcan's wrath, he was now putting space between himself and the other two.

But Vulcan turned his attention to Thomas. "Before I deal with him, I have something to say to you. I want you to hear it now, because I suspect you won't be in any mood to listen after I maul him. Then her. And after that, I'll contend with you."

If Vulcan was waiting for a response from Thomas before continuing, he got nothing.

"I chose this place because I want you to be in sight of Mytikas without reaching it. My patience has run out. The three of you will die knowing that your goal was beyond your grasp. It's symbolic, you understand."

Vulcan stumbled forward with a lurch. Luka had hit him in the back with a harmless but unignorable blast of water that now puddled at Vulcan's feet.

"Enough with the speeches. Besides, *you* were the goal, not some mountain peak that has meaning to you, but not to the rest of us," Luka said. He shrugged off his backpack and shook his hands out at his side, then balled his fists and licked his thumbs like he was some absurd street brawler.

It was the bravest thing Lea had ever seen. Even David had better odds against Goliath.

To her left, Thomas' stoic expression hadn't changed. He hadn't moved since taking his place beside her. Anger sprouted inside her. Luka was going to die for Thomas' cause — well, to be fair, they all were — but Luka would die first. It was going to be gruesome and horrible, and Thomas couldn't even bring himself out of his funk. Just like with the pastor in Hornberg. He was supposed to be the one with even better superpowers, but a hell of a lot of good that was if he wouldn't use them.

Vulcan roared and yanked his hammer out of his belt. "Enough with your petty insults."

She hadn't heard what Luka said, but it clearly struck a nerve.

He closed in on Luka with unexpected speed, raising the giant hammer high over his head and bringing it down with both hands. Luka dove out of the way and rolled, skittering across the loose rock. The hammer obliterated a rock just behind where Luka had been.

As Vulcan swiveled to go after him again, Luka scrambled up a boulder, nearing the highest point of the peak. Lea knew he didn't have a strategy. He was just reacting, trying to avoid having his ribcage turned to jelly.

Lea raised her hands over her head and brought them down with a flourish. Lightning crashed onto the stone between Luka and Vulcan, but much closer to Luka than either of them would have liked. He dove for cover much too late for it to have been effective.

"You continue to impress, Lea," Vulcan said. "My offer still stands."

Luka yelled at her from behind a rock. "Let's maybe not do that again. No sense having two of you trying to kill me."

She didn't know what to do. Nothing else in her arsenal seemed like it would make any difference. She looked around for something, anything she could use as a weapon.

Vulcan advanced on Luka, overturning the stone he'd been hiding behind. Luka bounded off again, but Vulcan snatched him by the back of his shirt and ripped him off the ground.

Lea charged at Vulcan and punched him in the back several times. But she was nothing more than a nuisance. He turned while still holding Luka aloft and shoved her to the ground. "Stay," he commanded, as though she were a dog. She popped up with as much defiance as she could muster. The shove hadn't injured her in any way, but it reinforced just how outmatched they were.

Luka kicked Vulcan in the chest. He grunted and, with his other hand, grabbed Luka by the throat. Luka's face reddened.

He sputtered as his arms and legs flailed. He pulled at Vulcan's clutched hand but couldn't pry even a finger away.

A torrent of flame burst past Lea and struck Vulcan squarely in the back. Lea looked over her shoulder to see Thomas slowly approaching with two streams of fire pouring from his hands. *About time. Welcome to the fray, Thomas.* The blaze didn't seem to cause much damage, but it had distracted Vulcan from crushing Luka. That was effect enough for now.

Vulcan whirled around, releasing Luka's throat and using him as a shield. Thomas immediately extinguished the flame. "Has it come to this, Thomas? You have rejected me all these years, only to die on this mountain? This place where I have spilled the blood of so many of our ancestors. I will soon add you and your friends to that number. It's a shame, really. You could have done wondrous things beyond your ability to conceive them now."

Thomas stood with his jaw set, his face glowing in the early morning sunlight. His hands were tensed at his sides, a gunslinger waiting for his moment.

"Thomas," Luka said gruffly, still suspended in the air. "Do you remember the day you burned me?"

That's the last thing you want to say to your best friend?

Thomas nodded.

"Remember why you fell?"

He nodded again.

"Lea," Luka said, letting her name hang in the air for a moment. It had been a weird ride for them, and they might be running out of track.

She waited for the rest of it, knowing full well that it might be something absurd, but hoping for something memorable.

"Blow me."

Lea nearly smiled. *Oh, I see now. This better work.*

Vulcan guffawed. "Strange last words, boy. I like your style.

Spiteful until the end. Too many get sentimental and conciliatory in the face of their mortality."

Luka expelled a blast of ice onto the ground underneath him. It rushed outward like a tide, encircling Vulcan. Thomas launched a ball of flame at Vulcan's head, causing him to flinch. While his balance was shifted, Lea hit Vulcan with a vicious gust of wind, knocking him back. When he tried to steady himself, Vulcan slipped on the ice underfoot. As his arms flailed, he flung Luka, who smashed into a boulder and landed roughly. Vulcan crashed to the ground, face down.

One shot. Lea called down lightning as she had before. Vulcan rolled onto his back and away from the bolt. The air shimmered with heat from the lightning as it missed its target. Admittedly, it would have missed even if he hadn't moved.

Luka jumped up off the ground, limping a bit.

Thomas called, "Luka, his hands."

Luka ran toward Vulcan, two streams of ice jetting toward him, and froze his hands and forearms to the ground to keep him from getting up. *How long will that hold?* It was already popping and cracking from the strain.

"Ning!" Thomas yelled.

A fat panda with an armful of bamboo plopped onto the mountaintop beside his summoner.

"Thomas, you seem to be in the midd—"

"Throw the bamboo down, Ning."

"There are ordinances that disallow my interference."

Vulcan was using his legs and back to buck against the ice and break its hold on him. Luka continued to pour it on him. Lea worried about how long he could sustain it, and the toll it would take.

"Do it! Now!"

"I am not allowed to affect your physical environment." Ning sat down with a huff. "Besides, you do not need me for this."

Thomas' expressions shuffled like a playlist from anger to

confusion to worry, before finally landing on comprehension. He squatted and flattened his hands on the stone at Vulcan's sandaled feet. A bamboo shoot emerged under each hand, causing small fissures where they embedded themselves. Thomas withdrew his hands as the shoots propelled themselves upward into fully matured stalk. When Thomas signaled, they bowed into arches, speared through the air like living javelins, and struck Vulcan's thighs, impaling him to the stone.

The ancient god roared in agony.

Thomas wasted no time in starting on a second set of bamboo while Vulcan writhed on the ground, trying not to move his legs and unable to free his hands. Two more shoots arced through the air above Vulcan and drove through his shoulders. He gritted his teeth and groaned.

"Don't let up," Thomas said to Luka.

Lea stood by, uncertain what to do, stricken with disbelief at how things had unfolded.

Thomas leapt from where he'd been standing at Vulcan's feet and landed on the giant's chest. He reached down to the pouch on Vulcan's belt and withdrew a chisel. "Lea, bring me his hammer."

Vulcan's eyes flared in recognition of what was about to happen. Thomas placed his hand just left of center on Vulcan's chest. "Is this what you used on Oma?" Thomas whispered. Smoke and an acrid smell arose from the leather jerkin that Vulcan wore, as the hide smoldered and burned away from Thomas' palm.

Lea handed the tool over. Thomas gripped the chisel in one hand. Soon, it glowed red with heat, sizzling against Vulcan's skin. He bared his teeth at the boy, who raised the heavy hammer over his head.

"You can't do this," Vulcan said with a grimace. "Agatha will die."

"We'll take our chances."

Thomas brought the hammer down on the glowing chisel with a dull ping. The metal cut through flesh and scraped against bone before getting lodged.

Luka had become too absorbed with what was happening and stopped what he'd been doing. Vulcan raged against his restraints. He broke his right hand free of the ice and grabbed for Thomas, catching hold of him, but not before Thomas brought the hammer down again, driving the chisel in all the way to the head.

Vulcan pulled Thomas close. "You have no idea what you have wrought." He clutched Thomas, even as his eyes grew dull.

When the strength ran out of Vulcan's hand, Thomas pushed it away, and it flopped onto the god's chest. Thomas jumped down and stepped away from the body. Lea and Luka congregated around him. Vulcan's life poured out of him, pooling onto stones of Mount Olympus. When the flood stopped, a deep rumbling began, and the mountain quaked beneath their feet. Boulders crumbled into shards. Shale flowed down the mountain in a rocky avalanche.

After several minutes of turmoil, everything fell still.

Luka said, "That can't be good, right?"

21

LEA

THE TRIO STOOD atop the eerily quiet mountain, the husk of an ancient god at their feet, and waited for something else to happen. Things felt somehow incomplete.

"Between the lightning and the earthquake, I don't think we have to worry about any other hikers for a while," Lea said.

"That's good, because we have the world's largest corpse to deal with," Luka said. "I kind of thought he would have used können against us. And can we talk about that lightning for a second?"

Lea crossed her arms but didn't stop him.

"You nearly barbecued me. Did you know electricity has a smell? I didn't either. But I do now. That's how close it was."

"I've never done it before, so I'd say you're pretty lucky to be here at all. It was a calculated risk."

"A calc—Unbelievable. Whatever. Your calculator may need some recalibration."

Thomas stepped away from them and went to sit with his back against an outcropping only a few feet from Vulcan's head. Lea nodded her head at him and whispered to Luka. "Maybe we can save this conversation for later."

Luka nodded and limped around the body to sit by his friend. He hugged his ribs as he sat, trying to alleviate the pain by applying some pressure.

Lea followed suit. She pulled her legs up to her chest and wrapped her arms around them. If she stretched her legs out, she could touch the shoulder of the god she had helped kill. She wasn't particularly comfortable being this close to him. For that matter, she wasn't particularly comfortable with the frequency with which she'd been killing people lately, either. That hadn't been on her Bingo card for this year. She didn't think anyone could fault her for either one, but that didn't stop the feeling that part of her soul was withering away each time.

"I have condemned her to die alone in whatever hole he has her stashed in," Thomas said bitterly.

"We'll find her, Thomas," Luka said. "It'll be okay."

"How?" he replied, anger underlying his quiet tone. "How do you think we're going to find her?"

For once, rather than continuing to talk when he didn't really have anything to say, Luka closed his mouth and looked down at his feet.

Lea pulled her jacket off and shoved it into her pack, giving herself something to do other than sit in the silence.

Finally, having had enough of pondering the gravity of their situation — and Agatha's — she answered a question that had been raised several minutes earlier. "His mageia was deeper than ours. I think he didn't have können like us. That's almost like surface level stuff. Vulcan moved in and out of ... I don't know. He opened portals to other places and moved himself and other things through them. He controlled volcanoes."

"We don't know if that's actually true," Luka said.

"What?" Lea asked in disbelief.

"We don't even know if it's true that he could control volcanoes and stuff. Sure, he was more powerful than us. But he definitely wasn't a god. So maybe the volcano stuff was just part of the legend."

They both looked to Thomas, inviting him to weigh in, but he was a thousand miles away, his eyes almost as empty as Vulcan's.

"I don't know," Lea said. "Maybe you're right, but something weird happened when he died."

"Well, one thing we do know — that panda is real," Luka said cheerily, patting Thomas on the back. "I'm not gonna lie, I was sure that you just made him up when you were a kid. Not like you were lying on purpose or something. Just like things got super crazy under that mountain, and your imaginary friend helped you get through it."

Thomas didn't respond. If it weren't for his chest moving as he breathed and the occasional blink, he wouldn't be exhibiting any signs of life.

"Anyway, what happened to him? I didn't see him after everything started."

"Probably left," Thomas answered quietly. "Ning isn't much for violence. He did the same thing when I was little."

Lea got to her feet and reached down to pull Luka up, then stepped to the side and did the same for Thomas. "Guys, we've got to figure out what to do. We don't have a lot of time, and we have a whole lot of corpse."

The trio looked at the body.

"I know you're trying not to say it," Thomas said. "There's only one way to get rid of it."

"Can you get it hot enough?" Lea asked.

"I melted stone."

"Right," she said, not knowing whether a fire hot enough to melt stone would be hot enough dispose of the bones too. And how long would that take? There wouldn't be any hiding the smoke either. There was no way this was going to work out well.

Thomas walked around to Vulcan's feet and laid hands on the bamboo stalks. They withered and shrank at his touch. The stalks left gaping holes in Vulcan's legs and shoulders as they retreated. Thomas whispered softly, but she couldn't make out his words and knew she wasn't intended to.

Thomas stood slowly and walked to Vulcan's side, retrieving the forging hammer and placing it on Vulcan's chest. He stepped back several paces and breathed deeply before raising his arms in front of him. He flexed his hands, delaying if only for a couple of seconds.

"That will not be necessary," a triad of voices spoke in unison.

Lea whirled around to her right, bringing up her hands in a defensive posture. She could not have anticipated what met her.

Three beings — she didn't know how else to describe them — stood at the forefront of a host of others like them. They had the most beautiful faces she had ever seen, each having a different complexion. But that was not the most striking thing about them. Not even close. Each was clothed in the bark of a tree. That wasn't the right way to see it. The tree was their essence. Though their faces were human, nothing else about them seemed to be except a shape that roughly evoked a woman's figure. Their hair was strands of vine and leaves, and where their torsos should have become hips and legs, a trunk extended toward the ground, evolving into roots that undulated around them.

The foremost among them carried an elaborate staff. It looked as though it had been grown rather than carved. White flowers with pink centers blossomed at the top of it.

"Come," the triad directed.

Luka, Lea, and Thomas did as they were told and gathered in front of the three dryads.

"We are the spirits of Olympus — Mytikas, Skala, and Skolio.

The others," they indicated the host behind them, "are its lesser peaks."

Their voices were mesmerizing. It was the most harmonious thing she had ever heard. The voices of the earth speaking directly to her. She had told the boys that Vulcan had the deep mageia, but these were even more primeval. She felt herself swooning, slipping into warmth.

"Do all the mountains have spirits?" Luka asked, his voice taking on the singsong quality of a hymn. He swayed in rhythm to the movement of the dryads.

"They once had. Many have now passed on," the triad answered. The host of dryads behind them hummed a mournful tune.

Lea yanked herself out of the comfortable quagmire, then reached over and pinched the back of his arm, hard enough to disrupt the enchantment that he was falling under. She looked at Thomas, but he stared vacantly at the ground before him, as he had before. Even the dryads' charmed tendrils had not grasped him.

"Hey," Lea yelled, stepping menacingly toward the triad.

Their beauty transformed into ferocity. They bared their teeth at her. Mytikas transformed her staff from a decoration to a weapon.

"Do not dare approach us, child," the triad hissed.

Luka grabbed Lea's wrist and wrenched her backward. She allowed him to pull her into place beside him, but her eyes still blazed. Wind swirled around her. "Do not seduce us with your enchantments."

The thing that had been drawing them dissipated. Lea breathed deeply, feeling only now that she had been suffocating in the most pleasant way. She let go of the wind that she had unconsciously harnessed. An uncomfortable truce lay among them.

"We need to get rid of his body," Luka said, gesturing at the fallen giant.

"We will deal with that, just as we have dealt with all those who fell before him. Many at his own hand."

Luka looked to Lea, a question in his eyes. She shrugged.

"Do not bother yourself over his body. You have much greater concerns to contend with."

Luka glanced sideways at Lea, who shrugged. "Like?"

"Who will assume the mantle of Hephaestus?"

"I don't even know what that means."

The dryads sighed in unison. They did not attempt to clarify their statement, and instead asked, "Did he leave a successor?"

"That's not something we discussed. We were a little pre-occupied," Lea said, letting her own frustration show. "Besides, I don't think he thought it would come to this."

"He had a long and uninterrupted history of prevailing in these contests. It is doubtful he had considered a scenario in which he was not the victor, particularly when pitted against three such as yourselves."

Lea's cheeks flushed again. They just killed a god, and now they were being insulted by tree-ghosts. "If you're done, we will get going. We have a hike ahead of us, and it's already been a long day."

"Who slew Hephaestus?" the triad asked, ignoring Lea's remarks.

Luka attempted to cover for his friend, uncertain where this line of questioning would lead. "We were all involved."

"No! There was only one."

Thomas stepped forward, looking up for the first time and meeting their gaze. His shoulders slumped. "I'll do what you want."

Luka whispered to Lea, "What do they want?"

Lea held up a finger, telling him to wait a minute.

"It is not so simple as that," the dryads answered.

"I am his descendant and the one who killed him."

"How do we kn—"

"Do not question me," Thomas commanded, stepping toward them again. He stood upright and did not look away from them after he had spoken. The person defying them had become something more than a man.

The triad retreated and cowered, murmuring among themselves. "He is certainly as impertinent as Hephaestus."

Thomas interrupted them. "There is something I want in return."

"What is it you would have from us?"

"Hephaestus was holding my mother hostage. Tell me where she is."

The horde of dryads hummed angrily behind Mytikas, Skala, and Skolio. "We are not yours to command."

Thomas knelt on one knee and placed both hands flat on the ground in front of him. Luka and Lea looked at each other with uncertainty. After several seconds, the mountain rumbled and shook. Thomas let the quaking continue for a full minute before he stood up and addressed the host. "I will remove this mountain to the sea, stone by stone. And you can preside over it there for the rest of time — the drowned dryads of the Aegean."

The dryads quavered, and the horde's tune faltered. The triad said, "The information you seek is not knowledge we possess."

"I can't tell you how tired I am of hearing that. Who knows then?"

"For that, you must seek out the oracle."

"Which oracle?" Thomas asked.

"There is only one."

"Fine. You're dismissed. You can return to deal with him after we're gone," Thomas said insolently, waving them off with the back of his hand. The dryads bristled and hissed, but rather than advancing on him, they turned their backs and vanished.

Thomas buckled and nearly fell to the ground, but Luka caught him under the arms.

"I don't feel right," Thomas said. "Something is happening."

"Come on. Let's get you off this mountain."

Lea looked one last time at the hulking corpse. She wondered if they had made a mistake in killing him and worried over the meaning of his last words. *You have no idea what you have wrought.*

22

EMMA

EMMA KNOCKED on the door and waited. Voices from inside permeated the threshold, but no one seemed in any rush to answer. When the door finally opened, she was greeted with a smile.

"Guten tag, Frau Brandt," she said.

"Hallo, Emma. Please come in."

She stepped aside, and Emma slid past her on the way into the house. She stopped inside the common room, and Finn's mother looked her up and down uncomfortably. "I remember when I wore skirts like that. I used to have a cute figure and long legs too. It doesn't last, so enjoy it while you can."

Emma floundered, trying to figure out the appropriate response. She decided not to go with the first thing that came to mind. *Did your legs get less long as you got older?* Not only because "less long" sounded weird, but sarcasm seemed like the wrong tact here. Frau Brandt hadn't sounded bitter about it, more matter of fact. And she wasn't old or dumpy or anything, but that wasn't much of a compliment. *'Hey, it could be worse'* probably *won't go very far either.*

Frau Brandt smiled at her. "I'll go get Finn."

Finn popped out of his room a moment later. "You ready to go?"

"That's how you greet your friend, Finn?" his mother prodded. "She's a beautiful fraulein, who can hang out with whoever she wants, and you come out with 'You ready to go?'."

At least she doesn't discriminate about who she makes uncomfortable.

With his back to his mother, Finn rolled his eyes in as exaggerated a manner as possible. Emma's cheeks puffed in a suppressed smile, trying not to give away Finn's response.

Finn bowed formally and stuck out his hand. When she presented her own, he grasped it in a vigorous two-handed shake. "It is kind of you to grace us humble plebeians with your presence. We are smitten with your generosity of time and spirit. And your demeanor is exceedingly handsome."

"Handsome?" his mother protested. "Is she a horse?"

Finn released Emma's hand and stuck his tongue out at her like an overgrown child. Straightening his face again, he turned to his mother. "As General MacArthur promised the Filipino people, 'I shall return.'"

Frau Brandt stepped forward, putting her hands on the side of his face and pulling him forward. She placed a kiss on his forehead. "Go before I decide to strangle you, my sweet idiot. I believe God may have made you too smart for your own good." Speaking to Emma, she said, "Please keep him in check and don't let him get away with too much."

"I will belittle him as much as is necessary," Emma promised.

"I like you," then to Finn with a wink, "I like her."

"Oh my gosh. You've known Emma her whole life. I don't know why you're acting like this. We should have left a long time ago." He snagged Emma's arm and pulled her toward the door. "Come on. Let's go before she says something truly regrettable."

With the door closed behind them, Finn apologized for his mother.

"What? I like her. She's sweet. Besides, she said she liked what I'm wearing."

Finn really looked at her, taking her in as if for the first time that day. He opened his mouth to say something but closed it again when nothing came out.

Emma smiled. Her heart fluttered at the realization she could have that kind of effect on a boy. Instead of letting the silence linger, she asked, "Where are we going?"

"Somewhere I can think. We need to brainstorm."

"Okay," she said slowly. "Is there one place that is better for that kind of thing than another?"

"For sure. There is *only* one place," he said cryptically.

"I don't love guessing games, Finn."

"The gelateria."

Emma raised her eyebrows in surprise. "That is not what I was expecting."

"You think there are better places?"

"Whatever gets your brain to start storming, I guess. I was just expecting a stroll through the park or a hike in the woods."

"I like gelato."

"I'm not complaining about the choice," she said.

"It sounds a little like complaining," he teased.

◊

"What are you going to get?" Finn asked as they approached the counter.

"There is *only* one correct answer." Emma said, turning his own phrase around on him. She turned to the owner of the gelateria behind the counter. "Schokolade."

She smiled at Finn.

He nodded. "I don't believe I've ever heard someone be so

confidently wrong before," he said, then announced his selection, "Mango."

Emma pretended to gag. "Have you never noticed that mango has a hint of the smell of death?"

The owner stopped scooping and glared at her. Emma grimaced. "No offense?"

"Have *you* ever noticed that everything you eat is dead?"

Emma put a finger to her lips. "I ... hadn't thought of it that way before. Besides, there's a difference between being dead and smelling like it. Sometimes, you boys smell like death, but you are decidedly not dead."

"Also, if your mango starts to smell like that, it means it's overripe. Mangoes have a very high sug—"

"Finn," she said as if it were a complete sentence on its own. "I was making a joke. I don't care about mangoes."

They picked a table as far from the only other patrons, an elderly couple, as they could find. Finn sat first, his back to the window wall. She slid onto the bench beside him. He looked at her curiously.

It was an odd choice, she knew that. But she chose not to address it. She was feeling a certain kind of way and didn't really want to think about it. She nodded toward the couple. "I hope I can be like them one day."

"Old with one foot in the grave?"

"Happily married and getting ice cream together after ... how old do you think they are?"

"From the looks of it, they might have been friends with Otto Von Bismarck."

She sighed. "Have you talked to any of the others today?"

He shook his head. "You?"

"Not today. Lea and I talked yesterday when they hitched a ride back to Litochoro after ... you know." Even this far away from anyone else, she wasn't really comfortable saying it out loud. *Hey, in case anybody is listening, my friends killed somebody yesterday. He was a really bad guy who had it coming for a couple thousand years, so it's totally fine.*

"And?"

"And they were going to stay there the rest of the day and get sorted out. Apparently, Luka took a pretty hard hit and Thomas is a mess. They were planning to figure out how to get to Delphi. I looked up how long it would take, and I think they probably didn't get there until late last night."

Finn said, "Why Delphi?"

"The dryads told them to seek the oracle," she answered quietly.

She knew that the mention of dryads would send empirical Finn into orbit. And he didn't disappoint. "Dryads?!" he hissed. "Are you kidding me? Are they just messing with us?"

Emma told him about Lea's account of their run-in with the wood nymphs. Finn listened with a heavy dose of skepticism. She would have thought that even with his disposition toward the tangible, after everything that had happened, he'd have an easier time accepting supernatural occurrences.

Finn diverted to a different topic. "You haven't heard from Thomas?"

Emma glanced at the phone that she'd laid face up on the table. Was she hopeful or resigned? She didn't know. He hadn't been returning calls or texts for most of the last week. She had considered texting him about nearly dropping her towel in front of Finn to see if that would elicit some interest, but decided against it. Maybe he was done and just didn't want to tell her. She shook her head and tried to swallow the lump in her throat. "He's going through a lot, I guess."

"Still, I'd have thought he would want to talk to you above anybody else."

"Yeah, well. Whatever," she said, flipping her hair over her shoulder. "Can we talk about literally anything else?"

"What do you know about American baseball? The playoffs have started."

Emma laughed and leaned into him. "Okay, I was wrong. Maybe not *anything* else. I should have known better with you."

He grinned. "Perhaps the topic at hand, then?"

"Let's start with what we know. Vulcan is actually Hephaestus, and he's Greek, not Roman."

"Was Greek," Finn corrected.

"You don't quit being your nationality just because you're dead."

"Okay. We also kn—"

"No, we're not moving off of this until you admit that I'm right and you were wrong."

"Fine. You were right."

"And?" Emma insisted.

Finn sighed before adding almost inaudibly and as quickly as if it were one word, "I was wrong."

"Alright, I think we can move on now," Emma said. "So if he's Greek, then wherever he's got Agatha stashed is probably somewhere in Greece."

"Probably," Finn said. "But with as long as he was alive, it could be literally anywhere."

Emma shook her head and turned to more fully face Finn. "This wasn't a new thing. He's been kidnapping women and stowing them away for ages. He would have started closer to home. So I think it's a pretty safe bet that he stayed there."

"Maybe" was all Finn would concede.

So frustrating.

"We don't have any evidence either way," he said. "Tell me again what Elle said to you."

Emma picked up her phone off the table. "I wrote it down before I left so I wouldn't get it wrong later. She said all she could remember was that it was the cradle of life. It wasn't warm or cold, and the sun only visited her."

"That's ... umm ... not very specific."

Emma grabbed his sleeve. "That's exactly what I thought."

"What do you think 'cradle of life' means?"

"Isn't it Mesopotamia? What is that — Iraq? Iran?"

"No," Finn disagreed. "That's the Cradle of Civilization. Mesopotamia."

"You don't think that's the same thing?"

Finn wrinkled his brow. "I don't think so. Where civilization was born may be a very different thing from where life came to be. Have you done a search on it?"

Emma typed *cradle of life* into the search engine on her phone. She used her thumb to scroll through the results, then flicked the screen back to the top. She looked back at Finn with skepticism written all over her face. "Dead end. The first half dozen results are all about a Tomb Raider movie."

"There were movies? I thought it was just a video game." Finn frowned. "What's after that?"

"A super boring book about fossils." She clicked a link. "Looks like it went out of print like twenty years ago."

"That's pretty obscure. Hard to believe that would have been on Elle's radar enough for it to be the one thing to stick in her head all these years. Humor me and look at the wiki page for Tomb Raider."

Emma raised an eyebrow at him, but did as he suggested. She mumbled as she scanned the page. "Second Tomb Raider movie. Released in 2003. Starring Angelina Jolie. Made a lot of mon—"

She stopped and stared at Finn.

"What?"

"Did you know?!"

"I'm lost," Finn said, holding his hands up.

"Part of it was filmed on Santorini. The Greek island."

"Whoa. Coincidence?"

"No way!" Emma said with a big smile. "This is it. This is

the answer." She threw her arms around Finn. She held on tight with joy and … something that she'd been denying for a while.

After the embrace lingered, Finn returned it, recovering from his initial shock. *The Tin Man was less tense than him.* The longer she held him close, the less the hug was one of celebration and more of an exploration of feelings. She was sure he could feel her heart pounding through her chest.

She loosened her grip on the hug just enough to pull her face away and lean her forehead against his. She took a deep breath, heart still in overdrive, and kissed Finn.

He broke away, but not with certainty. "Are you sure—"

She answered softly. "I'm sure I don't want to talk right now." She placed her hands on the sides of his face and pulled him back toward her. He didn't resist. But he was still rigid as a fossil.

She took his hand and slid it down her side onto her leg, where it remained unmoving. "Don't be a statue," she whispered and kissed him again.

He moved his hand timidly along her leg. *Good thing I shaved this morning.* When he found the hem of her skirt, he paused there and fiddled with the fabric.

Finn stopped abruptly and pulled away. "I can't. We can't do this."

"What?" Emma blushed. "I thought this is what you wanted."

"It was. I mean, it is. Just … not like this. I don't know what this is."

Emma swiveled in her seat, facing forward now. She didn't even want to look at him. A few seconds later, as the silence became a curtain, she scooted down the bench and stood up. "I have to go."

Finn, who wasn't accustomed to confusion, had never looked more lost. "I don't—what about Agatha? Santorini?"

"I'll handle it."

Emma walked away, not looking back. She let the door shut behind her without having any idea where she was headed, but determined to be away from here.

23

THOMAS

THOMAS LEANED down to pick up a rock the size of an egg. He stood up and threw it as hard as he could. It cleared the amphitheater and clattered against the trunk of a tree. "I am sick and damn tired of tromping around from one broke down pile of rocks to the next." He kicked at the ground and sprayed gravel in a wide arc in front of him.

Luka and Lea shared a look of frustration.

Thomas turned around in time to catch it. "What?" he yelled. "Somebody have something to say?"

Lea put hands down at her side and started to push herself up. Luka placed a hand on her forearm. "It's not worth it."

"Not worth what?" Thomas continued to goad them. "Huh? My mom isn't worth your time? You can go home whenever you want, you know."

"Dude, what are you even talking about?" Luka said.

"What I'm talking about is you wanting out of this. Well, no one is stopping you. I'll pay for your ticket home just like I've paid for everything else."

When Luka stood up, he was red-faced and as angry as Thomas had ever seen him. That was fine. Thomas was spoiling

156

for a fight. Luka stalked up to him, not saying a word, a rare enough occurrence on its own merit.

Thomas clenched his fists at his sides. Then he flexed them outward and clenched them again. The two stared at each other, predators sizing the other up.

Thomas said, "It ain't like you to have nothi—"

Luka swung as hard as he could, a right hook that caught Thomas in the left ear and dropped Thomas to the ground.

His ear buzzed like there was a gnat trapped inside it. He shook his head and sprang up. Before he'd even set his feet, Luka hit again. The same heavy right hand, this time landing in the hollow of Thomas' cheek.

He fell face down and shoved his hands out to catch himself just before the gravel smashed his nose. He looked at the horizon. It wobbled. Luka hit harder than he'd expected. It had knocked some of the vinegar out of him. But not all of it. Thomas straightened his arms, pushing himself up and pulling his legs under himself. He stood up unsteadily. The horizon hadn't straightened itself out yet.

Giving Thomas no reprieve, Luka swung around behind him and slid an arm around his neck. Luka had done this to him before, a choke hold. They used to think it was funny for Luka to nearly knock him out.

Thomas grabbed Luka's arm and pulled. He couldn't loosen the grip. His peripheral vision disappeared. His central vision followed suit as darkness swallowed the frame in front of him. With his last efforts, he tapped Luka's arm as he slumped to the ground.

When Thomas rediscovered his consciousness, he found himself sitting on the ground, propped against the steps of the amphitheater. Luka and Lea sat on either side of him. The clouds were ablaze with the golden light of the sun that had fallen below the peaks behind them. Marble ruins and a panorama of blue cascading mountains unfolded in front of them. Thomas' ear was on fire, and his cheek was so puffy he could see it protruding into the bottom corner of his peripheral vision. His head was too heavy to hold up. He let it fall against the step.

"You hit me," he said without looking to the side.

"Twice."

"And you choked me out."

"Yeah," Luka said, "but I only did that once."

Thomas smiled a small smile. The anger was gone for now. No, that wasn't right. It had subsided, almost like a tide that had gone out. It would be back. And when it returned, it would try again to pound everything into submission. "Something is happening."

Lea said, "That's a pretty weak apology."

Thomas scowled at her. A flicker of anger. He recognized and suppressed it this time, before the flicker became something more and found some unwitting kindling to latch onto.

"Who is that?" Luka asked, pointing at a woman sitting on a three-legged stool amid the six remaining pillars of the Temple of Apollo. "Was she there before?"

Lea shrugged.

Thomas shook his head. "I don't know. I didn't see her earlier."

"Should we go talk to her? Maybe she knows how we can find the oracle."

Lea said, "I … maybe. Sure, why not."

Thomas didn't object.

The trio filed out of the amphitheater and headed toward the solitary woman.

"How old do you think she is?" Luka asked.

"Can't tell," Lea said. "She could be forty or sixty."

Having traversed the temple grounds, they cautiously approached the woman on the stool, who appeared to be concentrating on something on the ground immediately in front of them.

Once they stopped in front of her, she looked up at them with a charming smile.

She appeared much younger than they'd first thought. It was the baggy, ill-fitting clothes that had added age to her demeanor.

"I am neither forty nor sixty," she said without accusation. "Though I am closer to one than the other."

Luka's mouth fell open. "You heard that? We were all the way …" he turned and pointed. "Oh, yeah. I guess we weren't that far away. Sorry about that."

"You have nothing to apologize for," she said dismissively. Her olive skin stood in stark contrast to her wild red hair. "What is youth for if not speculating about our observation of the world around us?"

"Are you …" Luka couldn't bring himself to finish the question. Even he didn't want to sound ridiculous in front of a stranger.

Her posture became more upright, and she announced with a flourish of grandiosity, "I am Pythia, priestess of the Temple of Apollo at Delphi."

Luka bowed. "We have been sent by—"

"Stop," Lea said. "How do we know you aren't just some gypsy who's set up shop here like some glorified grifter?"

"An insightful question, my dear. I see you are not one who is taken in easily."

Lea smiled, then frowned. "I'm not flattered easily either."

The woman on the stool shrugged, as if saying, *It was worth a shot.*

"We are looking for the oracle," Lea said.

"As are all who come this far," Pythia said with open arms.

This is a waste of time. "Let's go," Thomas said as he turned away.

Luka and Lea didn't move, caught in uncertainty.

"Wait," the woman said, pleading rather than instructing. "You are different from most. Tourists want a superficial tidbit that they can take away. A souvenir from their sojourn. They want a performance. But you are not like them. I see that now. Sincerity pours off two of you like water."

"What about me?" Luka asked, affronted.

"Why do you assume you are not one of the two?"

"Enough of this," Thomas said through gritted teeth. "Either you're her, and you can help us. Or you're not, and we will go elsewhere. But we have been sent to see the oracle."

Pythia dropped her cheery pretense. "What do you want of me?"

"I have slain Hephaestus."

Luka and Lea muttered to each other beside him, and Pythia's countenance shifted. This had taken a turn she had not expected. *No more games.* "But before I killed him—"

"We," Lea interrupted. "We, Thomas. All three of us."

Thomas turned to her and nodded. "I didn't want to put that on y'all. You know, in case … I don't know. Something."

"I know. But we were all there. We all did it."

"Before *we* killed him, he took my mother. No one knows exactly where or what happened, but I expect he carried her through a portal to some secret place. He killed my oma. He is responsible for my father's death. And he ruined my aunt."

Pythia stared at him, dumbfounded.

When she said nothing, Thomas continued. "After we killed him on Mount Olympus, the dryads came and told us the oracle would know where to find my mother. And I don't think we have much time. I can feel it. The earth is — this is going to sound weird — but the earth is angry."

"Have you seen the news?" she asked.

"I told you," Thomas warned. "No more games."

"No games," she said, smiling thinly. She held up a finger and reached into one of the pockets of her voluminous skirt, pulling out a phone. She flipped through it for a minute before turning the screen to the trio.

The headline read, *Italy's Mt. Etna Eruption Causes Rare Volcanic Storm*. The trio looked at each other with widened eyes. Thomas' heart sped up.

"Vesuvius billows smoke as well," Pythia said. "Seismographs are registering tremors to the east in the Aegean Sea. You say well that the earth is angry. If what you say is true, then you have slain the steward of the volcanoes. They are dogs without a master. One must arise to replace Hephaestus and commandeer the conflagrations, or Gaea will fall into chaos."

"Scheisse," Lea whispered.

"Who is Gaea?" Luka asked.

"The earth mother," the self-proclaimed priestess answered. She then cleared her throat and said, "Now, I must tell you something, and I believe it will cause you some displeasure. But hear me out. Pythia is the hereditary name given to the priestess at Delphi. The previous priestess — her given name was Elena — died nearly twenty years ago. She was extremely old. You would not believe me how old, if I told you."

"You'd be surprised what we can believe these days," Luka said.

Pythia continued. "I was her apprentice. After her death, I kept the candle burning for her successor. I waited months for the arrival of the oracle. None emerged."

Flames erupted in Thomas' hands.

Fear sparked in the priestess' eyes amid the reflection of the fire.

"You are a fraud," he accused.

Pythia replaced the fear with a stillness. "Do not be foolish and exhibit your mageia in this place. Have you not been warned about using it in the high places?"

Thomas balled his hands into fists, extinguishing the flames.

"What would you have me do? There was a need for an oracle, and none presented herself. So I became a placeholder." She shrugged. "When still none came, I maintained the position. I have been here ever since."

"You pretended to be something you are not," Thomas said.

"Is that not the human condition? Do we not all pretend to be something we are not? Either in the hope that we will become that thing, or because no one else has filled the void. There is only one oracle in each generation. I do not possess those skills. I am not her. But I will serve until she arrives. Think of me as John the Baptist."

The reference did not make an impression.

"No? None of you?"

"How do we find the actual oracle, then?" Lea asked.

"Do you think that if I knew the answer to that question, I would be here every day peddling my meager mageia at the whims of tourists, hoping that once in a very great while, something truly meaningful would cross my path? I assure you, I had greater ambitions than that."

"Greater ambitions than being the oracle?" Luka asked in amazement.

"She is—" she corrected herself, "I am a puppet beholden to certain conscriptions. Haven't you seen *Spider-Man?* 'With great power comes great responsibility.' It's not really my idea of a good time. I'd rather have a little power and a lot more independence. But as the fates would have it, I am just dumb enough to have both a little power and great responsibility."

"So what can the oracle do, anyway? Why are they such a big deal?" Luka asked.

"Do you know nothing of marketing? Exclusivity. There is only one. It's a pretty small club. As a practical matter, they have exceptional wisdom and were once consulted by kings. However, advising kings is a perilous occupation, so after a few generations of oracles were beheaded, they learned to be more ambiguous. But as ambiguity is rarely useful, they were sought after less. They have other talents as well. They can commune with spirits, and the rarest among them have precognition into the future. Or at least a future. There is some concern that, by speaking of what they envision, they actually change the future. At the very least, that is how they have explained away prophecies that did not come to fruition."

"Wait," Lea said, "tell me about the talking to spirits thing. Is just like dead people, or what?"

Thomas made the connection too, and his interest percolated up through his anger.

Pythia wagged her finger. "The mageia can take many forms. Some speak with the dead, others with spirits of the living over great distances."

"What about if someone was sick and unable to speak?" Lea prodded further.

All three unconsciously leaned in for the answer.

"That is … a very specific question. One might think you know more than you have let on. But I will answer. No, I have not heard of that before, which is not to say it is not possible."

"Time to go," Thomas snapped.

"Ciao," Luka offered as he turned to follow.

The false priestess held out a hand with her forefinger raised. "One more thing."

Each of the trio turned back to her.

"I am not the true oracle, but I am not without gifts." She looked directly at Thomas. "You are the heir of Hephaestus, the dimiourgós burdened with quelling the great conflagrations. As Gaea's anger undulates and shakes the mountains, so does your own."

Thomas' mouth had gone dry. He tried denying the truth of

what she was saying, but it resonated too deeply. "How do I stop them?"

Pythia once again put on a superficial smile and a cheery tone. "How should I know? I'm a fraudulent oracle sitting on a stool at a tourist attraction."

Lea tugged at Thomas' arm. "Come on. There's someone we need to talk to."

24

AGATHA

AGATHA SCREAMED in anger and flung her makeshift spear against the wall. It was a shrill, primal scream that she sustained at full volume for half a minute. She only stopped when her raw throat hurt so sharply that she thought she'd torn something. Breathless and exhausted from the effort, she bent over with her hands on her knees. Water that was now closer to the temperature of a bath dripped from her nose, clothes, and fingertips.

A wave of dizziness lashed out at her. She reeled and nearly toppled over.

"Tumped over. That's what they call it in Alabama," she said after regaining her balance. Casting off her inhibitions, she'd taken to talking to herself. "A girl needs to hear a voice sometimes, even if it's her own." Not that she had ever been particularly inhibited anyway. But here, her inhibitions served no purpose whatsoever, so she quit paying them any mind.

Agatha peeled off her sopping wet shirt and looked at her belly. She ran a hand over it and felt it grumble. "Oh, shut up." She moved her hand across and upward, and started counting her ribs. In recent years, that had taken a little more probing. Now she looked like Debra Messing.

As she dropped the shirt to the floor, her hand brushed the hilt of the knife she had made. She pulled it out and sat down. While time sloshed around like water in a bucket, one way she found to pass it was to sharpen her knife. There were several flat, smooth places on the cavern floor that were as good a whetstone as any.

The rhythmic movement and sound — six seconds away from her body at twenty-two degrees, and six seconds back — pulled her back to a different time and place. Her training with Oberhaupt some thirty years ago hadn't started that differently than a basketball coach who doesn't let his players touch the ball for the first week. The only time he permitted her to handle weapons in those first weeks was assembling and disassembling them. Learning the names of all their parts. Memorizing their feel by touch rather than sight. And hours upon hours of sharpening her knives.

Granted, the finest craftsmen had made those knives from German steel rather than from aluminum cans that they had melted down. Nevertheless, over the last week, she had honed it to a smooth, sharp edge. It was still rudimentary and thicker than she'd have preferred. And since it was aluminum, it wouldn't stand up to heavy use. But that wasn't its purpose.

This knife had only one function. She had created it for a singular task: penetrating Vulcan's hide and gouging a gaping hole into his black pig heart. And for that, it was entirely sufficient.

Even in her decimated form, she was sure she could muster enough force to get the knife where it needed to go. She tucked it back into the waistband of her underwear, wincing at the cold metal against her sensitive skin. Her pants had become so loose they barely held themselves up, much less a knife. She knew it looked ridiculous — the knife sticking out the top of her underwear and the blade protruding through the leg hole — but again, she'd laid down her inhibitions, so the absurdity of it didn't matter. What did matter is that the next time a portal opened up, she'd have her weapon close at hand. To that end, it worked, except for the times she sat down without first removing the knife. She wore a couple of reminders on her leg from those episodes.

Agatha moved across the room to the trash heap and scoured the aluminum cans for any forgotten morsels. If she didn't need the calories so badly, she wouldn't bother. Eating tiny amounts of food made her feel the hunger pangs more acutely. Whereas when she went without, her stomach stayed mostly quiet, only occasionally raising its head to rumble and remind her of its dissatisfied existence.

She had established a bit of a routine over the last week. Get out of bed sometime before the sun hit the second mark on the wall, the one she thought meant somewhere around nine o'clock.

Every day, the sun traced an arc along the cavern wall as it journeyed across the sky. She had devoted one of her days to tracing its progress as best she could, though the earliest entry points were too high because of the angle at which the light hit the wall.

After tracing the shallow parabola that she thought pretty closely resembled the shape of a wok, she went back and added evenly distributed marks that would give her some approximation of an hour having passed. Not that it mattered, except to the very fussy part of her brain that wanted to know what time it was.

To complete her task, she had fabricated a novelty-size pencil ... of sorts. Taking one of the slats from her cot, she split it lengthwise, then split it again so that it would be more comfortable to hold like the writing utensil she intended it to be. She burned the end of it using her können, and as she'd hoped, the charred end left definitive marks on the wall.

She wondered if her cave-dwelling ancestors had done similar things. Or had it not mattered to them? You rose when the sun came up and went to bed when it got dark, because there were big fearsome things that only came out at night. So you huddled in groups close to the fire. And daddy slept closest to the cave entrance. If any monsters came sniffing about, they'd have to deal with him first.

Of course, that was assuming he himself wasn't the monster. Because, as it turned out, some patriarchs were worse than any beast you could conjure up. And despite everything — all the decades of signals to the contrary — you still don't expect them to leave you marooned in a cave to starve to death. "Maybe that says more about me than it does him." She didn't know what she'd really expected from him. Maybe that if he was going to kill her, he wouldn't be so passive-aggressive about it.

So she got out of bed around mid-morning most days and went to her inlet. Saltwater wasn't ideal for rinsing her face, so sometimes she skipped that part. Regardless, at all costs, she avoided trying to catch her reflection on the water. She was in desperate need of a hairbrush. Raking her hand through her hair just wasn't cutting it. Her lifelong habit of wearing a hair-tie on her wrist had finally paid dividends. Now, she wore it up most of the time, which limited the worrying over mats and tangles.

The other thing that wasn't cutting muster was using a stick as a toothbrush. She saw people doing it on *Survivor* and had thought that it looked like it wouldn't make any difference. And now she could be sure she was mostly right. The upshot of being out of food was that she didn't have any use for a toothbrush stick anymore, or for the teeth themselves, for that matter. Of course, the downside was starvation.

"You win some, you lose some."

After her skincare routine, she would take a small drink of

water. That too would change after today. This morning's drink was the last of the water. She'd stretched it as far as she could. What pee she'd produced in the last couple of days was dark and stank. Her body protesting at its treatment. If her mind could have shrugged its shoulders at her body, it would have. She had never treated her shell as some sort of sacred temple. It should be used to harsh conditions. She had the scars to prove it. But her mind had to concede that even these conditions were an exception.

In the early days of her captivity, when there was still food in her containers and in her belly, she had gone fishing in the mornings. Maybe it wasn't right to call it fishing. She went swimming with a spear in her hand. But never once had she seen one large enough to spear. Only the tiniest of minnows, and those were impossible to catch. Once she familiarized herself with the underwater layout and mustered the courage to swim further, she also found what appeared to be vertical iron bars that kept her imprisoned on the island, cutting off the possibility of escaping even from beneath it.

She had plied her trade to the bars to see what would happen. But she had to contend with some limiting factors. They were far enough away from her inlet that she had only a very finite amount of time to work with once she was there. And swimming faster didn't help because it increased her heart rate, which meant that her body was consuming oxygen more rapidly.

Once at the giant grate, she tried a couple of different methods of destroying them. This, of course, took numerous trips for experimenting and spending what she had to assume was a tremendous number of calories. Even if it didn't pay off, she still had to try it. She wouldn't forgive herself for not trying.

At first, she tried heating the metal bars enough to make them pliable, so she could bend them outward and create a gap large enough to escape through. If she were surrounded by air rather than water, she thought this would have worked. But the water insulated the metal and wicked away the heat (or something like that — she didn't know the science of it, just the effect), preventing the bar from heating up along a length long enough to allow for bending.

Her next effort was super-heating a small segment the width of her hands. If she could get it hot enough, it would be soft enough to rip away. She would only have to do it six times to create a hole that would allow her to get through. But it would be one of those crossing the Rubicon moments. Once she was on the other side, she wouldn't have enough air for the return trip, and she had no way of knowing how far the ever-widening tunnel extended before she'd be able to surface. It may well have been a suicide mission. And as much as she hated the idea of drowning trapped under the sea, knowing that it would happen while she was trying to escape made it almost (but not quite) a tolerable death.

Anyway, it didn't work. Even though her knife proved that she could melt some metals, the bars proved impervious to her efforts. Whether it was the conditions or that their melting points were too high, she didn't know, and it didn't matter. She was stuck here.

But three days ago, things changed. Weird things had started happening, and she'd been unsettled ever since. About the time she was getting ready to crawl out of bed, the cave floor began quaking. Pebbles bounced around like Mexican jumping beans. Debris fell from the walls above her. She feared that the whole thing was about to collapse on her. She just hoped that if that happened, it would kill her immediately. It would be a real drag if it just maimed her, and she lay there under the rubble for days, waiting to die. Another reason to keep the knife on her. She scooted out of bed and across the floor, positioning herself under her skylight. Maybe if everything collapsed, it would fall straight down.

Agatha covered her ears when a thunderous grinding became

so loud she couldn't bear it. The floor rattled and her bones along with it. The arrhythmic vibration dealt her heart fits.

Beginning in the inlet, a chasm opened up, quickly spreading halfway across the cavern floor. The tremendous noise of the rocks breaking overwhelmed even that of the earth grinding against itself. Death was imminent. The walls groaned as they flexed.

The water level dropped momentarily as the crevasse filled. The seawater screamed when it hit the magma that gurgled up through the earth's crust. Great draughts of steam pummeled the cavern walls and rolled upward.

She had once shaved her head — if Natalie Portman could wear it well, why not her — and distinctly remembered opening the oven and feeling the heat roll up and over her scalp as it poured out of the oven. The waves of humidity were much the same here. Her hair frizzed instantly.

Just as suddenly, everything reached an equilibrium and fell still.

In the interceding three days, no more rocks tumbled down from overhead. The earth had not reached out further with its broken, crooked finger to swallow her up. But from time to time, it trembled in warning.

25

LEA

Lea listened to the boys try (and fail) to sing the lyrics from Guns N' Roses' "Paradise City," when her phone buzzed with a text from Lea. They had sprung a few extra dollars for a private room at the hostel, though private had taken on a new meaning when constantly sharing space with two boys for the last couple of weeks. Whenever this was over, she was going to lock herself in a convent with no human interaction for a month.

"They're ready," Lea called to the two would-be lead singers.

Luka meandered over, singing, "The grass is green and the girls hav—"

"No," Lea said. "I hate that word."

Luka shrugged. "What? Did I misquote the song?"

Lea rolled her eyes. Luka and Thomas gathered around her and waited for the screen to populate with images of their friends. Meanwhile, their own projections reflected back at them. One side of Lea's mouth curled upward in a smirk. "You know, boys—"

"No," Luka said.

Lea acted appalled. "You don't even know what I was doing to say."

172

"Doesn't matter. I know that look. It's all mischief. And it usually means someone needs to check their pocket."

The screen switched to Emma and Finn. Or more accurately, Emma and part of Finn. Everyone made their greetings. *They're oddly far apart.*

Luka said, "Finn, scoot over. We can barely see you."

He pushed himself over onto the sofa cushion beside Emma. But he did so without ever looking directly at her. *Something weird is going on here.* She was afraid that looking at Thomas to see if he was cuing on it would bring undue attention to … nothing? But it wasn't nothing. She knew that.

"Where are you now?" Finn asked.

"Back in Athens," Luka answered.

"Oh. What happened in Delphi?"

"Ran into a wall," Thomas said.

"Is that what happened to your face?" Finn said, gesturing at his cheek.

Thomas shot a look at Luka, who grinned and said, "Uhh. Friendly disagreement."

"Are you okay?" Emma asked.

"Yes," Thomas said curtly, and began fidgeting.

"We've been dealing with some heavy stuff around here," Lea said. "With our penchant for knocking off priests and gods, things have gotten a little off kilter. But we are sorting it out. Kind of. I think. What about you two? Anything new?"

"No," they both said simultaneously and a little too aggressively.

Liar, liar, pants on fire. Something definitely happened between you two. Not really that surprising. Spending a lot of time together. Absentee boyfriend. Boy with lifelong crush on girl. If Thomas figures this out, he's going to go all "Hulk smash" on everything.

"Enough with the pleasantries," Lea said, taking control of the conversation. "We've got business to attend to."

Finn nodded. "What did the Oracle at Delphi tell you?"

Luka said, "She told us she's not the real oracle. She kind of talked in circles and wasn't super helpful. And she said when the last oracle died, the new one never showed up."

"That's not all," Thomas said, looking directly at Emma. "She said some oracles can communicate with spirits and have unique wisdom and insights."

Emma visibly squirmed at his intensity, which must have translated even through the devices and with her being a couple thousand kilometers away. She said in a small voice, "I may never have been more than a passable heilerin, because that's not my true können, as it turns out."

Luka bounced up and down on the bed. "So we were right? You're an ... oracle?" He had looked from side to side before leaning in and whispering the last word, as if afraid to let out a secret.

Emma shrugged and seemed to get smaller. "Maybe? I don't know for sure."

Thomas' face reddened. He demanded in an accusatory tone, "How long have you known?"

Emma flushed and tears sprang to her eyes.

"Hey, man," Finn said. "How about you ease up?"

"Ease up?! We've been traipsing all over the Mediterranean while she's had the answers all along. That's what the dryads said. We have to ask the oracle. But it turns out, that's not some gypsy in Delphi. It's her."

Emma's tears spilled down her cheeks.

This is going well. "Hang on. We'll call back in a few minutes when everyone has settled back down."

"No," Emma said with determination, stiffening her posture.

Okay. Maybe my girl's got some backbone.

"Thomas, I need to ask you a question. It's going to seem kind of random. Okay?"

He nodded, and Lea could tell that he was trying to recompose himself. Whatever demon he'd been wrestling with since

Vulcan's death was wreaking havoc on his mood and ability to control his anger.

As soon as she had a second after they'd left the Temple of Apollo, she had made a note in her phone about Pythia's parting words to Thomas. She'd read them a dozen times since. "Thomas is the heir of Hephaestus. Something about having the burden of the great conflagrations. Somebody's anger shakes the mountains, and Thomas' anger will too."

That was the gist of it anyway. Maybe the anger was an indispensable part of whatever he had inherited. And maybe Vulcan couldn't control it, either. Was it possible that he wasn't a bad guy? That his anger was an inherent part of his mageia? *No, there's always a choice. It's just that it's not always easy or convenient. Thomas has a choice too. Then he'll have to keep making it over and over again. Like an addict deciding to stay clean. He has to keep making that decision. No equivocating. Where did that word come from? That had to have been tucked way back in her brain somewhere.*

Emma asked, "Did your mom — again, this is going to sound dumb, but there's a reason I'm asking — is there any connection between your mom and *Tomb Raider*?"

He looked at her with blank surprise. After a long silence in which everyone half winced, waiting for an eruption, he said, "Yeah. She wanted to be Lara Croft. I mean, she basically was … like Lara Croft meets the X-Men. She and Elle played the games to death on their PlayStation. Then when the movies came out, she says they went and saw them like five times in the theaters." He smiled in the telling of it, for what seemed like the first time in days. "Why?"

Emma told them about Elle referencing the cradle of life and the tenuous connection they'd made to Santorini. "It didn't really make sense at the time. At least not unless there was a line to connect the dots."

"And now we have a line," Thomas said.

"Rad," Luka added.

Lea raised her eyebrows. "Rad?"

"Yeah, I'm trying to bring it back."

Lea shook her head and refocused her attention on the phone. "How good do you feel about this?"

Emma looked at Finn. *First time she's done that today.*

He said, "It's all we've got. Emma says it's the only thing that's even remotely concrete that Elle has given us. It's like she's been mostly detached from her body for so long that she can't grasp anything. Or something like that. Right?"

Emma nodded. "We've done some quick research. The island of Santorini is part of the Santorini caldera, which is a group of four islands. They used to be all one big volcanic island, but somewhere around 1600 BC, there was an eruption — the biggest volcanic eruption that we know of in history."

Finn jumped in excitedly. "After the eruption, the middle of the island sank into the sea. Just ... poof." He reenacted a dome collapsing. "They think it might be the origin of the legend of Atlantis."

"Makes sense so far," Thomas said.

"Agree," Finn said, still riding the high from their discovery. "On a lot of levels. Obviously, there's the *Tomb Raider* thing that ties into Santorini. But it seems very on brand for Vulcan to have been imprisoning people in the ruins of a volcano. Maybe that's not a lot of levels. Just two. But still. This is it. It has to be."

"So what do we do now?" Luka asked.

"Tomorrow, you'll take a ferry from Athens to Santorini," Emma said. "Should take you about nine hours. Between now and then, I'll try to see if I can turn up any other details—"

"We," Finn corrected.

Mm-hmm. Girl, we're about to have a talk.

"Right," Emma said. "We'll try to narrow down a location. Even though Santorini is pretty small, it's impractical for you three to be scouring it for clues."

Finn chimed in again. "Yeah, and it's not just Santorini. Don't forget the other three islands. They're all smaller, though."

"Anything else?" Thomas asked, as sullen and stoic as ever.

You could have at least pretended you were excited. They're working their butts off to save your mom. She wasn't going to let this attitude thing ride for very long.

Disappointment and confusion inscribed themselves on Emma's face. "I—no, I guess that's it."

"Alright," Thomas said before getting up and walking to his bed on the other side of the room.

Indicating Thomas' vacant space, Luka whispered, "I'll tell you about it later."

"Let us know when you get to Santorini." Finn waved. "Ciao." He reached toward the phone.

"Wait," Lea said. "I need to talk to Emma. Alone."

Finn said, "Oh," but left his hand hovering near the phone, uncertain what to do.

"About girl stuff," she added ominously.

"I see. I'll wait in the other room."

Lea picked up her phone and left the room.

"What's wrong?" Emma asked

"Hang on," Lea said, walking out of the room. She looked for somewhere private to talk, pushing open the door to a room housing a flock of ancient computers that looked like they hadn't been touched in the last fifteen years. She flipped the light on and parked herself in a desk chair. "Spill."

"What?" Emma was clearly confused.

"I want to know what happened between you and Finn."

"I ... don't know what you're talking about," she said matter-of-factly.

"The hell you don't," Lea said with a grin.

Emma's cheeks flushed, and she broke eye contact with Lea.

That's what I thought. "Well?"

"Well, I would rather not talk about it."

"Then you should have done a better job of hiding it."

Emma's eyes glistened with fear. "Do you think Thomas or Luka noticed?"

"Ha! You would have had to hit them over the head with it for them to notice."

"Okay," Emma said, the relief obvious.

"So what happened?" Lea wasn't going to let this go. She was like a golden retriever on its first duck hunt.

Emma sighed. "I kissed him."

"Alright, now we're getting somewhere. *You* kissed *him*? Not the other way around?"

"Correct."

It was Lea's turn to sigh. "You know this is going to take a lot longer if I have to drag every phrase out of you."

"Fine. We were at the gelateria working on figuring out Agatha's location, and we made the connection to Santorini. And I got a little excited, and I kissed him?"

"Oh," Lea said with some disappointment. "So it was just like a little peck on the lips?"

Emma grimaced. "Umm ... no. It was ... pretty sustained. And it got a little handsy."

"Wow. Good for Finn. I didn't know he had it in him."

"Lea! Don't be excited about this. We were cheating."

"No. You were cheating. He was along for the ride."

"I know. I know," Emma groaned. "I feel bad enough about it already. Don't give me a hard time."

"You should definitely feel bad. But tell me anyway. What did you and Fondling Finn do next?"

"Don't say that. You make it sound gross. He pulled away, and it got weird. I left, and today was the first time I'd seen him since then. And now I have to tell Thomas."

Lea shook her head adamantly. "You do not need to tell Thomas. I don't know if you noticed, but he's kind of in a funk right now. Like a literal volcano waiting to erupt. So it was a one-time thing, right? It's never going to happen again? Then he doesn't need to know."

"Lea, I have to tell him."

"Easy for you to say. You're not the one in the blast radius."

"Blast radius? Who even are you?"

Lea shrugged. "I've been around too many of Luka's video games."

"Can you hand me off to Thomas?"

"You're doing this now?"

"Yeah, before I lose my nerve."

"Scheisse. Okay. Let me go find him." *This should be fun.*

26

THOMAS

THOMAS LOOKED up when Lea entered the room. She walked directly in front of him and asked, "What are you doing?"

"Nothing," he murmured.

"Quit being weird and sulky. Emma wants to talk to you."

"I don't want to talk to her."

"Too bad," Lea said, handing him the phone with the face up, showing that Emma had heard the exchange.

He glared at Lea. She shrugged and walked away. Thomas rested his forearms on his knees and cradled the phone in both hands. "Sorry. It's not you. I don't want to talk to *anyone*."

"It's fine. Don't worry about it."

"Is it?" he asked.

"Actually, no, it's not. But that doesn't matter right now. We need to talk about something. Are you alone?"

He looked across the room. "Luka's playing a game, so he's basically in another world."

Not satisfied with the answer, she asked, "Can you put earbuds in?"

Thomas reached back with one hand and shuffled through the side pocket of his pack, retrieving the small case holding his earbuds. He put them in, and the world around him grew silent as the devices paired with each other. All at once, he could hear her again. Quick, shallow breaths. Shifting positions, her clothes rustling. He watched her for a couple of seconds before telling her they'd connected.

It was kind of funny to say they were connected. They couldn't have been more disconnected over the last couple of weeks. "Did you ever see that cartoon *Aqua Teen Hunger Force*? It was on Adult Swim."

"No," she said. "But, Thomas, liste—"

He held up a hand. "Hang on. There's something I'm trying to say. There's a line in the show where one of the characters says something like, 'You don't have to yell at me. But do repeat what you just said, though, because something's going on in my head here.' And that's how I've been feeling. Even before I killed Vulcan," he said the last words quietly. Saying it out loud was a peculiar experience. "I'm really sorry th—"

"Stop. You can't apologize to me right now. You just can't. I have to tell you about something that happened."

So she did. She told him about all the time she and Finn had been spending together, working through logistics and problem-solving and brainstorming. About their excitement over discovering Agatha's potential location. And about kissing him. She took all the blame for it. Thomas remained silent throughout, asking no questions and showing no reaction. When she finished her telling of the events, he only stared at the screen.

"Thomas?" she prompted after several protracted seconds.

He refocused. "As far as I'm concerned, you two are done. You've done your part. And more, it sounds like. If Lea and Luka have questions for you, so be it. And *we* are definitely done."

Tears were already spilling down her cheeks for the second time that day. He thought it was less about the breakup. That had seemed all but inevitable for a while. It was more about how everything had gone, from really good to this. She was his first proper girlfriend. The first girl he'd — *No. Not now.* It hadn't taken long to sour either. She said his name once more, softly, almost beckoning, but was cut off by him pressing the red button at the bottom of the screen.

He set the phone on the bed beside him and pulled his earbuds from his ears. The barrage of sound that Luka's phone emitted bludgeoned his ears once more. "I'm going out for a bit."

"What do you want to eat for dinner?" Luka asked without looking up.

Thomas walked out the door without responding. He knew he was being rude, but he didn't care. Couldn't care right now.

He stepped out of the hostel to find Athens bathed in golden sunlight. The sun displayed a kaleidoscope of colors among the clouds, like kids forced to leave a party earlier than they want so they make spectacles of themselves to be sure they're remembered.

Thomas meandered aimlessly through the city, knowing that in some ways he was a tourist but hoping that he didn't look like one. He certainly didn't look like the Americans who stood out so conspicuously, or even the Canadians, who sewed maple leaves onto their bags, so no one would confuse them for Americans.

He detoured through the National Garden, which might have been fine in most other cities. But it was less impressive in contrast to the ruins it was in such close proximity to, which stood as ever-present reminders of the greatness that had once belonged to the weary city.

By the time he made his way to the few remaining pillars of the Temple of Olympian Zeus and the southern corner of the Acropolis complex, the sun had dropped below the horizon. Dusk had fallen over the city, whose lights combatted the darkness and obscured the stars. He kept the Acropolis to his left and made his way northward, just on the outskirts of the marble monuments. When he passed between a mosque and Hadrian's library, he realized he was only a few blocks from the Temple of Hephaestus. Had he been headed there all along? Maybe his subconscious self had known better than to clue him in on his destination.

Rounding the corner to the park's entrance, he found it closed and locked. The gate and fence were too tall to navigate. He looked around, considering his options. The fence to his left was waist high. Much more manageable. He walked over to it and placed his hands on the rail. *Just your usual tourist. Nothing to see here.* No one was paying any attention to him. It was going to be a bit of a drop to the ground on the other side.

Thomas swung his legs over the railing and prepared for someone to yell at him. When nothing happened, he lowered himself and twisted so that he hung from the wall by his hands. *Here goes nothing.* He let go and took longer to hit the earth than he expected, landing with a grunt and a thud.

He picked himself up and looked around. A couple of curious onlookers noticed him, but none seemed to do anything more than raise an eyebrow his way. Thomas hopped a low stone wall and scurried across the train tracks. After clearing the next wall, a quick jaunt across the grounds of the Temple of Ares and the ancient agora brought him back to the Temple of Hephaestus. If there were security guards monitoring the area at night, he hadn't seen any.

He was in such a different mental state than the last time they were here. Certainly not better, but undoubtedly different. As he stood in front of the temple and noted the missing piece of its facade, courtesy of Lea, he doubted his decision about coming here. To the extent that it was a decision. Something had drawn him here.

Pushing aside his uncertainties, Thomas stepped forward and brushed against the cable barrier. He'd forgotten about it and hadn't seen it in the diminishing light of dusk. He ducked under it and bounded up the disintegrating marble steps, pushing into the heart of the temple.

Once he walked into the inner sanctum, the world around him slipped into total darkness. He stood still and waited.

A shiver climbed up his spine. Thomas whirled around and saw nothing. Neither had he heard anything. He realized he was basically in a giant graveyard. But it was a city that was dead, not just its people. He stilled himself again in the blackness. Still, nothing happened.

As his impatience grew, so too did his rage that burbled beneath the surface. He allowed himself a small outburst and flung an orb of fire into the air, where he suspended it.

The fire illuminated a gilded chamber in which grand tapestries adorned the walls. Unlit oil lamps hung above them. Thomas sent this flame around the room, lighting the lamps. He then returned the fire to himself and snuffed it out. The marble altar stood in the middle of the room and the sculptures of Athena and Hephaestus on the far end, where they had been before and for thousands of years before that. Thomas hopped onto the altar beside its brazier and sat with his legs crisscrossed. If he were going to be here a while, he might as well get comfortable.

"I had not expected to see you again."

Thomas didn't turn around to find the source of the voice that had emerged behind him. He knew who it belonged to. "I wouldn't have put very good odds on it either."

27

———

THOMAS

Epitiritis, the temple's overseer, stepped within Thomas' field of vision and gestured at him with a look of disdain. "Do you not think this behavior is too irreverent to be exhibited within a temple?"

"Isn't it mine now?" Thomas said, picking up a chisel from the altar before setting it immediately back down when an image of it piercing Vulcan's chest intruded on his mind.

"I do not believe it is quite so simple as that."

Rather than engaging in coy answers, Thomas changed the subject. "I thought you said you were going to die after Vulcan did."

Epitiritis smiled grimly. "It is nigh. Duty beckoned."

"Me?"

The priest nodded.

"I have a few questions," Thomas said.

"I would have anticipated considerably more than 'a few.'"

"The oracle at Delphi told me — even though she's not the real oracle or whatever — she said that I am his heir. But my mom is still alive. I think. Shouldn't she be the heir? Or is she dead?"

"Not that I know everything concerning such matters, but I am not aware of your mother passing from this life. It could have happened without me knowing, but that seems improbable, all things considered."

"How am I the heir, then?" Thomas asked.

"These are not trivial things like kingdoms and crowns that pass from one generation to the next without consideration for whether the next head is worthy to bear it," the priest said defensively. "It is little more than happenstance that you, as the heir, are of Hephaestus' bloodline. Rather, your place as heir is a result of your constitution. A true divine right. Your characteristics mirror his own such that the mantle has passed to you. Like the prophets Elijah and Elisha. Elisha was not of the blood of Elijah, but he proved himself worthy of the other's mantle, and Elijah bestowed it on him before being carried to heaven in a chariot of fire."

"I don't know th—you know what, it doesn't matter." He slid down from the altar and crossed his arms. "I don't want it. I don't want to be his heir. I don't want his powers. He was a monster, and I want nothing to do with him."

"I am afraid, for your sake, that it is not so simple as saying you do not want it. A successor may not simply disinherit the mageia that has been bestowed upon him."

Thomas clenched his jaw and ground his teeth together, then asked, "Why not?" knowing he sounded petulant.

Epitiritis tilted his head and considered how best to answer the question. "Have you attempted to cast off your humanity?"

Thomas scrunched up his face. "What?"

"That is my point. You can no sooner cast off your mageia than you could reject your humanity. It is not a scarf to be discarded at your leisure. It is knit into your soul."

"Well, I don't want it."

The priest shrugged. He had said his peace, and it appeared that he would offer nothing else on the subject. They stared at each other until Thomas looked away and directed his eyes at the sculpture of Hephaestus. He hadn't thought it would be possible for him to hate the man more in his death than he had in his life, but that certainly appeared to be the path they were on. "I don't even know what I'm supposed to have inherited."

"I can show you, if you will permit," Epitiritis said.

Thomas nodded tentatively.

"You saw Hephaestus open portals?"

"Yes."

"This is one of the things that has been bequeathed to you. Open one now so we can proceed." Epitiritis held out a hand in invitation.

Thomas shook his head. "I don't know how."

"How do you call fire to yourself, Thomas? How do you grow and dismiss life?"

The boy recoiled. "You know about that?"

"I warned you that performing mageia in places of power would have consequences. Such places are never devoid of witnesses. Your acts were seen by a great host. You will no longer proceed in anonymity."

Thomas breathed in deeply. *Great.*

"I will do it on our behalf this time," the priest said. "My last time."

Thomas watched him intently, but there was nothing specific to be seen. It wasn't like he wiggled a wand in a particular way that had to be mimicked. Epitiritis held out his hand, and an opaque portal presented itself a few feet away. It was hard to even say that it opened. Instead, it seemed much more like it had been there all the while and he was just now seeing it.

The overseer of the Temple of Hephaestus entered the portal. Thomas followed.

When he appeared on the other side of the inky threshold, he stood on a mildly luminescent path that extended as far as he could see in either direction, with hundreds of branches breaking off the main trail. It reminded Thomas of the cardio-vascular system they had studied in biology. Arteries leading to smaller blood vessels that eventually gave way to the smallest capillaries.

It wasn't just the pattern that gave him that impression. Although there was no discernible source of light, everything thrummed with a deep red glow.

Energy pulsed discordantly around and through him, creating anxiety in the dissonance.

An eruption to his left sent globs of magma flying through the air. Where it landed on the path, the luminescence faded as the molten earth cooled into stone on top of it. He saw now that patches of blackness littered the paths. Eruptions, both near and far, claimed more territory.

"Where are we?" Thomas asked.

"The heart of the earth, where you are connected to every place you have ever been. And to those you have not yet seen, though those paths are not yet open to you."

"I can go wherever I want?"

"Not quite. You can go to any place you have been before, so long as you can call it to mind."

Every new bit of information was followed by a silence as Thomas pondered its implications and tried to figure out the next useful question. He already knew he could transport other people and things through. He'd seen Vulcan drag an igneous throne through a portal. What did he not know?

"How much time passes while I'm here, in this realm?"

"The usual amount," the priest said. "It depends how long you stay. Time does not stop here. This is a waypoint, a place of connectivity. It is not detached from the physical world it represents."

Thomas looked at his watch. The digital seconds flicked from one to the next. "How do I get there, the places I want to go?" He gestured at the innumerable paths before him.

"These are representative, little more than ornaments. Merely call to mind where you intend to go and open the door. Not a literal door, mind you."

"What about the lava?"

"That is quite real. And actually indicative of the situation. Should you attempt to disclaim your inheritance, the conflagrations will worsen and become catastrophic. Etna, Nea Kameni, Vesuvius, Vulcano — they have all sensed that there is no hand on the reins. They are gathering their full force and will unleash it. That will be the beginning."

"I saw what it did to him. What a monster he was. I can't be like that."

Epitiritis placed a hand on Thomas' shoulder. The boy's first instinct was to rip away from it. The last minister to take him under his wing had been no less evil than Vulcan. But he withstood the discomfort.

"Thomas, it was not Hephaestus' mageia that made him wicked. All are imbued with mageia — some greater and some lesser — just as all have a depraved heart capable of terrible deeds. But not all men are evil. What made him into what he became was that he stopped struggling against the darkness. And it is a struggle, Thomas. The darkness creeps into every crevice and claims more territory for its own as the light withdraws. You must not permit the light to retreat. Be vigilant against it."

"It's hard," he mumbled, his shoulders slumping.

"Undoubtedly. What is necessary does not come without substantial cost. It is the way of things. While the burden is yours to bear, there is no requirement that you do so alone. Look to the history of mankind. Few who did great good did so without companions." Epitiritis squeezed his shoulder lightly and let his hand fall away.

Thomas nodded. No doubt it would be easier to have and rely on friends, but that meant putting them in harm's way. Of course, if all the world's volcanoes popped their tops and sent the planet into another ice age after melting the continents to giant slabs of stone, that was less than ideal too.

Thomas held his hand out in front of him and splayed his fingers. A flame emerged. Thomas clenched his hand into a fist, vanquishing the fire. "Sorry," he said with an embarrassed smile.

"You need not apologize. Decide where to go."

"Should we go back to the temple?" Thomas asked.

"Go where you please. I have other matters to tend to."

Thomas sensed the finality in his statement. "I won't be seeing you again, will I?"

"I do not expect so. Regardless of your decision, I have fulfilled my obligations."

Thomas tried to think of some meaningful parting words. Nothing came to him, so he nodded and opened a door to another place. He looked over his shoulder before stepping through. The priest was already walking away.

Though the lights were on in the room, it was empty. Luka and Lea probably went out for dinner. At the thought of food, his belly growled at him. His phone lit up with a half-dozen messages. *Note to self: no cell reception in the belly of the earth.*

He texted on the group thread with his two companions — "Going to bed. Talk tomorrow." — then silenced the phone. Thomas pulled off his clothes and shoved everything off his bed onto the floor. He scrounged through his toiletries bag for his earplugs and sleep mask, which was still in its plastic packaging.

Thomas shut out the outside world, pulling his pillow over his face for extra security. Now there was only the cacophony within his head to contend with.

28

AGATHA

AGATHA'S LIPS CRACKED. She eyed the seawater in her inlet with lust. It would definitely kill her, either directly or indirectly, by making her sick and speeding up her dehydration. But the deep blue was so inviting.

She was already dehydrated when she ran out of water because of the limited rations she'd been permitting herself. She probably only had a day or two before her body began the process of shutting itself down.

If there was an upside to this, there were far more painful ways to go. With this, sludge would buil—no, was already building up in her blood.

She looked down at her arms, almost as though testing whether she could see her blood thickening and slowing down. She couldn't see them well since it was still dark out. The lantern had long since run out of oil. Not that there was really anything to see anyway.

A small amount of light bounced off the low-lying clouds and refracted a few of its waves into her cave. "Has to be a city, right?" she asked herself. "Close enough for some light pollu-tion, at least. There's nothing in nature that would do that. But not close enough to hear me." She had not heard the noise of people during her time here — this was Day 21 now. Only boats and the occasional plane.

Agatha had more pressing concerns than the source of the light and the inaccessible civilization it emanated from. The toxins in her blood would poison her organs. She was going to faint a few times before lapsing into an unconsciousness that she wouldn't come out of it.

The worst part of it — aside from death, obviously — was the helplessness. Not a position Agatha was accustomed to.

She had something she needed to do while she still could. Agatha stood up slowly from her cot. No hurried movements. Her blood pressure was already wonky, making everything go dark and dealing her bouts of lightheadedness when she got to her feet or sat up too quickly. She swiveled and faced the cot, using her shins to push it toward the wall as she shuffled her feet.

After ripping the bedding off the cot, Agatha pulled out three slats and used her homemade knife to split them lengthwise, as she had done before when creating her sun dial on the opposing wall.

She picked up her first oversized stylus and held it over her open palm. She burned the end to a char. Then, with a burst of flame, she set the cot aflame. Light now was more important than comfort for the short time she had left. Besides, she was going to be pretty uncomfortable with her body shutting down regardless of where she lay.

The flames danced on top of the cot, making the protrusions and indentions on the cave wall shift erratically. She stared at the wall for a long minute, trying to figure out what to say, hastening her process only when she remembered she had a finite source of light that would burn out before too long.

She reached above her head and began.

> *My sweet boy,*
> *I know you're not a boy anymore. But I'm not going to see you become a man. I will never see you again, and you are never going to see this, so I'm going to write all the things I always wanted to say to you but never did. I don't know why I held back before. You deserved to hear it.*

Agatha stepped back from the wall to look at what she had written. It sloped gently down to the right. That needed correcting. She held her partial slat out into the fire beside her to renew the char.

> *When you were young, I wasn't well. Maybe I'm still not. I spent so much of my life chasing hate, fueled by it, fed by it, that it took me a long time to learn how to love.*
> *Even with your dad, I didn't love him as well as I should have. We had good times. Wonderful times even. And if we had more time together, I think I would have learned to love him in the way he loved me.*

The light from the cot burned low, providing hardly any illumination. She flung an orb out to her left. It splatted against the wall and winked out. She had missed the bookshelf by a solid three feet. Even her coordination was already affected. Agatha took more careful aim, and the books and shelves burst into a blaze. "That should last me a while."

> *I didn't love you the way you needed, but I loved*

you with everything I knew how to give. You saved my life in ways that I never expected. Before you, I was fearless. But more than that, I was reckless. I threw myself into my work with fury and passion, but I left a trail of fires and smoldering ashes everywhere I went. I suppose I know where that came from now. Then, I didn't. I only knew that my anger was the thing that burned most brightly and enabled me to do the things most people couldn't, so I leaned into it.

Once I became pregnant with you, though, things changed. We hadn't planned on you, and in many ways, I'm glad for that. I could not have been ready until I had no other choice.

Also — and I know pregnant women aren't supposed to do this — I ate so much chocolate chip cookie dough while you were in my belly. And in case we never had that talk, babies aren't really in their mothers' bellies.

Agatha chuckled at herself. "He would kill me if he ever saw this. Of course, dehydration is going to beat him to the punch." The writing forced had her into an odd crouch. Her legs would never last in that position. Her muscles were already shaky under the stress. She retrieved her pillow, glad that she'd thought to pull it off the cot, and dropped it on the ground, where she knelt and resumed the letter.

I literally ate bucketfuls of cookie dough. I felt bad about it and felt worse about how much weight I gained. But I couldn't stop.

I want to tell you about your daddy. I wish you could have known him. In many ways, you do, but you can't see it. You are his spitting image. There have been times as you've gotten older that I've had to do a double take when you entered the room. It's not just your beautiful face. You are kind and smart and brave like he was. I didn't know how brave he was until you went missing. There is nothing he wouldn't have done for you. Remember these things.

He isn't the only one who would have given every-thing for you. I know I haven't always done right by you. But I've done my best. Things just kept going side-ways for us along the way. I don't know if life will be easier for you going forward, though my dying wish will be only the best things for you.

I love you, my sweet boy.

Mom

Agatha sat down, exhausted, and shook her cramping hand. She had said both more and less than she had intended, but it would have to do. She had worn herself out. Leaning forward and stretching her arms out, she snagged the pillow that had been her kneeling pad, nestled it behind her head, and lay back. She realized for the first time that the pre-dawn darkness had given way to morning. A dreary, cloudy morning, but morning nonetheless. "Who knew that writing a letter would be such a chore?"

The earth rumbled gently. Nothing like the quakes of the last few days. This was more akin to laying on the back of a gargan-tuan snoring bear, but with none of the comforts that might afford. Still, she craned her neck to monitor the crack that had opened up. "The last thing I need is to wake up with my head on fire because the earth refluxed some lava."

Nothing came up. *Just a burp.* She was too tired even to keep talking.

Despite it all, a memory turned her lips up in a smile. There were times when Thomas was little and Joseph was at work that she was just so worn out, she couldn't even talk in response to the boy's thousand unending questions. She grunted. The various grunts meant different things, and the child was intuitive enough to discern their meanings. Either that or she couldn't be bothered to correct him if he misinterpreted it. It was hard to remember now. Grunting had made her feel like her cave-dwelling ancestors. *Ha! I guess some things come full circle.*

Still lying on her back, Agatha closed her eyes to the gray sky. She wondered if when she drifted off to sleep, it would be for the last time. How fast did organ failure happen? A matter of hours? Surely not days. Would her body do her the courtesy of quitting during her sleep? That didn't seem in keeping with her life experience so far. She needed to prepare for whatever the worst-case scenario was. That was what life had given her. She shouldn't expect death to differ.

She never thought she'd take death lying down. But here she was, literally on her back, conceding the point. She was too worn down to do anything else. Besides, what was there to be done? Cry? Rage against it? She'd done all that. It hadn't changed anything. She might as well be still and quiet and see if she couldn't enj—

Something smacked Agatha in the forehead. Her hand flew instinctively to her face.

Wet. Blood.

Oh no.

She pulled her hand away and opened her eyes.

Not blood. Water.

She turned her head to the side and saw a miracle. Droplets of water splashing into the inlet.

Agatha jumped to her feet, then froze so she wouldn't pass out, and to give herself a second to figure out what to do. She hadn't processed what to do next. Her synapses were firing a little slower than normal, though a sudden flush of adrenaline was doing its best to compensate.

She dashed over to her trash heap, regretting having used any of the cans to make weapons that had netted her no food and no revenge, and would now collect no rainwater. She clutched the four remaining cans to her chest and rushed to the area east of the hole nearest the inlet. Setting the aluminum cans in a tight pattern, she went back for her broken bowl and added it to the collection.

The first few heavy drops turned into a steady downpour. What she wouldn't give for a deluge like the cloudburst she'd been caught in the night she found that first body in Hornberg. But she didn't expect that here. The Mediterranean islands — assuming that's where she was — were too arid for that. She was lucky for even this.

Agatha grabbed her pillow and threw it down beside the cans. Stripping off her pants and shirt, she laid them out on the ground as well. She tugged at the waistband of her underwear before stopping. "Nope." The thought of squeezing water out of three-week-worn undies nearly turned her empty stomach. "I'll just have to die if that would've been the difference."

Looking around the cavern, the only other thing she spied that could collect water was the blanket she pulled off the cot before burning it. She had to keep the blanket dry. If a cold front followed the storm, she would be in a bad state with only wet clothes and nothing left to burn to keep her warm. She didn't have the energy and focus left to sustain her own fire long enough to dry anything without substantial risk of catching it on fire.

Agatha returned to the roughly circular patch of wet ground and slid down to her hands and knees. Rivulets of water meandered through the stone's undulations toward the inlet, pooling in shallow indentations along the way. She crawled along the cavern floor, slurping up every splash of rainwater she could find. A scene from *The Lion King* — which Thomas had watched about forty-two bazillion times — popped into her head. Simba eats a grub and says, "Slimy, yet satisfying." That scene had inspired a live reenactment by three-year-old Thomas when he unearthed a worm in the yard. He had not found it at all satisfying.

"Gritty yet satisfying." Not really satisfying, though. The first few drops of water had exacerbated her thirst to a nearly intolerable degree. And while the pangs of that had lessened somewhat, her awakened stomach growled at her. "Too bad," she reprimanded it. "You get what you get, and you don't pitch a fit."

Finding no more pools of water, she lay on her back with her head by the precious containers and opened her mouth wide. She was going to make it a few more days. Anything could happen in that time. Maybe Vulcan would even come back, though that seemed increasingly improbable.

The cold, uneven ground prodded at her bare skin. *Shouldn't have burned my bed.*

29

LEA

A BLOOD MOON arose out of the Aegean Sea as the ferry plodded slowly to the east. The trio sat in a closely arranged triangle of deck chairs. Lea reclined in hers with her legs draped across Luka's lap.

"You haven't seemed nearly as pissy today," Luka said in a way that only friends can speak to each other without drawing too much ire.

Even still, Lea thought she saw Thomas tense up before settling himself back down. That was an improvement in itself. The Thomas of the last few days wouldn't have bothered restraining himself.

A film of seawater covered the deck, though there was no visible spray coming over the prow of the ship. She dug into Luka's leg with her heel to get his attention. He squirmed and slapped her foot. "I know you thought it would be romantic to sleep on the deck under the stars, but we absolutely aren't doing that."

She put her hand to her hair. It was already frizzing.

To his credit, Luka didn't argue the point. Instead, he pushed her legs off and stood up. "I'll see if there are any sleeping berths left."

A rolling wave slapped the side of the ship, causing Luka to have to shift his balance unexpectedly. "Still getting my sea legs under me," he said. "By morning, I'll be a salty dog."

"A what?" Thomas said with a genuine smile.

"You know, a veteran of the seas. That's what they call old sailors like us."

"Go," Lea said, pointing. "And you better hope there are rooms. I won't be happy if I have to sleep on the floor of that big common area."

"It's not like you to be displeased with something I've done."

After Lea stuck her tongue out at him as he walked away, she pushed herself upright in her chair and folded her legs under her. "Do you want to talk about it?"

"Talk about what?"

"Emma," she said, sitting forward. "But you already knew that."

Thomas leaned away and crossed his arms. "Not particularly, no."

"Too bad."

Thomas huffed. "Fine. If you're going to force the issue, let's start with how long did you know before I did?"

"About three-and-a-half minutes."

He was looking for someone to dump his anger on, but that disarmed him somewhat.

He asked, "What happened?"

Lea rolled her eyes. "Don't ask like you don't know. And I'm not excusing what she did when I say this, but you basically ignored her for the past couple of weeks. Things had bent as far as they could, I guess, before they broke."

"Honestly, I … never mind," Thomas said, opting out of whatever truth he'd decided not to level.

"Say it."

"It's going to sound bad."

Lea acted affronted. "Well, you know me. I would never say something hurtful out loud, so I guess you'd better not."

Thomas sighed. "Okay. It's kind of a relief. I don't have the bandwidth to deal with it right now."

Lea pursed her lips and nodded encouragingly.

"What are you doing?" Thomas said.

"This is what my therapist does when she thinks I need to dig a little deeper and explore my feelings more. That's her term, not mine."

"You know you look like a confused duck, right?"

Lea shrugged. "Yeah, I thought it was weird at first too, but I guess I got used to it."

"I don't think I'm going to be signing up for therapy sessions any time soon."

Lea pursed and nodded again, but couldn't keep from grinning as she said, "Uh-huh. Go on."

Thomas grimaced, but he didn't shut her down.

"I … don't really know what to say."

"Let me help. Tell me if this sounds about right," Lea said. "You've been dealing with *a lot*. It's been overwhelming. Your friend got kidnapped. You were involved in the death of someone who had become important to you and who tortured your friend. On the same day, your grandfather murdered your oma and kidnapped your mom. You're at your wit's end searching for her. Then you killed your grandfather, who was also responsible for the death of your father and had kidnapped you. And ever since that happened, you've been on the verge of an eruption yourself. So excuse you if you don't have time to deal with girl problems right now." She took a deep and mildly exaggerated breath, having said all of that in one go. "How'd I do?"

"I think that about covers it. So maybe it wasn't totally her fault?"

Lea held up both hands. "Well, I'm not letting her off the hook that easy. I mean, she could have broken up with you first, before … you know. But, yeah, you can definitely see how it got there." Lea leaned forward and put a hand on Thomas' knee. "Now, let's talk about your feelings for me."

Thomas jerked his leg away. "What?! No. What?"

Lea flung herself back in her chair and bellowed a laugh that lasted a good minute. She put an earnest expression back on and sat forward again. "It's okay, Thomas. Lots of patients develop feelings for their therapists."

"Get out of here," he said.

As Luka walked up behind Thomas, Lea said, "Don't worry, I'll keep it between us."

"Keep what between you?" Luka said, sitting down in his chair.

"Oh, Thomas has a crush on me."

"What? No, I don't," he said frantically. Looking at Luka, he repeated, "I don't."

"Oh, okay. It's cool."

Lea's second round of laughter disintegrated. She folded her arms across her chest. "That's it?"

"Yeah. I mean, you're smart and hot and kinda mean. It's very … what's the word when something makes you have a lot of feelings?"

"Evocative?" Thomas suggested.

"It's very evocative."

She asked, "Did you get a room?"

Luka pulled the key out of his pocket.

Lea stood up and grabbed Luka's hand, urging him up. "Let's go. Thomas, give us a few minutes before you join us."

Luka's eyebrows lifted in surprise, and he grinned like the cat who ate the canary before being tugged away.

When Thomas knocked on the door, Lea was sitting on the bottom bunk bed, scrolling through her news feed. "Come in."

"You sure?"

"Yes, I'm sure. Come in."

He pushed the cabin's door open slowly. "I'm coming in."

"Luka's not even in here," she said.

"Oh. Where is he?"

"Handling some personal business."

"Geez," Thomas said, blushing.

"Hey." Luka entered the cabin right behind Thomas. He wore much the same expression he had when they left Thomas behind a half-hour ago.

Before everyone got situated in the cramped quarters, Thomas said, "We need to talk about something."

Luka's smile fell away as he plopped down beside Lea and pushed himself back against the wall. "That sounds ominous."

Thomas sat opposite them. "Yesterday, when I went out for a while, I didn't just go for a walk. I went back to the Temple of Hephaestus, where—"

"We know the one," Lea interrupted, wanting to press the story along.

Luka's eyes widened. "You didn't burn it down, did you?"

Thomas smiled wryly at that. "No, it's still intact. But I got a visit from the priest again. Epitiritis."

"What did he have to say?" Lea asked, without masking her suspicion.

"That y'all have to do everything I say."

"At least we know now that he's not a prophet," Lea said. "Or at least not a very good one. Because if you believe that, you're in for a world of disappointment."

"Kidding. He said the same thing as the oracle."

"Not an oracle," Luka said.

"Is there something else you'd prefer I call her?"

Luka shook his head.

"Alright then. He said I'm the heir, just like she did."

A silence fell on the trio, with no one knowing quite how to proceed.

"Aren't you worried that you'll … you know, be like him?"

You can always count on Luka to say the quiet part out loud.

"Kinda. Not as much as I was. The priest said Vulcan had a choice and gave in to the darkness."

"So he was kind of like the original Darth Vader," Luka suggested.

"Sure. Pastor Stefan said something similar. I asked him if he was worried about being Heinrich Pommerenke's grandson and carrying that evil around with him — obviously, this is before we knew he was a killer too. He said we all make our own choices. We don't bear the sins of our fathers. Those were his words."

Lea held a finger in the air. "Just to be clear, we are taking life advice from a serial killer and a priest who served a supervillain? Is that where we're at now?"

"I guess," Thomas said noncommittally. "That's not all. There's something I need to show you."

He stood up and turned toward the window. He extended his open hand in front of him.

When nothing happened in response, Lea whispered to Luka, "What's protocol here? Do we act like something really cool just happened?"

Doing his best Monty Python impression, Luka said, "Gosh, we're all really impressed down here, I can tell you."

"Shut up. I'm still working out the kinks."

30

LEA

THOMAS HELD his hand out in front of him again, steadied himself against the lilt of the ferry as a wave passed under it, and held his pose. A sable void opened. Still holding his hand out, he turned to them with a smile.

"Umm, what the heck is that?" Lea asked.

"A portal to another place. Want to go?"

Luka popped up heedlessly, narrowly avoiding scalping himself on the top bunk. His hand went to his head, where his hair had been disturbed, and his eyes reflected his realization of the close call.

"Help me up." Lea stuck her hand out. She was far less certain about this, but wasn't going to be the one to let her inhibitions hold them back. "Have you done this before?"

"Once."

"That's very reassuring," she said.

Luka asked, "You remember in *Harry Potter* how if they did their teleport thing wrong, they could get splinched and have a foot amputated or whatever? Is that a possibility here?"

Thomas shrugged. "Dunno. The priest wasn't big on instructions. Are we going or what?"

Just like a boy. Oh, look at this shiny new thing. I wonder what it does. We should definitely try it out on ourselves first, don't you think? For sure — that's a great idea. "On a scale of one to ten, how certain are you about this?"

Thomas stepped through the portal, leaving one arm on their side of the door as the darkness swallowed the rest of him. He gave a thumbs up and retracted his arm into the portal.

Luka looked at her with a gleam of excitement for the new adventure. Not that there had been any shortage of adventure in their lives.

"What's the worst that could happen?" he said.

"I know you asked that rhetorically, but there are a lot of answers to that question, and they're varying degrees of terrible. Just go."

Luka leaped through.

Lea stepped forward and submerged her hand in the murkiness. She had expected some kind of sensation on her skin. It looked so viscous, and it even clung to her arm the way milk climbs up the outside of a straw. She felt nothing. "Whatever." Lea stepped through.

She emerged onto an illuminated pathway surrounded by a crimson twilight. It was an otherwise barren landscape.

"Where are we?"

"As I understand it — and this is only my second time here — it's like an in-between place. A space between worlds. No, not worlds."

Luka burst into a few bars of a Dave Matthews song.

"You done?" Lea said impatiently.

"Yeah, it's pretty much all I know."

"That's all anyone knows, because no one's listened to Dave Matthews Band since the Oughts."

Thomas was still trying to put into words how to best describe the place. "It's like a hub. You can get from here to wherever it is you need to go. I think."

"You just go down this path?" Luka said, taking a few steps and leaving darkened footprints on the luminescent trail.

"No. The trail is mostly symbolic. To get wherever, I open another portal."

"You can't do that without coming here first?" Lea asked.

Thomas shrugged. "I'm kind of learning on the fly here."

Behind them, a roar preceded a wet, slapping sound and a burst of heat. Lea pointed with her thumb. "And that?"

"Not symbolic," Thomas said. "And there's a good bit more if it now than yesterday. I want to check something out." A moment later, he opened a door and immediately stepped through it. When he reemerged, he motioned them to join him and popped through a second time.

"Not big on explanations right now, is he?" Lea complained.

Luka sidled up next to the portal. "You coming?"

Lea strode forward, filled her lungs and held her breath as if she were about to dive into a swimming pool, and pushed through the doorway. She stepped out onto a mountaintop that overlooked an immense city abutting a bay. There was something familiar about this place. The stench of burning rotten eggs slapped her. Sulfur. She turned around to see a lake of lava undulating within the crater at the top of the mountain.

"Whoa!" Luka pointed west toward the large body of water. On an island, a volcano put on a stunning display of glowing ash and molten rock. The emission set the island's foliage ablaze wherever it landed.

"Epomeo." Thomas called the mountain by its name. "Don't know how I knew that. It's almost like I've always known it. But I haven't. Like how a parent couldn't forget their kids' names. Or something. I don't know. That sounds dumb."

Luka added excitedly, "Maybe when Vulcan's abilities and connection with volcanoes was transferred to you, his knowledge of them and their names were given to you as well."

Lea turned her head toward him. "That was … surprisingly insightful."

"I know your words made that statement a compliment, but when you say it like that, it's kind of an insult."

"I'm supposed to harness them," Thomas said. "That's what he did. He shepherded them. But right now, they're all going out of control. From here to Sicily. Nea Kameni, the volcano that destroyed Santorini. They are all on the edge of wrecking the Mediterranean. And that's just here, right around us. I can't even grasp the magnitude of this yet."

"We're here for you, man," Luka said. "You don't have to do this alone."

The corners of Thomas' mouth turned down and when he spoke again, there was an edge in his voice. "I'm not trying to be mean, but what can you possibly do to help? I am in this alone. There's no one to show me how to do it, and there's no one else who can help."

"How are you feeling?" Luka asked, patting Thomas on the back.

I forget how compassionate he can be. It's always covered up by ridiculous antics.

"Not great, if you can't tell," Thomas bristled. "The world is literally burning down around me. I'm supposed to stop it. And there's nothing I can do about it."

Lea watched with horror as the angrier Thomas got, the more agitated Vesuvius became, spitting globs of lava down its sides. The eruption on the island to their west intensified. Beyond the horizon, a red glow emerged. *This isn't going to help the climate change problem.*

Luka turned Thomas abruptly by the shoulder.

Lea's hands went to her mouth. *He's gonna punch him again.*

Luka embraced Thomas in a big bear hug. "It'll be okay," he whispered. "We'll figure it out."

Thomas didn't reciprocate the hug, but he let it happen. He

even rested his chin on Luka's shoulder. As his anger subsided, so too did the intensity of the volcanic activity in their vicinity.

Lea let the moment play out a minute before asking. "So what's the plan?"

Luka released the hug and placed his hands on Thomas' upper arms. "You got this."

Thomas nodded and took a half-step back. "My first priority is to find my mom. Hopefully, all this," he gestured down at Vesuvius, "can wait a couple more days."

"Hey!" someone yelled from across the crater. It was followed by a string of commands in Italian and the arrival of a couple more people.

"Time to go," Luka said.

Thomas raised up his hand, and Lea slapped it down. "Below the ridge so they can't see it."

Thomas nodded. "Good thinking."

"But how will we explain disappearing?" Luka said.

Lea answered, "One, we won't have to because we'll be gone. Two, I don't care."

The trio took several steps off the lip of the mountain and stepped single file through the doorway that Thomas opened into the in-between place.

As they settled their hearts from the sudden excitement, Luka said, "I sure wish we could see their faces when they can't figure out where we went."

"I think you're giving them too much credit," Lea said. "No way they were going to trek all the way around the top of that mountain just to scare off some teenagers who had already bolted."

"Maybe," Luka conceded. "Back to the ferry?"

Before Thomas could answer, Lea spotted movement a good distance behind the boys. It was almost wraith-like in its stealth. She pointed in its direction. "What is that?"

Thomas and Luka turned. The figure must have sensed the

attention. She turned to face them and looked so familiar. She was in sweatpants and a frumpy t-shirt.

Lea whispered, "Did you know there were other people here?"

"I haven't seen anyone before," Thomas said. "And the priest didn't say anything about anyone else?"

Luka asked, "What's on her shirt?"

Yeah, that's the important thing here, her clothes.

Thomas' squint was followed by a smile. He yelled, "Elle," and took off running toward her.

Elle fled. Her running was unnatural. Everything about her was off. It was like her feet weren't actually propelling her. The running motion was a reflex rather than a necessity.

Luka and Lea fell in behind Thomas. Elle turned back once and when she saw the trio of pursuers, terror seized her face. "Please, no," she pleaded. "Haven't you taken enough?"

Lea grabbed Luka's wrist and slowed down, forcing him to do the same. "What's happening?" he asked.

"She doesn't know it's Thomas. She thinks he's somebody else."

Thomas gained ground quickly, still calling after her. When she stopped and turned toward him, he skidded to a halt. His hands went to his knees, and he gulped air. "Elle, it's me, Thomas, Agatha's son."

"Don't let that name come out of your mouth," she hissed, anger replacing fear, even if momentarily.

The ground at his feet began to churn. He jumped backward, colliding with Luka as he and Lea caught up to him. Thomas startled and whirled, ready to pounce, like a dog that had been struck unexpectedly.

Luka held his hands out. "Whoa. It's okay."

Thomas pointed at the ground.

Wind gusted around them. The ground spun in an expanding radius, waves of stone and dirt crashing outward. The trio backpedaled to avoid being included in the maelstrom as a lava flow was pulled into the mix.

"Is she doing that?" Lea asked. "It's kind of awesome."

The air filled with debris as the tumult widened and grew more violent. Luka yelled, "We need to get out of here before someone gets brained with a rock."

Thomas hollered, "Elle!"

She either did not hear him over the din or ignored him. Either way, she stood completely still in stark contrast to the melee she had created in the gulf between herself and Thomas. Lea tugged at his arm, and he relented. They jogged backward a safe distance and stopped. Elle had not yet quelled the storm.

"If this is a real place," Lea said, "and obviously it is since we're here, then how is she here?"

"I don't know."

"I mean, her body is still in Germany, right?"

Thomas shook his head. "I don't know. Y'all know as much about this stuff as I do."

Luka said, "I've had about enough of this funhouse. Can we get back to the ferry?"

Thomas looked at Elle one more time.

"You have to let her go for now," Lea said.

Thomas nodded.

"Hang on," Luka said. "Is this going to work? The boat's going to be in a different place than when we left."

"I think so."

"Nice," Lea said.

"Look. I don't know how all this works," Thomas said defensively. "But I think it's going to work. The priest basically told me that I have to visualize where I want to go. He never said I had to know its coordinates or geographical location. Besides, if you think about it, nothing is ever in the same place, depending on your perspective. The earth is always orbiting the sun and rotating." He sounded more confident as he spoke, but it may have been the confidence of a conman for all she could tell. "So maybe the ability to open a door to a place is tied to my subjective connection to it, rather than some specific point in time and space."

"Okay, Einstein, let's see what you got."

Thomas splayed his hand in front of himself and opened a door to another place. "Lady's first?" he offered with a grin.

She strode up to it and stepped through, surprising both boys.

31

THOMAS

A FRENCH FRY fell out onto Luka's plate. He immediately snatched it up and shoved it back into the gyro that he kept within striking distance of his mouth. Lea shook her head and tapped at her mouth. Luka mirrored the action with his napkin, wiping away a glob of tzatziki sauce.

"Have you always been such an animal?" she asked.

"Have you tried these things?! It might be the best thing I've ever eaten in my life."

"You may need to get out more," she said. "Because I am not eating some giant hunk of unidentifiable meat that spins in a circle all day where all the bugs and bacteria can get to it."

"Your loss. Thomas, you want to get another one with me?"

Thomas held up both hands in surrender. "Two is my limit."

"Be back in five." Luka stood up and knocked the sand off his backside, showering Lea with it.

"Dude!"

He pawed at her hair briefly before she slapped his hands away and dusted herself. He grimaced. "Sorry."

Thomas and Lea allowed the quiet that followed his departure to persist. The steady crash of waves against the beach lulled him into a stupor. He was still tired from the ferry ride. He hadn't been very successful in getting any quality sleep after the events with Elle. Not to mention trying to sleep on a boat isn't just something a person can do without being accustomed to those motions and your body waking up freaking out with every unexpected roll. They checked in to the hostel early and caught a nap until lunchtime, but he still found that he was drowsy. Naps weren't a fair exchange for a night's sleep.

"Done," Lea said, setting her phone down on the towel beside her. "We can pick up the mopeds in a few minutes. They'll probably be ready by the time Luka's done eating."

"I don't know where he puts it all."

"Me either. And I kind of hate him for it. If I ate like that, I would be a cow." She wiggled her toes, that were buried in the sand. "Perissa was a good choice. It's quiet and pretty here."

"I had to stay on this side of the island. I couldn't stare at that volcano the whole time we're here waiting for it to blow its top."

Lea looked back over her shoulder, where a plume of black smoke reached up toward the wispy clouds. "Yeah, I get that."

"As it is, I keep waiting for my phone to tell me that the Ring of Fire wrecked hundreds of thousands of miles of terrain and killed millions on four continents."

"That's not on you, Thomas."

"It kind of is."

Lea looked out over the crystalline sea and didn't argue the point a second time.

Luka plopped down beside her, a third gyro in one hand and baklava wrapped in wax paper in another.

Lea patted him on a belly that was already protruding because of the volume of food it contained and which he pooched out even further. "You need to hurry. We've got to take a tour of this island and see if we can turn anything up. Also, if you get sick on the moped, I don't think we get our security deposit back."

Luka shoveled the meat-filled pita down but insisted that the other two take the baklava. Thomas and Lea halved it and gushed about how good and sweet it was. Luka groaned with regret at being too full to eat it.

On the walk to the moped rental place, Luka asked, "We're just getting two, right?"

"Umm, no," Lea protested. "Not unless you're riding passenger."

In the spirit of compromise, Luka offered, "What if they have one with a sidecar?"

Lea quoted from *Garden State* to remind him what kind of people ride in sidecars.

"We'll get three," Thomas said.

At their destination, they exchanged signatures and Agatha's credit card for the vehicles. They headed north, following the beachfront along the perimeter of the island. Thomas quickly realized that whatever they were looking for — and none of them had any indication of what that might be — wasn't going to be anywhere near the beach. There were far too many people. No way to keep anything a secret with tourists crawling all over the place for most of the year.

He tried to enjoy the next hour. The warm salt air rushing over him. He worked to push out the anxiety and dread of the obligations that he'd been saddled with, along with the idea that while they were geographically closer to Agatha, they felt no closer to finding her. He had real questions about whether she was still alive after more than three weeks.

He wasn't particularly successful in clearing space from the oppression because he found no lasting goodness to replace it. When he did create room for other thoughts, Emma came waltzing in. Like everything else, that too had turned bitter.

When the trio rounded the northern tip of Santorini, the beaches gave way to cliffs that rose out of the sea. Cliffs that had once been parts of hills that were connected to the other islands within the caldera. Until the volcano had spewed their foundation out of its mouth and the land between had fallen into the deep blue.

Lea signaled to them and pulled her moped to the shoulder of the road. She turned it off and pulled her helmet off.

"Did you see something?" Luka said after he stopped behind her.

She pointed to a set of stone steps that wound down from just beside the roadway all the way to a rocky promontory at the water. There was no house or fixture attached to it, and no apparent reason for its presence. From the top of the steps, the sea was the color of a sapphire's heart, and it was hard to imagine that anything was wrong in the world when you were at a place like this, until your gaze rose upward to meet Nea Kameni again. Besides the smoke, helicopters roamed the skies and dozens of boats that had been loaded with scientists bobbed just offshore, everyone wanting their shot at studying a volcano that had sunk Atlantis and been dormant for most of the last thousand years.

At the bottom of the serpentine steps, the trio congregated on a landing cobbled from stone. Lea untied and kicked off her Doc Martens. Luka sat on the ground with his legs extended and leaned back on his arms like he was any other person here on holiday to catch some rays. Thomas was frustrated that this entire expedition was a wast—

Lea shimmied out of her shorts and peeled off her tank top. The boys froze and gawked.

Luka broke the spell first. "What are you doing?"

"What's it look like?"

"It looks like you're getting naked."

"You wish," she laughed and turned to face them. "I'm going for a swim. I'm hot."

"Yeah, you are."

Lea threw her shirt at his face. Thomas, realizing that he'd been staring, finally averted his gaze.

"Am I embarrassing you?" she asked with a grin.

"No," Thomas' voice cracked as he answered. "No, it's just, you know."

"What?" she said, reveling in the discomfort she was causing.

"You're in your underwear."

Feigning frustration, she said, "It's no different from a bikini. Covers the same parts."

"It's different. It's normal to be seen in a bikini. I'm not supposed to see you in …" Thomas gestured at her torso.

"My bra and underwear," she sighed. "You can't even say it." Lea reached her hands around to the middle of her back. "If it bothers you so much, I can just take it off."

Luka cleared his throat. "Fine by me," he said, as if there were any doubt.

Thomas disagreed. "Maybe best if you don't."

Lea cackled and ran to the edge of the landing and leapt into the water. Luka jumped up and stripped down to his boxers before making the same jump. Thomas heard the splash and then laughter when Luka surfaced. He stood awkwardly and uncertainly on the landing and noted that at least he'd been distracted from his worries for the last few minutes. *And all it took was a girl undressing in front of me. Probably can't count on that happening all the time, though.*

Thomas untied his laces and removed first his shoes, then his socks. *Gotta make hay while the sun's still shining.* That was one of Joseph's expressions that had stuck in his mind all these years. And now was one of those times. They had things to do, but none of them could be done right this second. So he should at least enjoy the moment.

He pulled off his shirt, folded it, and laid it on top of his shoes, then followed suit with his shorts. But not without some hesitation. What was worse — dealing with wet shorts for a couple of hours or running around in boxer-briefs? It was a much closer call for him than it had been for Luka, who appeared to have given it no thought at all. *Typical.*

Thomas ran and jumped to the right of where his friends had gone in. As he soared in a downward arc, he saw his friends entangled in each other's arms and wondered momentarily about the physics of trying to tread water while making out. He turned his freefall into a jackknife and inconvenienced them with a splash.

When he emerged from the water, there was no land to be seen. Walls of water arose on either side of him. Thomas felt panic for the briefest moment before the rolling wave pulled him out of the trough and onto its crest. He was no further from land than he'd expected to be. After his stomach unknotted itself, he located his friends who hadn't been overly bothered by his splashing.

Thomas dove under the water and kicked toward them. As he grabbed each of their legs and yanked downward, he spotted something shiny on the seabed. He was going to need more breath than he presently had to get down to it.

Luka and Lea were sputtering and separate when he surfaced.

"Blödsinnig," Luka grumbled.

"What happened?" Thomas asked innocently. "Rogue wave?"

Lea lurched toward him, but he took a quick breath and dove under again. He swam down to the object, glittering even in the weakened light that permeated through five meters of blue water. At three meters, he cleared his ears to relieve the pressure, and continued kicking his feet, pushing toward the bottom.

It was a spoon, an old one by the looks of it. When Thomas reached out and grabbed it, he immediately let go. It was so hot that it burned his hand, red but not blistered. Only then did he see that the sand beneath it had blackened and turned to glass. The glass ran in a roughly straight line. He swung himself around so that he could see where it went. The streak run due south. He scoured the sea floor and saw similar black streaks running toward the same central source, a web of glass.

Thomas kicked his feet, pushing himself toward the surface. He already knew where they led, but he wanted to lay eyes on it. He broke through and spied a smoldering Nea Kameni. Should he try to reach out to it somehow, like through telepathy? No, that was dumb. You couldn't share thoughts with a mountain. How did it work? His skills as a schopfer and in creating fire were straightforward. He just *did* them. But this was different. Somehow.

He swam over to Luka and Lea to tell them what he'd seen. It sucked all the life out of the afternoon. The trio paddled over to the steps that had been carved out of the platform long ago. Lea sat down in the middle of the landing with the boys on either side of her. Seawater pooled around the three of them as they dried off.

Lea said, "Agatha's not on Santorini."

Thomas nodded. "I agree. Too crowded. Too many tourists. There's just a lot going on."

"What's that big island to the right?" she asked, pointing to her right.

Luka said, "Thirasia. There are some towns there, but the southern part is pretty empty."

"Alright, so the volcano island is Nea Kameni," Lea said. "It's always teeming with tourists, and now scientists are crawling all over it."

"Too obvious," Thomas added. "He'd want somewhere less conspicuous. Not much less. But some."

"What's the one next to it, then?"

Luka raised his hand. "Oh, I know this one too. Palea

Kameni. There are some hot springs in an inlet and a church on the beach, but almost nobody goes to the interior of the island. There's nothing there but some goats and chickens that this one guy raises. He lives on the island by himself."

"That sounds promising," Lea said.

"Nice," Thomas added. "How'd you know all that?"

"Finn—I mean a friend of mi—"

"It's fine, man. You can say his name."

"Okay. Well." Despite the assurances, Luka looked uncertain about how to proceed. "My friend told me about it. He thought it might be useful."

"So, how do we get there?"

"Rent a boat," Lea said.

"Can either of y'all drive a boat? I know I can't," Thomas said.

Neither gave any immediate response.

Finally, Lea shrugged. "How hard can it be?"

32

THOMAS

THE TRIO PILED out of the taxi at the marina in Vlychada. "I can't believe you would rather have ridden in a taxi than walked here," Luka complained.

"What are you even talking about?" Lea said as their ride motored away. "That took us six minutes. It would have taken thirty to walk."

Luka shrugged off the criticism. "It's such a nice morning. I just thought it would be nice. Besides, the boat rental place doesn't open for another five minutes."

Thomas walked away from the conversation and swung his legs over the low wall that stood on the side of the road. The marina below him was still asleep despite its dozens of sailboats, yachts, and other watercraft. The sun warmed his back and neck, and he let his friends' bickering drone into the background. This was the day that everything would come to a head. He could sense it. Never mind that he had thought that several times now. And been wrong each time. If he kept believing it, he was bound to be right, eventually.

Luka put his hand on Thomas' shoulder for support as he

straddled and then sat down on the wall. "Lea's gone to take care of the rental. Should be back in a few minutes."

"Okay," Thomas mumbled, staring out across the water.

"You alright, man?"

Thomas shrugged. "If we don't find her here, we're not going to find her. And even if we do, she might be … you know."

"We're gonna find her," Luka assured him, "and she'll be alright. I just know it."

"You hope. You don't know," Thomas corrected.

"Of course, I hope. It's all we have to hold on to. But it's not like hope is some string that's going to break if we put too much weight on it. It's strong. Maybe the strongest thing there is. Hope is what we have that the animals don't. Hope can handle the big problems and the small things. Don't give up on it, because it's not going to let you down."

Thomas turned to look at Luka, a smile creeping across his lips. "That was pretty deep."

Luka blushed. He pushed away the hair that had fallen into his face. "I guess."

The jangling of keys caused them to turn simultaneously. Lea walked toward them with the boat keys held out in front of her.

"You did it?"

"Well, Lea would have been too young to rent a boat. But, fortunately for us, Mila Reinhardt of Frankfurt is twenty-five."

Luka reached for the keys. "I'll drive."

Lea snatched them away. "Afraid not, young man. Give it a few more years and you'll be old enough." She patted him on the head with a devilish grin. He swatted at her hand, but she pulled away too quickly and headed for the steps that led down to the marina. Lea led them to a boat with a white and blue hull.

"It won't win any races, I can tell you that," Luka griped.

"All we need it to do is get us to an island," Thomas said, stepping aboard the vessel.

Lea walked around the console, her boots sounding particularly heavy on the fiberglass. Luka boarded and started to sit down, but Lea warned him off. "Huh-uh. Untie the ropes."

"How do I do that?"

"I don't think it's some fancy knot. It's basically wrapped around the cleat a few times. Just get it undone so we can go."

Luka muttered under his breath and knelt at the cleat on the bow.

"Look at you using boat terms," Thomas said. "Pretty soon you're going to be talking about starboard gunwales and whatnot."

Lea pushed the ignition, and the engine burbled briefly before springing to life. "It's pronounced gun-whale, not gun-uhl or whatever you said."

Thomas smirked. "Whatever you say, boss."

"Look at me," Lea instructed in her best Somali pirate accent and pointing two fingers at her eyes. "Look at me. I'm the captain now."

"Hey, Captain," Luka called. "You're leaving black marks all over the boat with those giant boots of yours."

"I'm the captain now," she repeated more assertively. Lea shifted the boat into reverse. The transmission engaged with a clunking sound and the propeller began churning water. She eased the throttle down and backed them slowly — very slowly — out of the slip. Once they were fully clear of the dock, she turned the wheel until they were pointed at the opening to the marina.

Lea shifted into forward and pushed the throttle. The boat jetted forward, and the bow flared up out of the water. Luka, who had been standing in front of the helm, stumbled to the side and tumbled backward toward the stern. Thomas clutched at his cushion. Lea yanked back on the throttle and brought the boat to a standstill near the marina's entry. It rocked as waves projected out from it in all directions. Boats bobbled in their slips, thumping against their bumpers.

Luka jumped up and stared at Lea.

In her best public service announcement voice, Lea said, "And that's why we should all be wearing flotation devices."

"Try again," Luka said. "You don't get to act like this was some safety exercise."

"So that's what happens when you push the accelerator too far forward," she offered.

"Throttle," Luka corrected.

Lea nodded. "When you throttle the accelerator."

Thomas said, "Close enough. Let's go … a little slower this time, if you don't mind."

"My offer to drive still stands," Luka said.

Lea returned her hand to the throttle and eased it forward, motoring them out of the marina and into open water. After clearing the last of the buoys, Luka said, "You can open up the throttle again if you want. But you might want to adjust the trim too."

"How is it you suddenly know so much about boats?"

"Watched a few videos so at least one of us would know what we're doing."

Lea mimicked her earlier action and pressed forward on the throttle, but with less suddenness. She alternated between speeding up and adjusting the trim until they were at a comfortable speed and angle. "Now that I know *how* to go, I need to know *where* to go."

Thomas pulled up a map on his phone. "Go west for like nine kilometers. Just kind of follow the coastline. That'll probably take about fifteen minutes. When we pass the lighthouse — that's at the tip of the peninsula — we'll turn northeast and basically go for another ten minutes until we get there."

If it weren't for the icy ball of anxiety that had taken up residence in his belly, the twenty-minute boat ride would have been one of Thomas' more enjoyable life experiences. The Santorini coast alternated between rocky cliffs and sandy beaches, like it couldn't decide what kind of island it wanted to be. A few other watercraft had crawled out of their berths, but only a fraction of what their number would have been a couple of months ago at the height of tourist season.

As they rounded Santorini's southern end, Palea Kameni came into view, along with the invigorated remains of an ancient volcano spewing smoke and occasional ash on the other side of it. Midway between their present location and their destination, another rock jutted out of the sea, smaller than the other islands, with no beaches and no fanfare.

"What is that?" Thomas yelled back to the others, pointing and trying to be heard over the wind.

Luka held raised his arms to his side, palms up. He didn't know.

Thomas shuffled to the helm so he didn't have to holler. "Why didn't we know about it before?"

"Finn didn't mention it, and I guess we couldn't see it from where we were. It was on the other side of the island. Isn't it on the map you were looking at earlier?"

Thomas pulled out his phone and fiddled with the screen until he'd pulled the map up again. Sure enough, there it was. An island without a name until you pinched out to where it was the screen's only occupant. "Aspronisi," he read aloud.

"Does it matter?" Lea asked.

Thomas didn't know. He had long surpassed his threshold for determining what carried significant weight on this journey. He was down to hopes and half-measured guesses. Agatha would have called them wild-ass guesses. That's what she said when it had gotten to the point that he was doing math home-work that neither of them understood, and he eventually threw an assortment of numbers and letters down on the page. "That's not a solution. It's just a wild-ass guess." Now, her survival was going to come down to his ability to guess well enough.

33

AGATHA

AGATHA CROUCHED at the inlet and dipped her shirt in water that was so hot now that it was nearly boiling. At the first sign of another lava vomit from the crevasse, she bolted across the cavern. When she stopped, she tied her shirt around her face. Trying to breathe through the wet shirt felt a bit like being waterboarded, but that was still a better alternative than inhaling more of the noxious fumes that her particular vent in the earth's crust was putting off.

She and Oberhaupt had once tried their hands at waterboarding to … encourage some people to relinquish information. What they realized relatively quickly was that as zauberi, they had tools at their disposal that the CIA didn't. It was really impressive how creative the hexeri branch was with their brands of mental and emotional manipulation. It only took one exhibition for Agatha to understand that she should always keep those folks at arms' length, but treat them politely and with deference. Before becoming a parent, she hadn't been truly scared of much, but the hexeri were definitely on that short list.

"Turns out the prospect of burning alive in lava is on the list too," she said, her voice muffled by wet fabric and croaky from smoke inhalation.

As the environment inside the cave became more volatile, she wished for her cot, which could have given her another eighteen inches of clearance in case molten rock started spilling across the cavern floor. She felt better about not having it when she realized the cot was all bamboo and cloth, and the lava wouldn't even have to touch it for the bed to reach its flash point. *It would've been a really comfortable funeral pyre. Or at least moderately comfortable.*

Her memory flashed back to the last time she'd been underground with funeral pyres. Joseph and the moldering, broken bodies of a couple dozen children and small creatures that Thomas had reanimated to save her from Vulcan. *See you soon, Joseph. I hope. Unless this is the end of everything. Hoping it's not.*

She'd resorted to just thinking her thoughts rather than speaking them aloud because of how scratchy and uncomfortable her throat was from smoke inhalation. With any luck, she would pass out from that before the heat roasted her like a Thanksgiving turkey. As last requests went, that was a pretty grim, but that's where she was at now.

The earth rocked and shook. Not one of the tremors from before. If she'd been standing instead of sitting on her bed, she was sure it would have knocked her off her feet. She thought she could hear the tectonic plates grinding against each other.

Glowing magma burst up through the widening crack. She flung herself on her side, turning her back to the disruption and covering her head with an arm.

Fat lot of good that's going to do me. Agatha sat up to watch globs of molten rock being lofted into the air, followed by waves of it pouring over the lip of the crevasse and spreading across the floor of the cavern. The initial blast subsided, but unlike previous occurrences, the flow of lava into the cave did not. There was a constant sizzle — not a sizzle, a roar — as lava invaded the inlet. The sea screamed its objections and filled the cavern with steam.

Tendrils of lava slithered through low spots on the cave floor. Thousands of years of storm runoff had created natural avenues that now directed a different form of traffic. As Agatha watched the stream overflow its banks in a torrent of destruction, she realized she would soon lose her opportunity to change locations. If she was going to move, now was the time.

She bounded for the small promontory in the middle of the cavern. While she ran, there was a thunderous concussion. The earth around her shook. She lost her balance and went sliding across the floor. Not an earthquake like before. Something had struck it. Something large. A sheet of water passed over the hole at the top of the cave, some of it falling in and contributing to the humidity as it cooled the lava that it landed on.

"What the heck?" Then she remembered the tsunami that had devastated southeast Asia so many years ago. That had started with an earthquake in the Indian Ocean.

Agatha picked herself up and finished the jaunt to her new resting place. It wouldn't be long until it was its own island. She could probably count down the seconds to her fiery demise after that happened.

"Agatha," a familiar voice called softly.

She whirled and fell to her knees at what she saw. Tears filled her eyes and fled down her cheeks, leaving streaks in the layers of accumulated grime and ash. She opened her mouth to speak, but found herself unable.

Agatha wiped her eyes with the palms of her hands and cleared her throat. "I don't know how you did it, but it must have been a lot of effort just to come see the end."

Elle said, "Perhaps."

"You look—I'm not sure how to say it without being rude."

"You have changed," the older sister smirked. "I've never

known that to stop you before. As I remember it, you mostly go out of your way to be impolite."

"Got soft in my old age," Agatha said. "Where the heck is your body?"

"That old thing? Haven't had much use for it since …"

Agatha didn't press the issue. "How are you here?"

"There have been cracks."

Agatha looked at the crevasse that continued to emit lava. "You're telling me."

"They began when *he* died."

"Who?" Agatha asked, but quickly connected the dots. "Oh, Vulcan? Dead??" She covered her mouth in surprise. "What happened? I thought he decided to leave me here to die."

"I don't know, but he is dead. And there is an heir. I've seen him."

Agatha's eyes blazed with a balance of fear and fury. "Who?"

"I don't know for sure. I saw him once. He invoked your name."

A new crackling noise to her left distracted Agatha. Her blanket and pillow had gone up in flames, leaving small scorch marks on the cave wall beneath her letter.

Her sore throat constricted, and her heart skipped a beat in anticipation of the question she could hardly bear to ask. "Thomas? Is it Thomas? Is he okay?"

"I can't say."

Agatha let the question linger, hoping that Elle would provide more information. When it became clear that wasn't the case, she said, "Let's go back to how you got here."

"It's a long story," Elle said.

"I've got nothing but time." She gestured at her increasingly hostile surroundings. "Not a lot, obviously. But there are few other ways I'd prefer to spend it than with you. So maybe cut to the important parts so I get to hear it all before I start looking like a roasted marshmallow — all crusty on the outside and gooey in the middle."

"You're still disgusting."

Agatha shrugged.

"After he died, the interstitial space began to hemorrhage. Obviously, that has carried over to this world. Things are not well. When a crack opened up large enough for me to slip into, it sent me to the only place that I had a strong enough nexus to get through."

"I … don't know what most of that means. But if you got in, can't you — are you here to get me out?"

Elle shook her head. "I couldn't have gotten in if I'd been attached to a body. I didn't come here intending to leave."

"Oh," Agatha said, unable to hide the disappointment in her voice.

The earth shuddered again, and the volume of lava flowing into the cave increased, like blood pouring from a wound that had been pried open. The heat intensified, and Agatha's eyes stung. She adjusted her makeshift mask as though it made any difference. There was nowhere for her to retreat to. Even if she could get to the water, it was too hot for her to get into. Shellfish had better odds of survival at a shrimp boil.

Agatha looked at the apparition that stood across from her. "I sure wish I could give you a last hug. Or even hold your hand."

"You misunderstand my purpose here, sister. You've been taking care of everyone for so long that you can't imagine someone else taking care of you. But it is my time."

"I don't understand."

"My name is no accident. There is no happenstance, not even the nickname you taunted me with as a child. Do you remember it?"

Amid the chaos, Agatha sorted through nearly five decades

of memories, trying to find the right one. Eventually, she whispered, "Elle Strom the maelstrom."

Elle nodded. "Yes, that was the payoff for all the National Geographic shows you watched. You could not have known then — or perhaps you did, through intuition — that you had named my ability. And now it is that ability that will be your salvation."

"I still don't understand," Agatha said, though she was beginning to have a sense of what Elle was about to do. For the second time that day, she slipped down to her knees. "Please don't do this. There is another way. I'll be okay."

"There is no other way," Elle said as her disembodied spirit levitated high above the cavern floor. "The heir is coming. Be ready. I do not know his intentions, only that he seeks you."

The cavern convulsed and groaned, sounding like it might collapse around her. Agatha looked up instinctively, locating her window to the outside world. There was no way to position herself under it because of the lava flows, and no way to guarantee that if the place did collapse, it would fall straight down.

Elle raised her arms above her head, looking for all the world like a goddess. A smile slipped across Agatha's face. Even if these were her final few minutes, she was so glad this version of Elle was her lasting memory as they crossed over to the other side of the veil, not the fragile, helpless body that was incapable of doing anything for itself.

The stone, water, and lava that were beneath Elle tore away from the ground and spun upward, mixing in a torrential slurry. Elle pushed herself off the stone floor, dragging more of the elements with her. Wind whipped at Agatha as the vortex grew. She wrapped her arms around her legs, though she suspected there was little need to protect herself. The cave drained of its molten layer as Elle drew more of it within her storm.

With a last look at Agatha, Elle flung her arms down and drove through the center of the maelstrom into the earth. Agatha covered her ears at cacophonous destruction.

A crater devoured the earth on the far side of the crevasse. Magma and seawater raced to fill it, reaching a tenuous equilibrium before they breached the banks. Rocks plummeted to the ground from the arched cavern walls as they shifted their loads and acclimated to another change.

Before long, everything grew still and quiet. Agatha was again left alone. But this time, she knew her wait was not indefinite. It had an expiration date. For better or worse, Vulcan's heir was coming. In the meantime, she would mourn the loss of her sister, whom she thought she had lost so long ago.

34

THOMAS

THOMAS WATCHED to his right as the rogue wave picked up size and speed before smashing into the caldera-side ports and cliffs of Santorini. Even at this distance, the wreckage was clear, the only consolation being that it would have been far worse on the beach side.

He refocused his attention on their task when they approached the channel between Nea Kameni and Palea Kameni. The smaller, mostly uninhabited island was on their left.

Lea slowed the boat and said, "Tell me where I'm going."

Thomas looked up from his phone and pointed to a feature ahead of them. "That place where the rocks stick out at like ninety degrees to the shoreline. On the other side of that is the hot springs. Let's start there."

When they rounded the outcropping, Lea shifted the boat into neutral and idled the engine. The cove that would normally be cluttered with swimmers was occupied instead with dead fish and boats full of scientists and news crews. The hot springs were literally boiling. Beyond the small chapel having been converted to a temporary research facility, Thomas didn't spot any signs that the scientists had gone into the interior of the small island. Cliffs surrounded the hot springs cove on three sides by cliffs. If they could find another entry point to the island, they would still be out of anyone's sight lines and hopefully avoid drawing any attention.

"That can't be good," Luka said.

"I guess we're not going to dock here?" Lea suggested.

Looking at the map on his phone again, Thomas said, "There's a beach on the opposite side of the island. Take us around."

"Should I just make a u-turn?"

Thomas shook his head. "Go on around the northern end. We'll see if we can spot that hermit guy's house. That might help us narrow our search." He felt like he should qualify everything with *I guess* and *maybe*, because that's what all of this amounted to.

"Search? What search?" Luka said. "This island is small enough that I think I could piss across it."

Lea patted him on the shoulder. "As usual, you give yourself too much credit."

Thomas grinned and let the dig lie without piling on.

Lea shifted the boat into forward and got them going, accelerating more smoothly on her third attempt. She took them around the lava field that made up the island's northeastern corner. While none of the lava was new, fissures had opened and were venting smoke. *Won't be long until this one's blowing too.*

The boat rounded the northern end of the island without their seeing any evidence of human occupancy. As they rounded toward its western face, Luka pointed at some animals silhouetted atop a cliff. "Goat!" he yelled over the noise of the wind.

Not far from where Luka had spotted the animal, Thomas thought she saw a flat straight line of ... something peeking briefly over the ridgeline. But it was gone before his brain synthesized what his eyes had spotted. Something from a science class jumped out at him — *nature doesn't make straight lines* — so if he had seen something like that, it was most definitely made by a human. He noted roughly where it had been as they pressed forward.

Beyond the sheer rock walls that made up most of the island, Lea found the gray beach that Thomas had mentioned and sped toward it. It certainly wasn't the touristy sandy beach that Greek islands were known for. This one was all smashed bits of rock and shards of shell that had been ground against them. The beach slid out from under walls of stone that arose behind it.

Lea slowed the boat so they could look for an entry point. It was not an encouraging sight. Broken rock and gravel mounded from the beach to the cliff walls that offered no route to the scrub-covered terrain above them.

Thomas spotted what might be an option and said, "Take us down to the far end."

She adjusted the throttle and took them to the end of the beach, where the cliff angled closer to the water and the pile of broken rock reached higher. The two nearly met in the middle, like puzzle pieces that didn't quite fit each other.

"That might be doable," Lea said.

"It wouldn't be any fun," Luka added, "but I think it's possible. Maybe."

The beach ended at an ancient flow of igneous rock that looked like a monstrous webbed paw stepping down out of the heavens into the water.

Thomas said, "Before we commit to this, let's see what's around the corner."

Lea nodded and turned the boat back out to sea to navigate around the giant paw. In doing so, the trio found exactly what they'd been hoping for — a small cove protected on two sides by sheer walls with a small beach that rose gradually to the more level ground at the top of the island. A small boat with an outboard motor strapped to the back of it had been pulled onto the beach.

"Eureka!" Luka said.

Lea cocked her head to the side and gave him a contemptuous look.

"What? Isn't that what you're supposed to say when you find what you're looking for?"

"I'm pretty sure no one has said that in the last thousand years. But you do you, I guess."

Lea slid the boat into the cove and onto the beach, where it came to rest with a soft crunch. Thomas opened the anchor locker and tossed the anchor and coil of rope onto the sand. The three hoisted themselves over the side of the boat and onto Palea Kameni.

Standing alongside one another, they inspected the sloped pass that would take them to the top of the island.

Thomas grimaced. "It's a little steeper than I thought."

"Nothing about this whole trip has been easy," Lea said. "Why start now?"

Thomas strode off the beach and onto the shale and scree that made up the slope. As the angle of the pitch increased, he reached out for scrub brush to help pull himself along. It was a dicey proposition though, since their roots had little soil to take hold of. Too much pressure, and if they let go, he'd go tumbling onto the others that were following in his wake. He envied Lea's clunky boots, because at least they weren't filling up with dirt and rocks like his sneakers were.

Thomas paused to look ahead. He detoured to a route to the left that involved gravel and a slightly steeper climb, but avoided the cliff walls they would run into by forging ahead. Despite the morning's balmy temperature, sweat beaded on his forehead and ran down his face.

He dragged himself to the top and sat down. When the others joined him, Lea sniffed at them. "You two stink."

Luka leaned toward her and took a whiff. "Well, you're definitely all roses and sunshine." He whispered hoarsely to Thomas. "Not really. She smells very musky."

Lea shoved him a little harder than she'd intended, causing Luka to lose his balance and tilt outward. Lea's eyes widened as she snatched his shirt and reeled him back in. "I just saved your life," she said as he situated himself again.

"I don't think it really counts if you're the one who nearly killed me."

After catching her breath, Lea got to her feet. "Which way were the goats?"

Thomas stood up and pointed north. Even though the island was only a kilometer long, its undulating terrain kept the trio from seeing any of the animals. "Of course, the guy who lives here may not be near the goats. They probably have free rein. I mean, where are they going to wander off to?"

"True," Lea agreed. "But there's not that much area to search, and wherever he lives should be pretty obvious, I'd think."

"Question," Luka said. "What are we going to do when we find him? Just ask, 'You haven't seen a god and his captive wandering about lately, have you?'"

"Honestly, I don't know," Thomas said. "I haven't gotten that far yet."

"Right. Nothing like a good plan."

Disregarding the comment, Thomas headed north. Lea fell in line behind him without making any suggestions.

Don't we have to assume that if he admits to knowing anything, he's probably on Vulcan's side? And if he denies knowing anything, how can we be sure he's telling the truth? Probably best if you think through your options on the hike, dude.

A bald head and shoulders crested the hill that the trio was approaching, followed closely by a torso and bowed legs. Thomas screeched to a halt. The scruffy old man's inordinately large eyes showed no surprise at seeing them. "Most of you keep to the beaches and don't wander about my island. You haven't come to steal my chickens, have you?"

"No," Thomas said. "We'd like to talk to you."

The old man grunted and squinted at the sun that was climbing the sky.

"Better you three than all those animals down there doing somersaults about some boiling water. Come. I'll make us some coffee. Then, we can talk."

He turned and ambled toward the end of the island where Thomas earlier thought he'd seen a straight line.

The old man's home could only properly be called a hovel. It had four walls and a roof, but it looked like something that the next storm would leave in a heap. The old man opened the door and entered without speaking, leaving Thomas to assume that he should continue to follow.

Once inside, Lea snooped around, trying to look inconspicuous. The small table and its one chair could not have been used for eating as they were cluttered with all manner of bric-à-brac. Thomas suspected it was a combination of belongings left by tourists and things that washed ashore.

The old man shuffled around the hovel, knocking things about in search of a fourth coffee cup. Only when he began rinsing them did Thomas realize there was no proper plumbing in the place. Attached to the ceiling above the discolored sink was a large basin of water and a length of flexible piping that ran down to the faucet.

What is the toilet situation? Nope. Don't even think about it.

The old man hadn't spoken to them since suggesting that they come to his place for coffee. It was both an oddity and a relief. Certainly no more odd than his physical appearance, especially his condor-like arms that looked as though they belonged to a man a foot taller. But he tried not to judge him for things beyond his control. Obviously, not super successfully.

After the man cleared space beside the burner for the cups,

he put the coffee grounds in his briki and filled it with water. The briki, with its gleaming copper, looked singularly out of place in the shack. He placed it on the electric burner and turned to face them as it heated.

Though he looked in their directions, he did not meet any of their eyes. It was like he couldn't look any higher than their chins. But mostly, he didn't look directly at any of them. The quicker they were done here, the better. Thomas' spidey senses were working overtime, telling him they were creeped out.

Luka, unable to bear the silence any longer, blurted out. "Why do you live on this island by yourself?"

"I am craven," he confessed. "Given to much temptation. Opportunity to succumb to it is much less here. I go to the chapel each morning. Tend to my goats and chickens. Keep watch over this place. I am its shepherd."

Thomas shivered both in surprise at his candor and because this kind of talk hit close to home for him. He had talked little about Pastor Stefan since all that had happened. He was still ashamed of being taken in by him.

"Oh," Luka said. "So, this is kind of like a monastery for you?"

"I think of it as a sanctuary," he answered without meeting the boy's gaze. "What brings you here? It is not the hot springs, I gather." He turned and tended to the copper briki, which had begun to froth.

Luka continued to lead the conversation. "This may sound like a weird question. But do you know a guy named Hephaestus?"

The briki clanged against the electric burner. The old man's hand trembled as he poured the black coffee into the small cups. Thomas looked at Lea. *She thinks something's off too.* The question hung in the air while the man distributed the cups one by one, giving each of them a small nod as he handed the cup over.

"I am Greek. Of course, I know of Hephaestus." He chuckled

dryly to himself. "I am old, but not quite so old as to have been around when the gods ran amok. Besides, I think you will find that Hephaestus is a name that many will spit on in these islands."

Thomas asked, "Why?"

"Let us go outside," the man said without offering the coffee he had poured. He shuffled past them toward the door. He looked first toward Santorini, then gestured in turn at each of the other islands. "This caldera was once one great island, until Hephaestus — if you believe in such beings — out of spite or malice or just because he had the ability to do so, destroyed it in a matter of hours and carried our cities and its people to the depths of the sea. Most of the islands' residents can trace their lineage back to that time. And so, the resentment has persisted."

"So you don't know him then?" Luka asked, persisting in his awkward interrogation.

The old man tensed and met Luka's eyes for the first time. A strange expression fell over the boy's face. "I do not. Nor can I. He is a myth," he said with a conviction he hadn't exhibited before.

"Okay, I understand," Luka conceded.

"Now, I must get about my chores. You can see yourselves back to your boat," the old man instructed.

When he turned away, Luka recovered himself and watched warily as the man ambled toward his residence. No one said anything, even after they heard the door squeak closed behind him.

35

LEA

AFTER THEY HAD TREKKED back across the Palea Kameni and come to the descent down to the beach, Lea couldn't let it lie any longer. "What just happened?"

"Nothing," Luka said. "What do you mean? I think he just kicked us off his island."

"No," she shook her head. "Before that. When he looked at you."

"Oh, that." Luka looked at the scrub grass at his feet. "I … don't know. It was weird. This is going to sound—forget it."

"Spill."

Luka sighed. "I felt like I couldn't look away. All of a sudden, he was taller and stronger. And he was … erect? Not like … you know. His posture. He wasn't all hunched over. But listen, I couldn't exactly see it, or not see it. It was weird. I might have it all wrong."

Thomas said, "It's an illusion."

"No," Luka said with a kind of confused confidence. "What I saw when I looked into his eyes felt more real than the rest of the time I was looking at him. Even though I could see the old body at the same time. I mean, when I was looking at him before, he looked real enough. Obviously. Or we all would have noticed. But when I saw the other version, then I could tell, you know?"

"I think Thomas is right and wrong. What we all saw is an illusion. Him walking around every day looking like Quasimodo is a glamour. But he slipped when you pressed him about Vulcan. Something about looking him in the eye let you see into the illusion."

"But why go to all that trouble?" Thomas asked.

"That's a good question." Lea turned around and stalked back the way they'd come.

Luka called to her. "I don't think that's a good idea." When she didn't slow down, he jogged to catch up. He pulled at her arm. "Lea, this is not a good idea."

She yanked away and kept walking.

Thomas pulled alongside her and said, "What are you going to do?"

"You asked a question, and I plan to get us some answers. We came out here for answers. Right now we have none, but we have a guy who let slip that he has some kind of können when Luka started asking questions. So that seems like it's worth investigating. Any further objections from you two?"

Neither raised any.

When they got to the old man's dwelling and stalked toward its only entrance, she was glad it had no windows. She did not want anything to give away their return. They rounded the corner and stopped in front of the door. Luka stepped forward and raised a hand to knock. Lea grabbed him by the shirt collar and snatched him backwards. He started to protest, but she quickly raised a finger to her lips.

Taking a half-step forward, she raised up her right leg and smashed her boot into the door handle. The rotting frame splintered, and the door flew inward.

The old man was hunched over something on the floor with

his bare back to them. Tattooed across his torso was an enormous owl in mid-flight, its wings expanded so that their tips wrapped around his ribs. Its open beak carried flesh from the disemboweled woman who drooped from its talons.

Only after looking past the tattoo did she realize what he was huddled over. Four cloven-hooved legs stuck out around him, and the man had buried his face in the soft part of its neck where its throat had been cut. He stood slowly. Before turning around, he raised his arm to wipe his face. When he lowered the arm, it was smeared a deep red. The same blood that dripped from the knife that he clasped. He growled, "You should not have returned. I did not give in to my temptations before."

When he turned around, the glamour dissolved. He was a man of strength and power, much taller than the bent old man they'd seen before. Most striking were his glacier-colored eyes.

"Who are you?" Lea asked.

He hissed at her, revealing teeth that he had shaved to points. "You can demand nothing from me. There is power in a name, and I will not give that power to you."

"Fine. If you will not tell us who you are, tell us what you do here on this island."

"Obviously, I am a goatherd," he answered smugly.

"No," Thomas said. "The old man tends to the animals, but not you. You are something else."

"You speak truly," he said.

Lea pushed her hands through her hair, trying to figure out how to get to the heart of the matter instead of dancing around its perimeter. His eyes flicked down to her exposed neck, and his gaze stayed there a moment too long.

When they were here before, she thought he'd been a skeezy old man who'd checked her out a few times. She realized now how wrong she was. This was far creepier. His lust for her was almost palpable.

"Do you know why we are here?" Thomas asked.

Lea let her hair fall back across her neck, curious about what effect it would have. The man broke his gaze from her and tilted his head in Thomas' direction. "How could I? You have not said, and the only questions you have asked are about … him."

"Hephaestus."

"Hephaestus," he repeated with a snarl.

"You know him then?"

"I am tethered to that monster in ways that you cannot imagine. But no one has come seeking him for many centuries. Why you? Why now?"

Thomas looked to Lea with a question in his eyes, seeking guidance. She shrugged almost imperceptibly. They were on uncertain ground here. His guess was as good as hers.

Filling the gap, Luka decided for them. "I'll tell you what we want — there is a place where Hephaestus takes his captives, where he holds them until he decides what to do with them. Do you know where it is?"

The man barked a false laugh. "You ask me to reveal a three-thousand-year-old secret, of which I am the keeper. That I cannot do."

"Okay, let's talk about you then. What are you?"

"Do you know of the stryga?"

Luka shook his head.

His face darkened, and a glimmer darted across his eyes. "Then it is no matter." He pounced toward Lea, who was caught off guard. Luka intercepted him, jamming his shoulder into the man's ribs. The force pushed them toward Thomas and the wall of the hovel. Thomas jumped backward to avoid being embroiled in the collision. Luka and the man struck the wall with a thud. The hovel trembled and dust fell from the ceiling.

When they hit the floor, the man's knife skidded several feet from the combatants. Lea dashed for it.

The man rolled on top of Luka and raked gashes into his ribs with his taloned fingers. Luka yelled in pain, and the man drew himself closer to Luka, who shifted his hip to throw the man off. The bite that was intended for his neck landed instead on the muscle above his shoulder. Luka howled.

Thomas circled around behind the man. He shot in, reaching under the man's arms and wrapping him tightly around the chest. The man was almost too broad for Thomas to clasp his hands together. He tugged. But the man tightened his grip on Luka's ribs.

At a loss for what else to do, Lea yelled, "Hephaestus is dead!"

The man went slack. Thomas was applying so much force that the two of them flew backward and crashed into a pile of clutter. The man broke Thomas' grip and rolled away, popping to his feet. He heaved several deep breaths.

Lea glanced at Luka, who looked like he'd been mauled by a tiger. He pressed his hands against his sides to staunch the bleeding, but it still dripped freely from the wound in his shoulder.

Thomas scrambled up off the ground. The man held up both hands to Thomas, indicating a ceasefire. "Hephaestus is dead?"

Lea nodded slowly.

The man's demeanor shifted. With a crooked grin, he said, "I wish you would have mentioned that sooner."

Lea shuddered upon seeing his teeth stained with Luka's blood, making his smirk all the more insidious.

Thomas asked, "What does that mean?"

The man held his arms out. He was almost jovial now, like this was some kind of performance. "I am not beholden to a dead Hephaestus. Dead men have no secrets."

Lea wrinkled her brow, trying to process the sudden turn. "What, so just like that, you'll answer our questions?"

The man considered her query for several seconds.

A scuffing sound over her shoulder told Lea that Luka was pushing himself upright. He grunted in pain.

"Yes," he answered. "But first, to whom do I owe my gratitude?"

"Me," Thomas said gravely. "I killed him, and I am his heir."

"Congratulations are in order, perhaps? Or better still, maybe you can do something about Nea Kameni before we are all buried under ash?"

Thomas shook his head. "I don't know how."

"In that case, I'll gather my—" he stopped and looked around the meager dwelling. "No, I won't be taking anything with me."

"Do you owe nothing to me?" Thomas said.

The man answered a question with a question. "Do we have oaths between us?"

"No."

"I agree. We do not. Did Hephaestus leave a testament bequeathing my bonds to you?"

Thomas shook his head.

"Well, in that case, I owe you nothing."

He asked quietly, "Where is it? Where does he keep them?"

The man pointed to his left. "Aspronisi. The white island. Now if you don't mind, I'll be going."

Lea stood between him and the door. As he stepped toward her, she looked again at the dead goat and at Luka's wounds. She recalled the tattoo and the man's words to them about temptation. "I have a final question for you."

He paused in front of her.

"Will you kill again?"

Without hesitation, the man answered, "Almost certainly."

"I understand," she said. "I feel like we all got off on the wrong foot here. Come, give me a hug, and let's part on better terms."

From her right, Luka objected.

She shot him a look that quieted him. She reached behind her neck with her right hand and pulled her hair off of her shoulder. The doubt that had clouded the man's face gave way to greed. He closed the gap between them and leaned down, burying his face in the hollow of her neck. She wrapped her arms around him and pulled him tight.

Lea felt his tongue and teeth scrape against her skin as she plunged the knife into his back and through his heart. He gasped and pulled away. With his momentum already going backward, Lea crooked her leg behind his knees and shoved his shoulders.

He fell, landing on his back and driving the knife in until the hilt embedded in his flesh. He thrashed several times, trying to get his feet under him. Lea kicked them out while Thomas stood above his head. Luka looked on the scene with shock. The man's movements became more spastic, then stilled completely.

Lea went to Luka and squatted in front of him. "Can you get up?"

"Was that necessary?"

"Yes. Can you get up?"

"You just killed that guy," he insisted.

She stood up. "We can talk about the ethics of it later. Give me your hand."

Luka peeled his right hand off his ribs and grasped Lea's outstretch arm. Blood trickled again as soon as he let go. When his torso flexed as she pulled him up, the trickles became streams.

Lea ordered, "Thomas, find something we can wrap around him."

Thomas spun in a circle, then strode to the bed and pulled the sheet away. There was too much fabric to use without it being unwieldy, so he held his hand to the top of the sheet, burning through the hem. He tore it lengthwise and carried it to Luka, keeping it off the floor so it would not drag through any of the several pools of blood that littered the place.

Lea took the sheet and handed a corner to Thomas. "Hold this against his chest." Addressing Luka, she said, "When I tell you, let go of your sides and pull your shirt up. It's gonna hurt like hell, but you gotta to do it fast. Ready?"

Luka bit his lip and nodded.

"Go."

With his jaw clenched, Luka reached down to the bottom of his shirt and pulled it up to his armpits. He grunted and his breath caught. Lea used the sheet like a giant bandage, wrapping it around his chest several times. With the last pass, she shoved it under his shirt in the back, looped it over his shoulder, and tucked the corner in at his chest.

When she had finished, she stepped back to look at her work. "It's not as tight as it should be, but it'll have to do until we can get back to Santorini. You can let your shirt down now."

"No," Luka said. "Agatha first."

Lea looked to Thomas for help.

He said, "Listen, Lu—"

"No. Agatha first."

"Okay," Lea conceded. "Agatha first." She looked around the place, her gaze landing on the bodies. She said to Thomas, "You know what you have to do?"

"Yes," he whispered.

"We can leave no trace of what happened here. None," she said, trying very hard to avoid saying what she was alluding to.

"I understand. I've done this before. You two get to the boat, and I'll catch up. Them first, then the house."

Lea nodded in agreement. "Oh," she said. "The knife."

Thomas grimaced but didn't disagree. "Help me turn him over."

Lea and Thomas squatted down and rolled the body onto its belly. The tattoo was mostly covered in a darkening well of blood. Lea reached for the half of the sheet that Thomas had discarded a few minutes earlier. She wadded it up and dropped it onto the body, then stepped on it with one booted foot. "Grab his shirt. It's behind you. And pull that knife out. I'll take it with us. We can drop it into the sea."

Thomas complied, though it took him two strong yanks for the blade to release its grip on the man. He handed the weapon to Lea, who coiled the shirt around the weapon.

"Ready?" she asked Luka.

"You're a little better at all of this than I'm comfortable with."

"Me too," she said.

Luka shuffled out of the door. Once she was outside with him, Lea draped his right arm around her shoulders so she could support him as they walked. They turned and stopped before going. Thomas had already begun his work. A bright blaze illuminated the interior of the hovel. The last image they had of him as they started for the boat was Thomas retching after being smitten with the acrid smell of burning fur and clothes and flesh.

36

―――――

LEA

LEA HAD the engine idling and the anchor back in its locker when Thomas appeared at a run. He didn't slow when he reached the lip of the island's surface. He hit the shale at full tilt and skated down, somehow managing to keep himself upright. Once he hit the sand and gravel, he sprinted into the water and high-stepped to the boat. After Lea helped pull him aboard, she returned to the helm and set about putting some distance between them and the smoke that was rising to the sky.

"We good?" Lea asked.

"We're good."

He doesn't look like he's good. "You okay?"

Thomas shrugged. "Had to be done. You know where you're going?"

"The only island left."

Lea maneuvered the boat out of the cove and headed southwest in the open water between Palea Kameni and Aspronisi.

Luka stood up from his seat at the front of the boat to join Thomas and Lea. "You know, the last time I was wrapped up like a mummy like this was when you tried to barbecue me."

Thomas smirked. "You know how some people, when you

see them, you think to yourself, I'd really like to hit that guy? I think maybe you're like that."

"Yeah, that checks out," Lea said.

Thomas looked to his left and then over his shoulder behind them. "Most of Aspronisi is going to be visible from the other islands. Take us around to the far side. Hopefully, that will give us some cover."

She adjusted their course to go around the north side. They covered the three kilometers that separated the two islands in a matter of minutes. She brought the boat to a stop beside a flat rock just offshore of Aspronisi.

"This place is like a fortress," Thomas said. "How tall do you think that is, fifty or sixty meters?"

"At least," Luka said. "Maybe more."

Lea agreed. "I don't see a way up."

"Get us as close as you can, and kill the engine," Luka said. "I have an idea."

Lea did as Luka had proposed. Thomas dropped the anchor. With the tide out and relatively little wind, the small boat bobbed lightly beside the rock, out of sight of the rest of the caldera.

Luka dropped into the water beside the boat and made a strangled screeching sound. Thomas and Lea hurried to the side where he'd gone in and looked down.

"Salt water. I didn't think."

"Dummkopf," Lea said.

Using mostly his right arm, Luka pulled himself out of the water onto the flat rock, where Thomas and Lea joined him after they'd jumped in. Pink-tinged water dripped from his ripped and sodden shirt as he waited to tell them the plan he'd come up with.

"Alright," Lea grumbled, "you've let the tension build. We are eager to hear your plan. Get to it."

Luka grinned and moved to the westernmost end of their

rock, which was adjacent to the lowest section of the island's plateau. Lea and Thomas followed like confused ducklings. He turned to face them. "I'm going to make an ice bridge from here to there."

Lea's and Thomas' heads swiveled from where Luka was standing to where he proposed to attach the bridge. Thomas said, "Actually, that's a pretty good idea. Can you do it?"

"Dude, if Elsa can do it, so can I."

"Elsa? From *Frozen?*" Lea said incredulously. "I hate to break it to you, but Elsa is animated and never did—"

"Don't you dare talk bad about Elsa," Luka said. "She was my hero growing up. I wanted to be just like her because we had the same powers. Then I got older and realized I could never be like her..."

"Because she's a cartoon?"

"No, because she's hot." Luka burst into laughter that immediately made him grab his ribs and inhale sharply.

"You're gross and you deserved that," Lea said. "Can you get on with this bridge of yours before I decide to maroon you on this rock?"

"Yes, but it's going to take all three of us. I have plenty of water to draw from, but I don't know how far I can project the volume we'll need to make it stable. I may not be able to finish it and attach it to the island until I'm on it. Lea, can you create some wind to push the arch outward?"

She nodded.

"Where do I come in?" Thomas asked.

"Steps. I need you to make steps so we can actually go up the bridge. Can you handle that?"

"Sure. Fire and ice. Classic combo. What could go wrong?"

"That's the spirit," Luka said enthusiastically. "Okay, here goes." He cracked his knuckles and held his hands out in front of him, pointed at the ground. A flurry of ice coagulated on the rock at his feet and began mounding. Luka took several minutes to make a solid base that was a couple of meters wide.

With the base done, he directed the flow of ice in an upward arch toward the island, being sure to keep the top portion as flat as possible while also keeping the angle from being overly steep. He revolved around the structure as he built it. "This is going to take a little longer than I thought."

"It's fine," Lea said. "Don't worry about the time."

After the bridge rose about twenty meters into the air, Luka paused his work. "You're up," he said to Lea. "I'm going to do the same thing I've been doing, but you're going to have to push it, because I can't get it up any higher."

Lea smirked and opened her mouth to speak.

"Don't. I know what I said."

She withheld her comment, but the smirk remained. Luka extended his arms above his head and looked over his shoulder at her. She nodded. He projected ice upward, and she blew gusts of wind so that it carried upward and adhered to the part of the bridge that he had already built.

The process became much less efficient the taller it got. The second segment of the bridge took twice as long to build as the first twenty meters had. Instead of continuing to push upward, Luka adjusted the angle of his hands and began working downward. A stalagmite emerged from the bottom of the arch until they heard it groaning and popping.

"Stop," Luka yelled.

Lea cut off the wind. Luka hurried to the edge of their flatrock and hastily built a pillar of ice at the base of Aspronisi, just above the waterline, directly below the edge of the arch. As quickly as he could, he grew the pillar, focusing more on building its height than its width.

Lea whispered to Thomas, "I don't know what we're going to do if this doesn't work."

"It's going to work."

She suspected he had less confidence than the words themselves imparted.

After a harrowing few minutes in which the bridge groaned at its weight, Luka connected his pillar to the portion of the column that he had begun under the arch. He spent several more minutes building the support column. The arch ceased its protests and appeared to be no longer verging on collapse. Luka lowered his arms stiffly and returned to Lea and Thomas, his shoulders slumped.

"That's as much as I can do from here."

The trio looked up. The arch only reached about two-thirds of the way to the plateau.

"Scheisse," Lea said. "Is that it then? We're done?"

"No," Luka said, affronted and surprised at the question. "I just can't do the rest from here. We have to go up there and build it as we go."

Thomas' eyes widened and most of the color drained from his face. "Is this a bad time to mention my fear of heights?"

"Yes," Lea said flatly.

Thomas swallowed hard. "Let's do this before I have to think about it too much. Will it hold?"

"It should, at least until the tide comes back in and melts the bottom of that pillar."

"It should. Nice," Thomas repeated. "How do we do this?"

Luka looked at his structure again. "You have to go first and make the steps. I'll be right behind you, then Lea. They don't have to be deep or evenly spaced, just … enough. Once we get to the end, you'll have to squat down while I finish. I won't be able to go around you. But I think I can do the last part in one go. I tried to make the ice gritty and not slick, so we don't … you know. It's tall and there are rocks below us."

Thomas muttered to himself as he made his way to the base of the arch. He experimented with sending an orb of fire ahead of himself, but it took too long and didn't generate enough heat.

Next, he placed his palm just above a place on the ice. It gave way under the heat, forming a ledge deep enough for a toehold, but not much more.

"Like that," Luka says, looking over his shoulder. "Alternate them right and left. It doesn't have to be the entire width. That'll save time."

Thomas climbed the arch. Everywhere he placed a hand, a melted place emerged that became alternately a handhold, then a foothold. Progress was slow but steady. Lea trailed the procession, noting to herself that water was dripping from the structure. The bright autumn sun warmed both the air around them and the ice beneath their feet. She didn't mention it. Not yet. There was nothing to be done about it.

When they reached the top of the arch where progress had halted, there were a couple dozen meters left to build. They weren't quite level with the plateau, so that the last segment would have an uphill grade. Luka said, "You can stand up now if you want."

"I'm good," Thomas said as he crawled, clinging to the sides of the arch. "You could have made this a little wider."

"Not unless you wanted it to take all day."

Thomas stopped about a meter from the end of the arch. "This good?"

"Can you get a little closer?"

"No."

Lea stifled a laugh. *He can face down a murderous god, but get him a few meters off the ground and he wilts.*

"That's fine," Luka said. "I can finish from here, I think."

Luka resumed building. Over the next half hour, he affixed the arch to the plateau. During that time, Thomas' only movement was to hunker even closer to the ice when the slightest breeze wafted their way. Lea monitored the water dripping from the ice and counted how many seconds it took for it to hit the rocks below. As best she could tell, if she fell, she would have four long seconds to think about it before she became a messy red patch.

"Let's do this," Luka said. "Thomas, you're up."

"Okay," he said weakly. He willed himself forward on the meter-wide bridge. One hand, then another.

"Focus on what's right in front of you," Luka encouraged. "You can do it."

Thomas crawled forward, making holds and steps for the two who followed him. He shuffled along on hands and knees until reaching the island and collapsing on his belly on Aspronisi's white pumice. When Luka and Lea joined him, they sat on either side of him.

Lea patted him on the head. "Good boy."

"If she's not here, and I did that for nothing, I'm going to kill her."

37

LEA

THE ISLAND WAS SMALL, not more than a couple hundred square meters. It wouldn't take them long to cover the plateau looking for signs of Agatha. Lea stood up and reached her hands down to the two boys. Each clasped her wrists, and she tugged. Once they were on their feet, she said, "Let's finish this."

Seconds after they fanned out, Luka whistled and pointed at a place where heat shimmers disrupted the air. They approached cautiously and stopped well before they could look directly down into the hole in the ground.

Thomas looked at Lea with a single question in his eyes. She didn't know the answer, but she could find out. She cupped her hands beside her mouth and yelled, "Agatha?"

A fireball rocketed past them from inside the cave, causing them to dive for cover.

Lea jumped up, checking her arms for new abrasions. Thomas wore the broadest grin she'd seen in weeks.

He called, "Mom?"

Time stopped while they waited for a response. Or an infinite amount of time passed. It was hard to say.

An eternity later, a hoarse voice called back, "Thomas?"

He jumped and raised his hands over his head in victory. "Yeah, mom, it's me." He stuck his head over the rim of the hole to see inside. Lea and Luka followed him, but it was too dark to see anything except the red glow of lava. Their eyes couldn't account for the contrast between their bright surroundings and the darkness below.

This time, the voice that called up to them was stronger, but laden with suspicion. "How do I know it's you and not someone else? I was told to expect someone else."

Lea looked around, suddenly concerned they weren't the only ones looking for Agatha.

The air split with a loud crack, followed by a thunderous crash, coming from the western end of the island. Luka ran back the way they'd come.

Agatha yelled, "What was that?"

Luka turned with widened eyes. He jogged back, saying nothing, and just looked down at the hole in the ground.

"Well?" Lea prompted.

"That was the bridge. It collapsed."

"Okay, we can build another one. Should be easier from up here."

Luka shook his head. "Onto the boat."

Lea took a step to go see for herself. He grabbed her wrist. "It's a submarine now."

"Scheisse."

Agatha yelled again, "What's happening?"

Thomas said, "Our escape plan just ... uhh ... hit a snag."

"I still need to know that you're you."

Thomas consulted his friends. "How do I prove that I'm me?"

Lea said, "You have to tell her something that only you would know. Like a memory that only you and she have."

"Okay," Thomas said. He rubbed his temples like he was trying to massage a memory to the surface. After a minute, he looked up with a half-grin. "I've got it." Looking down into the hole, he said, "You ready?"

"If this takes much longer, I'm going to get swallowed up by lava, so can we maybe get on with it?"

"When I was little, you told me your farts smelled like lavender."

A surprised cackle rose up from the bottom of the hole. It devolved into sobs. "Okay, baby boy, I believe you."

An embarrassed Thomas avoided his friends' eyes, but he couldn't hide the sniffling and throat clearing that followed.

Luka called, "Are you able to get out of there?"

Lea shook her head in disbelief at the question.

"Luka, is that you?"

"Ja."

"Do you think that if I could get out of here on my own, I'd still be down in this cave?"

It was Luka's turn to be embarrassed.

"How are we going to get her?" Lea said.

Thomas wiped his eyes. "I have an idea." He looked around the barren plateau as if confirming something to himself. "It'll take me a couple of minutes." Before anyone could respond, he opened a portal and dashed through it.

Luka nudged at the white pumice with the toe of his shoe. They otherwise waited in silence.

After several minutes, Agatha yelled, "What's going on up there?"

Luka said, "Umm … Thomas disappeared. He said he'd be back."

"Disappeared? What does that mean?"

"Like, he opened a door and went through it."

When they got no further response from Agatha, the silence resumed.

A portal opened. Thomas popped through, entangled in a

giant vine. "Kudzu. From the woods behind our old house in Alabama."

"Couldn't you have just done the thing with your hands?" Luka splayed his hands like he was pressing them against the ground.

Thomas smirked. "Yeah, probably."

"You wanted to play with your new toy, didn't you?"

Thomas looked suddenly embarrassed at the transparency of his actions. "Kind of." He dropped the kudzu and searched for a broken end, which he held to the ground and covered with his hands. Roots crawled out from under his hands and buried themselves in the pumice. When Thomas grabbed the body of the vine, the end uncoiled itself and slithered into the opening to the cavern.

Once it reached its full length, the vine grew until Agatha said, "Okay, I've got it."

Thomas set the vine down. "Can you pull yourself up?"

"No. I'm basically just skin and bones down here."

"Grab the vine, and we'll pull you up."

"Hold on. Let me get my clothes on. It's hot as balls in here."

Thomas flushed red again. "That's her alright."

"I'll volunteer to go down there," Luka offered, wiggling his eyebrows at Thomas.

"Let's be clear," Lea said. "We're on the verge of rescuing your best friend's mom, and you're using the opportunity to try to see her naked. Did I get that right?"

"When you put it that way, it sounds bad."

Thomas cocked his head to the side. "Is there another way to put it?"

Agatha called up, "Okay, I'm ready."

Thomas and Luka picked up the vine. When it went taut, they pulled. Their first couple of efforts were disjointed and resulted in little progress.

"You have to get in sync," Lea said.

"We know," Luka replied. "Just getting a feel for it is all."

On the next attempt, Luka made a more concerted effort to synchronize his pull with Thomas. They raised Agatha half a meter off the ground.

"That was good!" Luka said.

"Yeah, well, now we have to do that like a hundred more times."

When Luka and Thomas heaved on the kudzu, the sharp edge on the lip of the cave sheered the vine in two. The boys tumbled backwards, and Agatha crashed to the cave floor with a thud and a grunt. Lea ran to the opening. "Are you okay?"

The answer was a long time coming. Luka and Thomas joined her in waiting. "Mom?"

"Yep. Okay. Had to test my systems. But I can't do that again. Can't hold on."

Lea peeked at Thomas, whose concern grew. "New plan. We're coming down to you."

"I'm sorry, what?" Lea said. "We're just going to go down into the lava cave?"

Thomas looked from Lea to Luka. "I'm going down there to get her. If we can't get her to us, I'm going to her. You two can do whatever you need to."

Luka put a hand on Thomas' shoulder. "I told you from the start that I'm in this until the end. Let's go."

"Fine," Lea said. "Whatever. I'm in."

"Good," Thomas nodded. "You're first."

"I'm first what?"

Thomas knelt down to the remnant of the kudzu vine and placed his hands on it again. The severed end slid toward the opening and coiled itself as it grew. Having reached the critical length, the vine slid into the opening and unwound.

"You're the first to lower yourself down. You're the lightest."

"Not with those boots, she's not." Luka said. "They're probably ten pounds each."

"He's right, actually. We need your boots."

Lea said, "I'm not gonna lie, I don't really care for how you think you can just tell me what to do and expect me to do it." When Thomas said nothing else, Lea sat down and untied her boots. "I'm doing this because I want to, not because you told me to."

She handed the boots to Thomas, who set one down beside him and placed the other under the vine on the lip of the opening. "That should keep it from breaking and causing us to plummet to our deaths. Luka, go stand on the vine."

Luka complied more readily than Lea and walked to where the vine had rooted into the pumice.

"You're up," Thomas said.

She scooted to the entrance and dangled her legs over. "Is there an easy way to do this next part?"

Thomas shrugged.

"Great," Lea mumbled. She grabbed the vine and gave it a yard yank. She didn't know what she was expecting, what was a good or bad sign. *Here goes.* Lea lowered herself over the edge and wrapped her legs around the dangling vine.

Thomas squatted and peered down at her. "You good?"

She grunted as she began her descent into the darkness. One hand at a time, she lowered herself toward the cave floor. Once she got out of the sunlight, Agatha's dire situation became clear. Lava was overtaking the cave. *It's not just Agatha's situation anymore. It's mine too.*

She reached the ground a couple minutes later, her arms and abdominal muscles burning from exertion. Before she even released the vine, a surprisingly strong arm wound around her and dragged her backward, while another hand covered her mouth. She felt a blade pressed against her sternum.

After she let go of the vine, Thomas called down, "Are you okay?"

Agatha whispered, "Tell him you're fine and it's his turn."

"Yeah, mostly." The pressure of the metal increased against her chest. *This is not how I expected this to go.* Agatha maintained a backward pressure on her that kept her off balance. "You're up."

"Good girl," Agatha whispered.

A pang of betrayal ripped through Lea. *But what the heck was I supposed to do?*

Thomas' lower half swung over the edge, then the rest of him. He shimmied down much quicker than she had. As he got to the bottom, he said, "I did it with my eyes closed so I wouldn't hav—"

His smile at his achievement disintegrated. He opened his mouth to speak, but closed it again. Lea watched his posture change subtly. He was like a leopard now. This was definitely a boy who'd been dealt a hard hand. He didn't even flinch at the possibility of having to combat his own mother.

"You're his heir," Agatha accused.

"Apparently. I didn't choose it."

"That doesn't matter. It only matters that—"

"You're wrong," Thomas said defiantly, angrily.

Agatha took a quarter-step backward, pulling Lea with her. *This is going well.*

"Choice is all that matters. It's all that keeps me from becoming a monster."

"If you are the heir, aren't you already like him?"

"You are his daughter," Thomas said. "Are you like him?"

The statement landed like a haymaker. Agatha was shaken. The pressure against her chest slackened. Lea whirled away, though she couldn't go too far and avoid the lava.

"What's going on down there?" Luka yelled. "Can I come down? Is Thomas clear?"

No one answered him.

Thomas approached Agatha slowly. As he did, her arms fell to her side. He wrapped her in an embrace. The knife clattered to the floor. Agatha buried her face in Thomas' shoulder and wept.

"Guys?" Luka called again.

"Yes, come down," Lea hissed up at him. "Just shut up."

"Why? What's going on?"

Lea covered her face in frustration. *We're wrecking a moment, dummy. That's what's going on.*

Thomas whispered, "I'm not like him. I'm like you."

"But what if I am like him? Look what I did to Lea."

Lea sidestepped into Agatha's line of sight, feeling very much a third wheel. "I'm okay. That's not even the worst thing that's happened today."

Agatha groaned. "I'm so sorry. Come, give me a hug."

Thomas swiveled and opened his embrace to include Lea, who stepped into the hug.

Thomas asked, "How did you know about Vulcan?"

"Elle. She … or at least some part of her, came here and told me. She's gone now."

Thomas nodded. It was just the two of them now.

"Did y'all do it? Vulcan?"

He nodded again. Agatha squeezed them harder and kissed both Thomas and Lea on the cheeks.

"I'm feeling a little left out over here."

Agatha released the other two. "Come on, you can have a hug too."

Luka winked at Thomas over Agatha's shoulder. "And a kiss?"

She pushed him away and patted him on the shoulder. "Don't push it."

"Fine. Well, on the way down, I noticed that we have a problem." Luka gestured at the lake of lava that had refilled the cavern. "Anybody have any ideas?"

Thomas opened a portal beside them. "Let's go home."

Agatha cast a sidelong glance at it.

"It's okay," Lea said. "Luka, go first. Show her."

Luka paused before going through. "What about the boat?"

Lea answered, "I think that ship has sailed."

Luka dropped his jaw dramatically. "Look at you making bad puns! I'm so proud. Just for that, I'm going to let yo—"

"Nope. Don't. Whatever that was going to be, don't say it. Just go."

Luka hung his head and walked through. Agatha followed him, taking a deep breath before stepping into the portal.

"Go on," Lea said to Thomas. "You next. I'm right behind you."

As Thomas went through, Lea really looked around the cavern for the first time, noting some sort of calendar on one blackening wall and a letter on the opposite wall. Tears welled in her eyes as she read it. She pulled her phone out of her back pocket and snapped a picture of it. She didn't know if Agatha would want Thomas to read her farewell letter, but she'd at least give her the opportunity to make that choice. Lea stepped through, and the portal closed behind her.

38

THOMAS

AGATHA PULLED the car to a stop at the end of the dirt road deep in the woods, where they had never seen another person. She opened her door and said, "Don't forget the coffee cans."

Thomas rolled his eyes and got out of the car. "Please don't call them that. Just be a normal human."

"Oh, I think we both know that ship sailed a long time ago."

He opened the door to the backseat and retrieved the urns they had buckled in before they left the house. "Fine. If normal is out of the question, I'll settle for you calling them urns."

He shoved the containers into his backpack and caught up to Agatha as she entered the woods, making her way toward their magical oasis. "Hey, Bones, you sure you're up for this?"

"Don't think that you're too old for a spanking."

Thomas grinned. As much as anything during the nearly four weeks that his mother was gone, he missed this the most. The bantering back-and-forth. Was that an odd thing to miss more than anything else? Probably. But if it was an oddity, at least it was — to borrow from *Hitchhiker's Guide* — mostly harmless.

As orange and red leaves fluttered to the ground around

them, Agatha said, "You know it hasn't even been two months since we were last here?"

"It feels a little more like two lifetimes."

Agatha shivered when a stiff breeze blew through the woods.

"You should have worn a jacket," Thomas said. "You're a little short on insulation right now."

"Probably. But I just wanted to feel the coldness." She rubbed her arms. "I think I still smell like sulfur."

Thomas took a whiff in her direction. "You can probably do with another shower. I don't think we're going to be sneaking up on any animals today."

They walked in silence for a while as the flora evolved from plants native to the Black Forest to those that a younger Thomas learning how to use his abilities had grown here. Fond memories of successes were interspersed with recollections of trying and failing time and again to improve his skills. And there was also the time he'd threatened to kill her, and she hadn't even flinched.

The chatter of small creatures increased as more of them noticed Agatha and Thomas and told others of their return. They were stewards whose subjects reveled in their visits.

"Lea showed me the letter you wrote," Thomas said to Agatha as she walked ahead of him on the narrowing trail.

"What letter?"

"On the cave wall."

"Oh, that. Yeah, that was there when I got there."

"Huh," Thomas smiled. *Never change, Mom.* She may have been emotionally vulnerable when she was at the point of death and unlikely to see him again, but now that the window had closed on that, so too had the brief glimpse into her heart. "It sure was oddly specific to have already been there." *Might as well try to make her a little uncomfortable.*

"Yeah, I thought so too. Weird, right?"

"So that part about babies not being in their mothers' tummies — what did that mean?"

"Well, Thomas, when a man and a woman really love each other, he takes his—"

"Sorry. I'm sorry. I'll stop."

"That's what I thought," she said, not hiding the smugness in her voice.

The creek that burbled beside their path would lead them to the clearing that they sought. But some time before reaching it, Thomas asked, "Are you going to date Luka's dad?"

"Wow. Okay. I wasn't expecting that," she said without turning around. "And I really wish there'd been some segue between this conversation and the last one."

Thomas retraced the trail of breadcrumbs in his mind, trying to go backwards a thousand steps to figure out what the last conversation had been. When he got there, he said, "Gag a maggot. No. Very unrelated."

Agatha laughed.

He couldn't remember how long it had been since he'd heard her laugh like that. But that didn't mean things were back to normal. Not yet. Was that even a thing they could aspire to?

The hike through the woods was a labor for her. He had never seen her physically weak before. That part would probably resolve itself soon. She'd been eating everything in sight for the last three days since they'd been home.

Once in the clearing, Agatha turned to face him, hands out with her palms up. He swung his pack around and unzipped it. He pulled out one urn, then the next, and handed them to her.

Agatha waggled the containers. "Who's who here?"

"Has anyone ever commented about how irreverent you are?"

"It's always been one of my best qualities. So?"

Thomas sighed, "Steel is Oma. Copper is Elle. What are we going to do with them?"

"Dump them in the creek."

Thomas cocked his head. "Can you do that? I mean, is it legal?"

Agatha tucked the steel urn under her arm and unscrewed the lid on the copper urn. "Do you care?"

He considered it for a second and decided that he didn't care. He shook his head.

"Good. Here." She handed him the opened container.

He looked inside at the ashes. Calling them cremains seemed ridiculous. They were ashes, just like the ash pouring out of the dozens of volcanoes that were still beyond his grasp.

After Agatha unthreaded the lid on the steel urn, she asked, "Any last words for them?"

"I … don't think so," Thomas said with a frown. "Can I do it later?"

"Sure, you can talk to them whenever you want. They can't hear you or anything weird like that, but if it makes you feel better, go for it. I already said my peace to them. You may not know this, but I recently went on sabbatical and had a lot of time to myself to think about what I had to say to everyone."

"And what do you have to say to me?"

"You need to figure out how to keep the world from being burned alive by volcanic eruptions."

Thomas' mouth became a thin line. "That's not nice."

Agatha shrugged. "It's next on the agenda. Come here and kneel beside me."

Thomas and his mother knelt at the edge of the creek and poured in the ashes, making murky the otherwise clear creek. The gray cloud flowed downstream until it was carried out of sight under a canopy of trees.

Agatha stood to her feet and reached down to Thomas. He took her hands and pulled himself up. "Now, on to the other pressing matter."

Thomas took a deep breath and blew it out slowly. "Okay." He gestured with his hand and opened a portal to his right.

Agatha shivered and released a guttural noise.

"Possum walk over your grave?"

"No," she said. "That still gives me the creeps."

Thomas gestured for her to step through.

"Fine," she said testily, and entered the portal. Thomas followed, closing it behind himself.

In the dim cavernous space, his fears returned with all the suddenness of a thunderclap. The earth erupted all around them, a calamity of chaos. Ash choked the air and lay over the ground like a gray snowfall.

"What's the deal with this place?" Agatha asked, her voice laced with concern rather than irreverence.

"This was his realm. You know how he called himself the lord of conflagrations or whatever? This place was how he controlled it. But I haven't figured out how to take control, and everything is kind of going haywire."

"I'm going to ask you some questions, because I need more information. And I want you to try not to get frustrated with me."

Thomas nodded.

"Where are we? Like, literally, where are we?"

"I wish you'd started with something more concrete like, 'What's all this molten liquidy stuff all over the place?' Because I know you think you were starting with a simple question, but … I don't think it has an easy answer. There was a priest who indicated that this was the belly of the earth. But that's not quite right."

"Didn't say you saw Elle here? She said she had been in the place between worlds. Does that mean anything to you?"

"Yes. Perfect. It fits my theory about what it is. Ready?"

"I guess?"

"I think it's a pocket dimension that may not literally be in the middle of the earth, but is somehow adjacent to or connected to the earth. Because this lava is real. It's connected to our world. What happens in here mirrors what happens on earth. So that fits what both the priest and Elle said. Emma's been here, too, I think. She may have some ideas."

"Are y'all going to reconcile?" Agatha asked.

"Can we not do that right now?"

"I'm just saying. From everything you've said, you were being a bit of a jerk. So maybe you should give her another chance."

"Mom! You're supposed to be on my side."

"Baby boy, I'm always on your side. And—"

"Except when you pull a knife on my friend," Thomas said with a smirk.

"One time. That happens one time and nobody wants to let it go. Anyway, part of being on your side includes telling you when you're being a moron."

"Are we done with this?" Thomas said impatiently.

A nearby eruption hurled magma in all directions. Thomas yanked his mother toward him and turned his back to shield them from the projectiles. When a heavy glob of magma struck him in the back, he and Agatha went sprawling. They skittered across the path a couple of meters before coming to a stop. Thomas jumped up and ran to Agatha. "You okay?"

She stared at him wide-eyed as he pulled her up.

"What?" he asked.

"Turn around," Agatha instructed.

Thomas did. Although his shirt had mostly burned away in the back, his skin was intact. Red from the impact, but not melted away like it should have been. She spun him back around.

"It didn't burn you," she said with bewilderment.

"Maybe …" he couldn't think of a plausible suggestion and let the sentence disintegrate.

"This magma is like your fire, I think. You are impervious to it."

Thomas strode to the edge of the path and knelt beside a growing lava pool that was fed by a stream running from the crusted lip of the nearest opening. He held both arms out in front of him.

"Wait!" Agatha said franticly. "What are you about to do?"

"Test your theory."

"And if I'm wrong?"

He paused to consider it. "Then, best-case scenario, I look like Anakin at the end of Episode III and you get me a Darth Vader suit."

"I'm not kidding."

"I know," he said, and plunged his arms into the lava.

After a long minute, a shockwave of energy pulsed outward, resonating through the cavernous realm. It nearly knocked Agatha off her feet as it passed through her. Still, Thomas remained where he knelt. Slowly at first, then all at once, the eruptions subsided. A tranquility returned to the place. After several more minutes, Thomas stood and turned to face Agatha.

"How did you do it?" she asked.

He shrugged. "I just did it. Same as I grow things. I don't how know to put words to it."

"Fair enough." Agatha looked around the suddenly quiet space. "What now?"

"Lunch?" The worry in Thomas' eyes belied his light tone.

"What's the problem?"

Thomas broke eye contact. "It's just that … I'm more like him now. What if—"

"Wait." Agatha held up both hands. "Aren't you the one who told me the priest said that Vulcan only got consumed by the darkness after he stopped resisting it?"

"Yes."

"And aren't you the one who told me the stryga thing said

that he wasn't beholden to you and oaths he'd sworn to Vulcan didn't carry over to you?"

Thomas nodded.

"And don't you think you can take from those things that you have some choice in how all this turns out?"

Thomas sighed. "I guess."

"Oh, and one more thing. You were preaching at me about your decisions being your own and not having to bear the sins of your ancestors and deciding your own fate."

"Alright, alright," Thomas said. "I get it."

"Do you? Because I can keep going if you want."

"Please don't."

Agatha looked at him for a long couple of seconds and raised her eyebrow at him. "You good now?"

Thomas nodded.

"Good. Let's talk about lunch." Agatha's eyes grew greedy at the mention of food. "I'm ravenous."

Thomas opened a door that they stepped through and onto the clover-covered meadow.

"Oh, one more thing," Agatha said.

"Yes?" Thomas said, now on alert. *One more thing* was never good.

"I checked my credit card statement this morning...."

Thomas' eyes widened, and he looked down at his wrist. "Look at the time! I gotta run. I've got ... things." He opened another portal and jumped into it, leaving Agatha standing alone in the woods.

She smiled and bent down to pick up the empty urns. "That's okay," she said to the empty space. "You have to come home sometime."

AUTHOR'S NOTE

A few months ago, my mother asked me if something terrible had happened in my childhood that she didn't know about. My parents have read all the books in The Zauberi Chronicles and my short stories. It's safe to say that they were a little squeamish that some of what they'd read had come from the mind of their son.

Immediately before my mother asked me that question, I had just given her the synopsis of the next few stories I plan to write. So rather than provide assurances that things would get lighter and cheerier, it became clear that I was doubling down on the same kinds of stories you and they have been reading.

Stories that are certainly dark and sometimes grisly. My parents had concerns about the source of these tales. But the answer is no. Nothing terrible ever happened to me. Not in childhood and not as an adult. But my writing has always been dark, dating back to my first forays into poetry and creative writing as an angsty teenager, and extending to the present.

Those early poems got me in trouble when I left my writing notebook laying around. The adults who found it *had concerns.*

The fallout from that episode engrained in me a sense of shame about the nature of my writing. I'm still digging out of that hole more twenty years later, and have only recently come to terms with this aspect of myself.

I am not morbid or unhappy. But I am interested in the grislier side of humanity, so that is what I write about. What draws my attention and curiosity is how people respond deeply unsettling events.

A couple of years ago I was listening to an interview with horror writer Michaelbrent Collings. He said that he often writes about the things that scare him the most. That makes a lot of sense to me. And in reading The Zauberi Chronicles, you can probably pick out some of the things that produce the greatest fear in me.

Writing gives me a way to explore those fears and work through them. To experiment with how I might respond when confronted with the kinds of deeply unsettling events that I pitch my characters into.

Writing also gives you a way to go on those adventures with me and with the characters I've created, some of whom will go on to other adventures and some of whom have met their demise in the pages of these books.

Much like it is difficult to say farewell to a beloved character (and sometimes even to a loathsome one — looking at you, Vulcan), it has also been difficult putting a wrapper on this trilogy. Writing these three books has been a significant chapter in my life. One that started on August 31, 2020, when I penned the first words of what became *Vulcan Rising*.

I had wanted to write a novel for more than half my life, and The Zauberi Chronicles finally opened the door to that opportunity. What I didn't know then was what lay behind the door — a torrent of other stories. I have so many ideas for novels and short stories that I hardly know when I'll write them all. I likely won't. But I'll do my best to put a dent in them.

And I feel like it's only fair to warn you now. They mostly won't have happy endings, but they will have hope and love, while exploring both the best and worst that humanity has to offer.

277

May 23, 2022

ABOUT THE AUTHOR

J. W. Judge lives in Birmingham, Alabama, also known as The Magic City. In his day job, he is a lawyer, practicing commercial litigation.

Forging Bonds is the third book in The Zauberi Chronicles. It follows *Vulcan Rising* (Book 1) and *Seeking Sanctuary* (Book 2).

If you enjoyed *Forging Bonds*, sign up for Judge's newsletter for information about the The Zauberi Chronicles and other stories he's working on. You can also follow him on social media for updates, developments, and news about other projects. If you'd like to reach out to him by email, please do so at jwj@jwjudge.com.

Please help others find and enjoy *Forging Bonds* by leaving a rating and review on Goodreads or your preferred retailer, or by sharing about it on your own social media.

WORKS BY J. W. JUDGE

Fiction

Vulcan Rising (The Zauberi Chronicles, Book 1)

Seeking Sanctuary (The Zauberi Chronicles, Book 2)

Forging Bonds (The Zauberi Chronicles, Book 3)

The Murder Tree (A Short Story)

Non-Fiction

Write Your Novel One Day at a Time: How to Write a Novel While
Having a Career, a Family, and a Life